FOUND

Lesli Weber

Copyright © 2024 Lesli Weber

All rights reserved.

ISBN: 979-8-218-47263-4
ISBN-13: 979-8-218-47263-4

To Mike, always.

Prologue

When all else fails, go to Mars.

Michelle squirmed, trying to find the position of least resistance. Interplanetary transports were statistically safer than airplanes, but, somehow, the seats were even less comfortable.

"Ladies and gentlemen, we are beginning our descent into Mars Colony. Please remain seated with your seatbelts securely fastened until otherwise notified. Thank you."

Michelle snuck a glance at Phil as she snugged down the safety harness. He tore his gaze away from the viewport just long enough to make eye contact before refocusing on the starfield outside. "Where've you been?"

She shrugged. "I didn't sleep very well last night." The twin berths were serviceable, but not more than that. "I was just trying to sneak in a little more before we land."

"Before you see *Dave* again, you mean," Phil teased in a singsong voice.

Michelle grinned. Her teenage brother wasn't wrong. Three months was plenty long enough to be literal worlds apart from her husband, especially when those three months made up half their marriage. Mars wasn't her first choice for a romantic reunion, nor to forge the next phase of their lives, for that matter, but at least Mars wasn't Earth; that was a point in its favor.

A sharp pinch at Michelle's hip made her jump. Phil was tugging on her belt rather than his own. "Hey." She elbowed him.

"Hmm?" He didn't even bother to turn her way.

She nudged him again. "Adjust your own belt, kiddo. Mine is fine."

"What?" Now he looked down at where their seats met. "Oh." When he looked up, his grin spread wide across his face. "Heh."

She couldn't stop herself from chuckling. "Yeah, 'heh'." The red glow of the planet looming large outside the window caught her attention. Phil followed her gaze.

"Mars, Shelle," he whispered. "We're going to live on frickin' *Mars*."

"Language," she murmured automatically. Her heart skipped a few beats; she was caught up in the view. Their future loomed increasingly larger with each breath.

The transport vessel began to shimmy and jolt as it broached the upper atmosphere. Michelle's jaw clenched of its own accord as her grip tightened on the armrests. She closed her eyes and began deliberately breathing through her nose. Beside her, Phil cackled softly with excitement.

Michelle filled her lungs completely then let it out in one great *whoosh*. This ought to be the last of it. The last of the almost unbearably rough road that had brought them to this place, of all places, to start over as a new version of their family. If she could just breathe through this final turbulence, just push through her discomfort one last time, then before she knew it, they'd be on the ground. Dave would be waiting and the three of them would go to their new home and start settling in, start establishing the Arensen-Collins household.

The squeeze of Phil's hand on hers made Michelle open her eyes and look at him. He was watching her carefully, and

FOUND

when they made eye contact, he smiled gently. She turned her hand over so that her fingers were grasping his and squeezed back.

They'd come through so much already. Their first interplanetary landing would be small potatoes.

"You're missing the view," she said, gesturing to the viewport with her chin.

Phil visibly relaxed. Shooting her another brilliant smile, he turned back to the viewport, eager to watch their official arrival at their new home.

1

Good wine was hard to come by on Mars.

So, though it was a poor substitute, Michelle sipped rose hip tea, courtesy of the colony's greenhouse plants, as she gazed at the seemingly endless vista. Dave sat beside her, absently rubbing her thigh, as they waited for Phil to finish washing the dinner dishes. The sun was setting behind Elysium Mons. The volcano hadn't erupted for millennia, but its inactivity did nothing to detract from its beauty. The entire landscape, from the lifeless, arid plains, to the jagged volcano, to the dusky sky, was an homage to hues of red she never saw together on Earth. As the dusk gave way to evening, double moons rose and illuminated the miles of desolation.

It was hostile, cold, and unforgiving. It was also one of the most beautiful things Michelle had ever seen.

Things were working out better than she'd expected. It was a huge change, uprooting their lives and starting over on Mars, given that Michelle's usual idea of adventure was eating breakfast for dinner. But the past eight months had allowed them the space they needed to heal. Phil was happier than she'd seen him in a year. Her insomnia had all but disappeared and she didn't feel as anxious. Dave was a positive, calming, and stabilizing influence on them both.

Michelle felt more hopeful this evening, their first Halloween on Mars, than she had for the past two years.

Dave's warm hand enveloped hers. While not a bulky man, Dave was quite tall, and his hand dwarfed hers. He gently tapped his thumb three times on her knuckles and lifted his brows, the silent way of checking in on her that he'd developed since Adam died.

Michelle squeezed his hand and nodded.

"Done," Phil announced, tossing the dishcloth aside on the counter. It only took a few steps to move from the small kitchen sink to the dining area where Michelle and Dave were waiting; Phil claimed his spot at the table in a heartbeat. "All right, let's play."

The living facilities were far from luxurious. For their family of three, they had a small, simple, two-bedroom, one bathroom unit with a kitchen/dining area and living room that, altogether, was about the size of her one-bedroom apartment back on Earth. It was cozy at best, but it worked.

So far, everything worked.

Dave released her hand and shuffled the deck, showing off a technique he'd learned during a college trip to Las Vegas. Once the game started, the time passed quickly. Hands were won and lost, trash talk was traded with gusto, and they all took turns answering the door when the few miniature ghosts and goblins who lived in the colony came to call this evening of October 31st.

Michelle had always loved Halloween, and since she'd

become the one handing out treats instead of hoarding them, her favorite part was the kids' reactions. Granted, these kids were getting fruit from the greenhouse instead of the candy of her own childhood, but they were trading that buzzy sugar bliss for the rare privilege of trick-or-treating on *Mars*. It seemed like a fair trade to her.

The evening quieted down after a little while, as there weren't that many children in the colony, and the three of them played uninterrupted for a couple of hours. Phil and Dave were both a bit competitive and the good-natured rivalry between them was entertainment for Michelle. Just before ten, Michelle yawned so big that her jaw popped. Rubbing her eyes, she laid her cards on the table. "I'm gonna call it a night, you guys."

"You can't, not right now. Look at the score!" Phil thrust a notepad at her; he and Dave were tied.

She looked at her husband.

"One more hand?" He gave her a hopeful grin.

Michelle was bone-tired, but between Dave's attempt at charm and Phil's desperation, she nodded. "All right, one more. But this is it, though."

"Yes!" Phil fidgeted in his seat. "Gimme the deck."

Dave handed Phil the deck and sat back in his seat, watching his brother-in-law deal the cards, then deal again as everyone traded some in hopes of improving their hands.

Michelle scooped up her cards and looked at the pitiful combination she held. "I'm out." She laid the cards back down on the table.

Phil eyed her suspiciously. "Are you just saying that 'cause you're tired? 'Cause that would make you a quitter."

She barely resisted rolling her eyes at him. "Oh, I'm absolutely a quitter." She flipped her cards over so that everyone could see that she had absolutely nothing. "When I have this good a reason to bail."

Dave looked at the hand she'd revealed and hissed. "Ouch."

"Not a quitter, then," Phil taunted. "Just a loser."

Dave hissed again. "Double ouch."

She shook her head, chuckling under her breath. "And one of you guys is gonna be a loser with me. So who's it gonna be?"

Dave and Phil locked gazes. Dave was the first to taunt. "Bring it, buster. I'm taking you out."

"I think you're bluffing." Phil squinted at his brother-in-law critically. "You bluffin'?"

Dave shrugged. "Guess you're going to have to find out."

"All right. You think you've got something, let's see it. You're going down, man."

"Oh, yeah?" Dave displayed his cards, spreading them in an arc in front of him on the table. "Straight flush, King high."

Phil's jaw dropped. "Shit."

"Language," Michelle murmured, though she couldn't have said it better herself. Phil was screwed.

Reluctantly, Phil showed his cards. A straight, Jack high. A strong hand.

Just not strong enough.

"Hello, loser number 2," said Michelle.

Dave sighed in mock sympathy. "You weren't even first loser."

Phil laid his forehead on the table and groaned. "I can't believe it."

"You have to play the hand you're dealt, grasshopper," Dave said in an overexaggerated voice of wisdom before grinning widely. "Too bad you dealt it to yourself."

The teen snorted and rolled his eyes. "Whatever. You're mine next time, Collins. And real wise men don't actually call anyone 'grasshopper'."

A laugh burst from Michelle. "I think he might have you there, babe." She stood. "All right, it's bedtime. C'mere, you." Phil got to his feet and gave her a hug and Dave a wave before heading off to his room, closing the door behind him with a click.

Michelle meandered over to where Dave still sat at the table, gathering up the cards. She came up behind him and rubbed his shoulders.

Dave's arms relaxed to his sides and he moaned. "That feels amazing."

Michelle leaned down and nibbled at his ear as she trailed her fingers along his chest and over his abdomen. "Oh, I can do better than this." She leaned in and whispered, "*Someone's* going down tonight, Collins."

Without missing a beat, Dave bolted up, grabbed Michelle's hand, and beelined it for their bedroom.

The next day started as the days usually did. Dave left for work at the crack of dawn, waking Michelle with a kiss right before he went out the door. Michelle then wrangled herself out of bed and woke Phil up on her way to the kitchen to prepare breakfast for them both. Breakfast wasn't a grand affair; the menu was pretty limited: protein ration, scrambled or fried, and fruit. Happily, though, the supply ship that came every twelve weeks always brought coffee with it, and it had only been three weeks since the last resupply, so there was still plenty lovely bitter, rich, elixir of life left.

Michelle had just plated the protein, which she scrambled today, with a side of leftover Halloween berries, when Phil appeared at the table, hair still wet from his shower.

"Morning, kid. How'd you sleep?"

Phil groaned. "Why's school have to start so early?"

"It's a time-honored way to torture teenagers," she said, setting a glass of water in front of him.

The left corner of his mouth turned up. "It works."

She hummed. "I know. I lived through it, too." She plated her own meal and sat down beside him. "You ready for your botany test today?"

"Yeah," he mumbled. "Don't know why I have to learn that stuff, though. I'm not gonna work in the greenhouse." He said it with a dismissive sneer, but the mischief in his eyes gave him away.

Michelle pointed her fork at him. "That's what I said, and now look at me."

He scoffed and finished the last of his breakfast.

"Already?" she said as he took his plate to the sink. "What are you, a vacuum?"

"It doesn't take long. It's not like the food fights back or something." He planted a quick kiss on her cheek and picked his backpack up from the sofa, slinging it over his shoulder.

"See ya," he called on his way out the door.

"Love you!" she called back, watching his long legs eat up the ground the way the boy himself devoured breakfast.

She polished off her protein and berries. With the guys successfully out the door, now it was her turn. She'd hit the shower and go to work, expecting that her scheduled eight-hour shift in the greenhouse would turn into ten hours or more, as it did more often than not. Michelle didn't love what she did, she had trained as a linguist, of all things, but at least the greenhouse work was useful here.

Utility was the only measure of value in the colony. Everyone had to do their share, pull their weight, or this, humanity's third attempt at colonizing Mars, wouldn't be any more successful than the first two had been. Except that it already was. This outpost had lasted for just over four years already, a little more than twice as long as its predecessor, Mars 2. Mars 1 had been such a short-lived endeavor it almost wasn't worth measuring.

Michelle smiled as she stepped into the shower. This time, the colony was going to be just fine.

And so were they.

2

The glorious symphony of color in the Martian sunrise lit the sky as Michelle walked to the greenhouse. While the planet's atmosphere and geology created stunning vistas on the other side of the transparent atmospheric dome, the climate was always temperate on this side of it. Today was November first, the time of year when the rain started turning to snow back home. Here, there was no rain, no snow, no heat waves, no cold snaps. Every day within the dome had the same weather as the day before. It could be hell on small talk.

But conversational acuity wasn't what had led Michelle to Mars.

Not long after Dave graduated, all of his hard work culminated in the once-in-a-lifetime opportunity to intern under Dr. Ellen Aiani, a brilliant visionary currently in charge of managing all aspects of the intradome atmosphere on the colony. To work with her, though, Dave had to leave Washington State and relocate to Mars for at least the next three years.

Michelle and Dave had been engaged for just over nine months when he was selected for the internship. If he accepted, and of course he would, Dave would have to be on Mars no later than four months after the offer, including the two-weeks it would take to get there. So the very next week, at a small, sweet, courthouse ceremony with Dave's parents and Phil as witnesses, Michelle became Mrs. David Collins.

She still went by Arensen, though, because Phil shouldn't have to be the only one bearing their family name.

Dave loved working with Dr. Aiani, and Michelle was glad for it, because her own situation wasn't nearly as rosy. Michelle was a trained linguist, a skill for which there was as much demand on Mars as there was naturally occurring water. But, while families were welcome in the colony, there was no capacity for waste. Everyone had to be useful, so Michelle helped out in the greenhouse. She also stopped in at the Records Department once a week to help them catch up on any backlog they had. Julius, the lovely man who ran Records, was a joy to work with. The perfect foil to Dr. Morgan.

Petra Morgan was at the forefront of her field, creating hardier, more resilient, more prolific plants through advanced genetic manipulation. It was fascinating work, producing eggplants that provided all the iron a body needed in a day, even if they did taste like chalk. But while Michelle respected the hell out of the woman for her professional achievements, she was glad that she was far enough removed from Dr. Morgan that she didn't have to work with her every day. Their typical semiweekly interactions were sour enough for Michelle's tastes. Dr. Morgan was consistently prickly and demanding, crude and rude and beyond arrogant. Dr. Morgan was an unwavering believer in her own superiority.

Michelle couldn't stand her.

Greenhouse staff didn't enter by the main door, but by the office door around back. Someone was always in the office, as was the case with most posts on Mars Colony. Every function was essential, so someone needed to be there day or night to instantly handle anything that arose. The wrong malfunction left to itself could spell disaster for the entire colony.

Emilio Barrigan was sitting behind the desk when she walked in. Emilio was one of the two poor souls who had the misfortune of working directly with Dr. Morgan on a daily basis, and Michelle had no idea how he maintained his easygoing attitude. At the sound of the door, he looked up from the display he'd been studying. "Hey, Michelle! How's it going?"

"Good, Em, thanks. You?"

"Same. Did you get to see the moon twins, not to be confused with the actual twin moons, last night?" Paige and Amelia Jacobs had dressed as Phobos and Deimos, Mars' moons.

Michelle grinned. "Were you able to guess what they were?"

Emilio barked a laugh. "Nah. I was thinking along the lines of a pair of eyeballs or something. Bonnie, on the other hand, knew instantly." Bonnie, Emilio's wife, was the head nurse and one of Michelle's better friends on Mars.

"How?" Michelle shook her head.

"Search me," he shrugged. "The woman's a wonder."

Michelle's heart warmed. Unlike her and Dave, who were just getting started, Emilio and Bonnie had been married for over 20 years and were still going strong. If she and Dave played their cards right, that could be them one day.

Em turned back to his monitor and changed the display. "OK, Dr. M's got you carrying on with nursing the winter greens today."

"That works for me," she said, grabbing her gloves and her tools. "Hey, are we still on for Saturday?"

He nodded. "As far as I know. Bonnie'll bring cookies."

"Excellent. Have a good one!" she called out over her shoulder as she walked through the office door that led into the greenhouse. Emilio would be gone as soon as his relief arrived, which would probably be in the next few minutes.

The door closed on Em's cheery, "You, too!"

Michelle passed the flowers and the fruit trees and made her way toward the back of the greenhouse, where the winter greens were planted. With a survey of her domain for the day, Michelle got to work.

She didn't see Dr. Morgan all day, so it was, by default, a good day.

At least until she got home.

Phil and the other kids met in the colony's classroom during the day. Their lessons were taught online from Earth, but there were two on-planet teachers, Ms. Kate and Mr. Karl, who helped the kids stay on track, answered questions, and basically functioned similarly to the teachers in the schoolhouses of the Old West. After school finished for the day, Phil and his friend Chris hung out together and did whatever it was teenage boys did on Mars after school. Sometimes they spent the afternoon at Chris' place, other times they hung out here, sometimes they were somewhere else altogether. Phil never caused any trouble, so Michelle tried to give him as much freedom and privacy as she could.

But today, Phil was home by himself. She knew because his stuff (and only *his* stuff; Chris' backpack and shoes were a familiar sight now) was dumped by the front door, despite her instructions to him countless times to take it into his room. One of his shoes was tucked under her chair at the table, the other on its side in the living room. Phil's detritus ran in a clear trail from the front door to his room.

His unusually silent room.

Hoping he wasn't coming down with something, Michelle rapped lightly on the door. "Phil?"

No response.

She knocked again. "Phil? Let me know if you're in there or not so I don't come barging in on something a big sister doesn't need to see."

Then she heard his voice, muffled and angry. "What?"

Michelle took it as an invitation and opened the door. Phil sat slouching on the edge of his bed. She could tell by the way his hair was mussed that he'd been lying down. "Hey," she said, reaching a palm toward his forehead. "What's up? You feeling ok?"

He knocked her hand away. "'M fine."

"Yeah? 'Cause you don't seem fine. What happened?" Michelle sat beside him, shoulders touching.

"Nothing," Phil snapped, glowering at the floor.

Michelle sat beside him in silence for a little while.

Then, so quietly it was almost a whisper, he said, "I just miss him."

Her heart broke.

"I know." She rested a hand on top of Phil's knee. "I miss him, too."

"But I don't *wanna* miss him!" Phil exploded upward, hands waving, pacing in the small space next to his bed. Michelle could now see the red rimming his eyes. "I *hate* him! I needed him and he... he just *left*! He *left*!" His face contorted, turning red with the effort it took not to cry. "I needed him and he was an asshole and he left me."

"I know."

His lower lip trembled as he stood alone at the end of the bed, defeated. "He left us."

"I know." Michelle rose and walked to him. "But I'm here. Dave's here, and I'm here, and we won't leave you." He let her wrap her arms around his shoulders and pull him in for a hug. After a moment, his arms came up around her and he rested his head against the side of hers, snuggling his face into her hair. She could feel his breath stutter as he inhaled, and she gently rubbed his back as he clung to her.

Their mother, Katherine, had been afflicted with early-onset dementia from the time Phil was only four years old. He didn't really have any memories of her outside of the care facility, no memories other than visiting her once a week, on holidays, and on birthdays. When she died eighteen months ago, Phil had been sad, but not devastated. Michelle had felt the loss more, though she'd been letting her mother go for years already. When a mother forgets who her child is, doesn't recognize her own 12-year-old daughter, it's hard for that child to become terribly attached to anything other than memories to anchor her affection to the stranger who gave her half her DNA. Michelle was twelve when Katherine had been committed, but her mind had been slipping away long before that.

Adam, their father, had more memories, stronger memories, than either of them. He loved Katherine more than anything else in life, and had made good on his vow to care for her in sickness. He was vigilant, dedicated, and devoted to her health and happiness as much as he possibly could be. And he did his best to be both mother and father to a young boy and a preteen girl as he watched his wife fade further and further from his grasp each day. It had been a heartbreaking eleven years for him. When Katherine finally, mercifully, passed away a year and a half ago, Adam handled everything from the funeral arrangements to probate to ensuring that his own will was arranged to make his passing as painless as possible for his children.

That came in handy when he'd taken his own life four months later.

Now, here they were, a year and a half later, the two of them, three with Dave, making a new life together, making a new family on Mars. Eighteen months was nothing in what Michelle had come to think of as 'grief time'. Sometimes, for no reason, when everything seemed to be going just fine, grief reared up out of nowhere and kicked you in the teeth. When it did, all you could do was hold on and try to breathe through it.

She let Phil hold on to her.

Dave had been there with them through it all, so when he got home and Phil remained stubbornly in his room, skipping dinner, it was no surprise Dave figured out why. "Did something happen, or is he having a gray day?"

"Gray day." Michelle scooped a couple of ladles of stew into a bowl for Dave, then for herself, and sat down, bringing both bowls to the table.

Dave glanced at the closed door to Phil's room. "Poor kid."

"Yeah." She stirred her food aimlessly, not very hungry but knowing she would be better off for eating.

"How are *you*?" Dave asked her, and some of the tension in her belly unwound itself. Sometimes just knowing she wasn't alone was enough to help. She hoped that was true for Phil, too.

"All right." She stirred her stew again and brought a bite up to her lips. "Mostly." She ate.

Dave watched her another moment then scooped up his own spoonful. "And how was work?"

Michelle tossed her husband a look of appreciation. Ever since Adam's funeral, Michelle had been adamant about not breaking down in front of her brother. The last thing Phil needed was to unload on her, then see her hurting because of it. He might never feel comfortable letting her in again. So she couldn't break here at the dining table, because Phil might walk in anytime. And although she and Dave been married less than two years, they'd been together since she was sixteen; he knew her well enough to know that if they started talking about it all, she might not be able to hold it together.

So he'd switched topics. Work was normal, steady, dull. Talking about work would let her pack all the crap away until another, more private time. "I managed to avoid Dr. Morgan all day, so it was an improvement over yesterday. And the romaine is finally starting to perk up, so all in all, I'd give it three and half stars. You?"

He grinned. "It was good. Dr. Aiani is a freaking genius. Her ideas are…" His free hand spun in the air as he took another bite. "She thinks of things that wouldn't cross my mind in a thousand years. It's an honor to be able to work with her, but Shelle, I'm telling you now, I will never, *ever,* be the scientist she is."

It was good to see him so excited. "Aw," she teased, "you're fangirling."

Dave nodded enthusiastically. "Yes. Yes, I am."

And he spent the next half hour telling her all about water cycling and humidity balancing and temperature consistency and other things that made sense when he talked about them, but which she wouldn't remember in fifteen minutes, even if she tried.

3

Phil had eventually emerged from his room to eat a late dinner, and Dave's gentle cajoling had eventually coaxed a smile out of him. He'd gone back to his room immediately after eating, but the fact that he'd come out to eat at all, and that he smiled, even once, gave Michelle enough confidence about his mental state that she was able to let herself go in the shelter of Dave's arms later that night.

Michelle was grateful that together, the three of them had the resilience, or hope, or fortitude, or whatever it was that allowed them to see and do what Adam had not been able to. They were carrying on.

Which required more effort some days. While most work days felt long, today was actually going to last longer than normal. She was one of the first to arrive at the greenhouse office, and she was scheduled to manage the desk after her regular shift ended at 17:00 until midnight, when Emilio would relieve her. She put on her gloves, gathered her tools, and entered the greenhouse.

The scent of lush, growing plant life enveloped her, and some of Michelle's worries moved to the back of her mind. The abundant verdant plant life stood in stark contrast to the vermilion landscape she could see through the dome's wall. The first rays of the morning sun were starting to pierce the sky, and the effect of the light with the red and green put her in mind of Christmas. A small smile grew on her face as she walked back toward her winter greens.

The moment she had a clear view of them, her heart dropped into her stomach. A pile of wilt sat limply where a patch of romaine had been yesterday. "Oh, no."

Carefully, she picked up a drooping leaf. This plant was healthy just two days ago. Not robust, exactly, but doing well after a shaky start. What could have happened overnight to bring it to this? They had to figure it out. If the romaine had caught some kind of plant virus, fungus, or other organism, the threat needed to be identified and contained before it spread to the rest of the plants.

They needed to fix this, fast, or they could lose everything.

And the next resupply ship from Earth wasn't due for nine more weeks.

Her inspection of the sad plants didn't show any obvious signs of predation; even under magnification, there were no visible bites taken from any of the leaves, no dust or powder that would indicate the beginnings of mold. So that left a microscopic organism or some kind of problem with the plants' nutrition, either soil, compost, chemical fertilizer, light, or water. Michelle inspected the other plants surrounding the romaine patch. Everything else seemed fine, so whatever it was, thankfully, appeared to be confined to this one species.

She was coming back from collecting a pH testing kit from the office when she spied Dr. Morgan leaning over the area of concern. As Michelle approached, Dr. Morgan looked up, and her sharp gaze was as accusatory as her words.

"What the hell happened here?"

"I'm investigating, but I don't know yet. I've ruled out —"

"Have you informed Ken?"

"Not yet, he hasn't —"

"Dig up the plot and put it in isolation," Dr. Morgan interrupted. "We can't risk the rest of the greenhouse in the event these plants are dying due to something other than mishandling." The doctor shot Michelle a little side-eye that she didn't even try to hide.

Michelle bristled. "Excuse me? These plants are being well cared for."

The Australian scientist's glare turned dismissive. "Dig it up and isolate it while Ken runs tests. Do you understand?"

Michelle opened her mouth to reply when Dr. Morgan held up a hand. "Never mind. Just do it."

Michelle turned her face downward, focusing on her feet, and her mouth twitched a couple of times as she considered what she wanted to say. In the end, she simply gritted her teeth and ground out, "Yes, doctor." She raised her face to meet the doctor's glare, and instead, all she saw was the woman's back.

Dr. Morgan was already too far away to hear her.

Michelle briefly imagined vaporizing the lithe doctor's retreating form, then turned back to the ruined plot and began the process of digging it up.

The thing that burned Michelle's gut was that Dr. Morgan wasn't wrong. She was rude as hell about it, but she wasn't wrong. However, there were ways to say things and treat people and ways not to. Despite all her education, clearly Dr. Morgan hadn't retained that part of her early childhood training.

"Wow, what did that lettuce ever do to you?" said a voice from over Michelle's shoulder.

She turned to see Ken, one of the greenhouse botanists, grinning at her. She realized that she'd been digging for the roots of one of the plants with unnecessary vigor. "I may have been thinking about something other than the immediate task at hand."

Ken chuckled. "You think?" He pulled up a seat to the bench and sat next to her. "Where are you at?"

She slid the testing checklist over to him. Though her degree wasn't in any of the sciences, she had been trained by the on-staff botanists and had proven herself competent at basic testing procedures. He reviewed her work and gave it a nod of approval. "OK. I'll start with pH testing on the opposite end of the plot and meet you in the middle."

"Deal."

They worked in companionable silence for a while before his timer went off. "All right, what do we have? I have 15 minutes to write a report for the good doctor."

Ken graciously ignored her derisive snort and together they reviewed the results they'd logged during their testing. At first, things looked normal, but then Ken pointed at one specific section of the test results. "Look here," he said, pointing at the column with his finger. "What do you see when you look at the pH results together, as a whole?"

She frowned, studying the numbers until she saw the pattern. "It's too alkaline at the edges of the plot, and it only gets worse as we work in toward the center."

Ken nodded. "What was it yesterday?"

She pulled up yesterday's records. "It wasn't monitored yesterday, but the day before it was exactly where it should've been."

Ken harrumphed. "We need to test the soil for contaminants. There are a few things that might have raised the pH that quickly. We need to identify what the culprit is."

She nodded. "I'll get started."

"Thanks. I'll be writing if you need me."

Michelle turned to her monitor and began seeking out tests to identify alkaline agents.

Michelle sat in silence with a colleague for the second time that morning, only this experience was far from the comfortable silence she'd shared with Ken in the isolation lab. Now she sat in one of the visitor's chairs in Dr. Morgan's office, watching the woman read the report Ken had submitted. He had run to the mechanics' building to retrieve a tool for one of the tests they were running, leaving Michelle to enter the lion's den alone when the beast summoned.

With a final tap of her index finger on her desk, Dr. Morgan peered at Michelle over the top of her glasses. "This is all you know?"

Michelle inhaled smoothly through her nose. "At this time. We are conducting further tests as we speak."

"The ones Ken recommends here?"

No, the ones I'll pull out of my ass if you'll give me a moment to stand up first. "Yes, doctor."

Dr. Morgan's thin lips pulled to the side in a look Michelle took to be disappointment. "Very well." She turned back to her monitor and began typing. After a moment, she looked at Michelle again as though mildly surprised to see her there. "You may go."

Michelle bit the inside of her cheek to keep from commenting on the senior scientist's patronizing tone. With another deep breath, her third in 30 seconds, she stood and stuck with the safest response. "Yes, doctor."

She was two steps from the door when the ground began to shake.

The sudden movement caught Michelle off guard. She stumbled into the wall shoulder-first and grabbed onto the door frame to stop herself from falling. She threw open the door and sat in the doorway. Over the sound of the ground rumbling, she faintly heard Dr. Morgan scrambling to shelter under her reinforced desk. Marsquakes weren't unheard of, so the dome, the buildings, even the furniture was built to withstand tectonic movement. Still, Michelle was willing to bet that Bonnie and her team would see more than a few bumps and bruises over the next few hours.

She didn't realize that there was anything unusual about this quake until a warm tingle passed through her body, right to left, like a large heat lamp had crossed over her. Then Dr. Morgan's voice carried thinly over the din. "Did you feel that? A tingling?"

"Yes," Michelle yelled. "What was that?"

"I don't — "

All the noise around her abruptly faded into a heavy

silence that permeated even her own body. Michelle couldn't hear herself breathe, couldn't hear her own heartbeat. The tingling in her body resumed, starting in the pit of her stomach and radiating outward. Her body felt heavy, weighed down. Dr. Morgan's hands popped up from underneath the desk and clawed for purchase as she scrambled up, stumbling to her feet and shouting something Michelle couldn't hear.

Dr. Morgan was glowing blue.

Michelle looked at her own hands to see the same eerie glow surrounding them.

Panic gripped her throat as everything disappeared into a field of white, and she lost consciousness.

Why was the light so bright?

Michelle winced and pinched her eyes more tightly closed as the light above her pierced through her lids and a sharp pain shot through her head. She groaned and tried to bring her hands to her eyes, to cover them, only to discover she couldn't move her arms. They were secured above her head. When she tried to move her legs, she found that they too were secured, spread-eagle, by something cold and hard around each ankle.

Her heart began to pound. Michelle ignored the pain in her head, turned her head to the right, and squinted her eyes open. Dr. Morgan was looking back at her.

The scientist was lying on what looked like a hospital bed without rails, hands locked to the mat above her head by two metal cuffs. Michelle's gaze traveled downward to look at the woman's feet, to see if they were bound like her own, and a lead weight filled her stomach.

Dr. Morgan was naked. Michelle looked down at herself to confirm that she, too, had been stripped of her clothes. The air was warm, the light bright, and most of the room was the same too-bright shade of white.

"Michelle?"

The whisper came from her left. She turned her head that way to see Bonnie lying there in the same predicament. "Bonnie. What..?"

The blonde shook her head. "I don't know. There was the quake, then a tingle, then I don't remember anything until waking up here."

Michelle nodded. "It's the same for me."

"And me." Dr. Morgan added.

"Who's that?" asked a voice belonging to a woman Michelle couldn't see.

Bonnie looked away from Michelle and spoke to someone. The room ended after Dr. Morgan's bed, and on Bonnie's other side was a floor-to-ceiling wall that ran half the length of her bed. Michelle could see another pair of feet on the other side of the wall, but beyond that, nothing.

A door a few meters away from the other side of Dr. Morgan's bed opened with a soft swish and eight figures entered the room. They walked very smoothly, almost gliding. They stood just under two meters tall, with long, thin limbs covered in flowing white robes. Their heads were narrow at the neck, growing in circumference toward a bulbous top, like a misshapen balloon.

Michelle's thoughts slammed to a halt.

They had no faces.

Rather, where their faces ought to have been was a

wrinkled, raisin-like, but otherwise featureless expanse of their lilac-tinged skin.

One of the aliens turned to face the others and began humming. It gestured to the row of women, and the others began humming as well. As they began to hum, some of the wrinkles on their non-faces vibrated. Each strange hum sounded like all the others to Michelle's ears. Something about the sound rubbed her the wrong way, like it wasn't really a hum, or a whisper, or like any sound she'd heard before.

Then she realized. Bonnie hadn't been in the room with her and Dr. Morgan, yet she was here. And, going by the tone of the moans, whispers, and muted chatter, there were other women deeper in the room. But —

Dave. Phil. Where are you? Are you safe? What have they done to you?

The humming group dispersed to various cabinets around the room and collected objects that could have been made of liquid opal by the way they glimmered in the light. They hummed at one another again, then turned as one toward Dr. Morgan's bed.

"Oh, fuck," she spat.

They walk-glided toward her and she began struggling against her bonds, grunting and swearing. Lavender hands reached out from within white robes to touch her bare skin.

Dr. Morgan writhed so hard she was lifting her entire center body off the bed.

One of them stopped Dr. Morgan's protesting movements by grabbing her at the waist and pressing her down onto the flat surface. Another approached her head. He... it?... hovered over her for a moment, then hummed something to his colleagues. Six of the aliens, moving quickly, surrounded her bed and descended on her as one, fingers the color of spring flowers grasping at her body.

Dr. Morgan screamed bloody murder.

Michelle's heart pounded in her throat. She couldn't see what they were doing, she couldn't see past the wall of alien robes to see what was happening, what they were doing to Dr. Morgan.

She wasn't entirely sure she wanted to see.

Dr. Morgan's screams turned into yells, threats, insults, and some startlingly inventive swearing. As abruptly as it had begun, the aliens stepped away from their captive and conferred in a huddle, humming intensely while standing roughly a meter from the end of her bed. Michelle's gaze swept over Dr. Morgan's quivering body. There were no visible cuts or bruises.

But that didn't mean she hadn't been hurt.

"Dr. Morgan."

Nothing but residual trembling answered her.

"*Petra*," Michelle called, her throat tight.

The older woman whipped her head around at the sound of her name. Had she not been bound, Michelle would have been genuinely scared of her. The snarl on her face was nothing less than feral, and the hatred radiating from her eyes struck Michelle dumb for a moment. After a beat, she gathered her wits. "Are you all right?"

"Of course I'm not all right!" Petra exploded. "I'm naked, trussed up like a plucked chicken, poked and prodded and experimented on like a lab rat. *Nothing is all right!*"

Michelle's mouth went dry and she struggled to swallow before she spoke. "What do you mean, experimented on?"

Petra shrieked in fury and writhed in her bonds.

"Petra!" Michelle's voice sharpened in her panic; the

aliens had turned to face her bed. "What do you mean? What did they do to you?!"

The other woman saw the aliens start moving toward Michelle. "Samples, scans, needles," she shouted in a rush.

Then the aliens were towering over Michelle, surrounding her, instruments ready in their hands. She began to hyperventilate, panic taking over her body. When one of the wrinkled aliens lowered a tool that bore a frightening resemblance to an opalescent drill toward her head, Michelle screamed.

"Arensen."

The voice sounded as though it were coming from the other side of a vast canyon, with a gentle wind trying its best to sweep it away. It sounded vaguely familiar, and Michelle had a feeling she herself was the Arensen in question, but she couldn't quite get her thoughts together.

"Arensen, wake up." A thick silence, then, "Wake up now." The voice was hard, demanding.

Should she wake up? She felt awfully heavy. Maybe she could sleep just a little while longer.

"Goddammit, woman, wake up! I need to know you're still with us."

Us? Us who? And was she with them? Why? What was happening?

The sudden memory of the quake, the aliens, the violation of captivity, flooded her all at once and Michelle sat bolt upright in terror, swinging her fists to ward off her attackers.

Only there were no attackers. And her swinging fists meant that there were no more restraints on her arms and legs, only a blanket lying in a rumpled heap on her lap.

Whose blanket was this? Did she have a pillow, too?

Michelle laid back down, pulling the blanket up to her neck, and closed her eyes. No attackers. Blanket. She could go back to sleep, pretend nothing had happened. Maybe it was a dream.

"No!" said the annoying voice. "No, no, no. Open your goddamn eyes and look at me, holy cartwheeling Christ!"

Michelle sluggishly turned her head toward the voice and slowly opened her eyes.

Petra Morgan sat on the edge of her bed, blanket wrapped around her thin body. Her tawny hair was mussed and tangled, giving the illusion of a Huckleberry Finn style straw hat atop her head. "Talk to me. Tell me your name."

Michelle frowned at her. "You were just saying it."

"Jesus. Just — Full name. Birthday. Husband's name."

"What?"

"For the love — just answer the damn questions!" Petra's voice was hard as stone. "Full name, birthday, husband's name. Right now." Petra rubbed her hands over her face and muttered something about ass farmers.

Michelle rolled and fought to prop herself up on her elbows, feeling at least twice as heavy as normal. "Um... Michelle Kay Arensen. 17th of July. David— " She broke off. *Dave. Oh, God, Dave. And Phil!* Fear for them bubbled in her stomach and threated to make her heave.

Petra nodded, satisfied. "Good enough."

The soft patter of Michelle's tears landing on the thin bed underneath her disrupted her already fractured focus. "What?"

"They gave you something," she replied darkly. "You've been out for I don't know how many hours. It sounds like some of us they took blood from, others of us they injected. Different substances, probably, based on how we three reacted." Her gaze swept down their small row of beds.

Michelle turned her head and followed Petra's eyes. Bonnie's bed was empty.

Michelle looked back to her remaining neighbor. "What happened? Where is Bonnie?"

Petra's naturally thin mouth thinned further. "Dead." The single word was blunt, but not unkindly said.

Spots danced in Michelle's vision. *Dead?*

"For Christ's sake, lay back down before you faint."

Michelle followed the good advice and closed her eyes again. "How?" she whispered.

A small pause preceded the answer. "Something they injected her with. Susan Perry died, too. I saw them take her body out."

Susan was a research and records aide with a young son, Seth.

"Whatever they pumped you full of knocked you out cold, but thankfully it didn't kill you. How do you feel?"

Michelle opened her eyes. Petra was scanning their surroundings, examining the door, the walls, and the cabinets with her gaze. She was paler than usual, tension making every plane of her face drawn and taut.

Michelle herself was still too groggy to be tense. Her tongue felt swollen and fuzzy, her throat dry and scratchy. She tried to swallow but couldn't work up enough saliva.

"Thirsty. My head is too heavy."

Petra grunted in reply.

Michelle chewed on her tongue to try to limber it up.

"How are you?"

Petra's pale green eyes darted to hers and held them steadily. After a beat, she said, "They didn't give me anything."

Silence rested between them, broken only by the sniffling and whispering of the other women.

Michelle wanted to join them in their weeping, but her body was too heavy, too awkward, to do anything but lie there, staring at the white ceiling. All she could think of was her family.

Where were they? What were the aliens doing to them? Were they alive? Unharmed? Tied down like she had been? If they'd been hurt, or worse, Michelle didn't know what she would do. Dave and Phil were her world, her anchors. They'd been all that kept her together over the past couple of years. Without them…

She couldn't bear to finish the thought. "Have you seen…" *Anyone I love?* "…anyone else?"

"No."

Was that good or not? Michelle couldn't decide, though the bleakness of the situation inclined her toward 'not'.

Suddenly, a belated realization broke through her brain fog.

She wasn't tied up anymore.

She could move. She could get up and walk away. She had to look for them. She had to find Phil and Dave.

With a groan, Michelle rolled to her side and pushed up to a sitting position. Not caring about the blanket that fell from her shoulders, she lowered herself off the bed and took a couple of wobbly steps.

She ran into something invisible but no less solid for being unseen and lost her balance. Her arms pinwheeled as she stumbled backward, her left hip colliding with the edge of the bed. She grabbed onto the mattress and clumsily collapsed onto the floor with a moan. Cradling her head in her hands, she began to cry with the pain, the body fog, the fear and frustration.

"What, you thought I was still here because I was having fun?"

Oh, piss off, Michelle might have said if she'd had the energy.

"Whoever these bastards are," continued the doctor, "they've figured out how to make some kind of transparent force field."

And there, sitting naked on the floor, trapped by a wall she couldn't even see, afraid for her family, afraid for the other women, afraid for herself, the enormity of the situation began to hit her in full force. She'd been kidnapped by aliens — kidnapped by fucking aliens — who were sufficiently technologically advanced as to have developed stable force fields in addition to whatever gimmick they'd used to take her from the greenhouse's office.

She wasn't getting out of this.

Maybe none of them were.

Michelle didn't feel herself getting cold as she continued sitting there, didn't feel the tears flowing down her cheeks, didn't even feel it when her body and mind started to clear up and return to normal.

All she felt was empty.

4

She lost track of time, sitting there, huddled in the corner with the wall pressing against her side and the foot-tall, empty white box she'd begun using as a bedpan at her back. Phil and Dave were missing. Bonnie and Susan were dead. She was naked and trapped. No matter how she tried, she couldn't make her mind work, couldn't form a coherent thought. What was she supposed to do now?

"You could start by getting your ass back on the bed."

Michelle could barely focus through her swollen eyes. "What?"

Petra sighed from her supine position on the sparse mattress. "You say that a lot. You asked what you were supposed to do. First, get back in bed and cover yourself." She looked over at the woman huddled on the floor. "You've got goosebumps."

Michelle hadn't meant to say anything aloud. Bereft and overwhelmed, she saw no need to get back in bed. Why bother? Her world had been upended. Everyone she cared about was gone, missing, leaving her drifting alone in an endless black void. What did it matter if she had fucking goosebumps?

She continued to sit, unmoving.

"Fine." Petra rolled onto her side, facing away. "Ignore me. But you're only making it easier for them."

Michelle frowned. Making things easier for them? The aliens? A realization began to take shape on the outskirts of her exhausted mind. She was wearing herself out, being hard on herself, when chances were good that her kidnappers were going to break her anyway, all on their own.

Was she inadvertently helping them hurt her? A heat flared in her belly. Dave would never stand for that. Dave would never let her put herself in a position that would end up hurting her. And Phil… would she want Phil to follow the example she was setting now? No, she couldn't let them down this way. She had to think of them. If she were permanently injured or worse, it wouldn't hurt only her, but Dave and Phil, too. She'd be damned if she was going to help her abductors hurt her family.

She reached up and grabbed the edge of the mattress. She was trembling. From cold, weakness, or shock, she didn't know. Pulling herself up took more effort than she'd expected, and when she finally crawled into bed and pulled the blanket over her, damn if it didn't feel like a reward.

She was lying there, nonplussed and unmoving, neither asleep nor awake, when the swish of the door sent a bolt of adrenaline right through her. She jerked upright, clutching the blanket to her chest and staring wide-eyed at the three aliens who had just entered. As before, they hummed together and made their way toward Petra.

Petra sat up, her fists at her sides clenched even more

tightly than her jaw.

This time was different, though. The group of three stopped at the foot of her bed. One tapped a rhythmic sequence into a pearly device. There was a small burst of what sounded like static, though Michelle couldn't tell where it came from exactly, and the other two laid one cube each on Petra's mattress before swiftly backing away. The first one tapped on his apparatus again and the three moved in concert to Michelle's bed.

They repeated the same sequence, placing two cubes on the foot of her bed, then moved on. They passed the empty bed that had been Bonnie's and stopped at the first one on the other side of the wall. It was still occupied by someone Michelle couldn't see.

Michelle scooted cautiously toward the end of her bed. The blocks sitting there weren't large, only three-by-three cubes. One was clear, the other a sort of rust color. She reached for the reddish one, and the moment her fingers brushed its surface, the top popped open to reveal that this cube was also clear. It was the thick gel within it that was red.

"Oh my hell," Petra said. She was hurriedly scooping the red gel into her mouth with two fingers.

Food..?

Michelle sniffed and couldn't smell anything at all, so she took a chance and followed Petra's lead. When the gel landed on her tongue, the texture of it nearly prompted her to spit it back out again. It was like eating play-doh. But the flavor of it…

She swallowed, then looked at the red gel, baffled. "It… it tastes like chicken..?"

Petra barked out a laugh through a mouthful of chicken-gel. "Son of a bitch, it does."

The absurdity of it both insulted her and threatened to make her break out in hysterical cackling. "It tastes like *chicken?*"

"The universe has a truly twisted sense of humor." Petra sucked the last of her gel off of her fingers. "Now, what do you suppose this might be?" she wondered aloud as she reached for the clear cube.

As with Michelle's cube, when Petra touched hers, the top flew open. This time, though, she was greeted with a liquid, a colorless, odorless liquid. Petra slowly raised the cube to her lips and touched the liquid with the tip of her tongue.

"Water. Jesus." Petra gulped hers down, and Michelle was right behind her.

They both froze as the group of three passed in front of them again, silently moving toward the door. As soon as the door swished shut behind them, the buzz of murmuring voices filled the room as Michelle picked up her water cube and began to drink.

One of the voices from the other side of the wall sounded familiar. It was Annabelle Carter, a colleague of Dave's.

Michelle swallowed the last of her water and called out, "Anna! Anna, it's Michelle. Michelle Arensen. Are you —" She broke off abruptly. *None of us are all right.* "Are you injured? Who's with you?" She bit her lip, hoping to hear the most unlikely of names.

"I haven't been able to move my right side since the first time they came, but I'm not in pain. Kate Biship is here with me."

Kate's high-pitched voice drifted across the room. "There's nothing wrong with me."

Michelle's heart sank a little, despite already knowing that Dave wasn't, couldn't be, there. "Petra Morgan and I are over here. No lasting ill effects from whatever it was they did earlier."

"Dr. Morgan," called Anna, "what's going on? What's going to happen to us?"

Petra shook her head, though Michelle was the only one who could see. "I don't know, but we have to be strong. We have to take care of ourselves, stay rested, stay fed and hydrated, and do whatever we can to resist them."

"But…" Kate's small voice trailed off. "*Can* we resist them?"

"Yes," Petra answered without missing a beat. "Can we stop them from doing whatever it is they're going to do? Probably not," she admitted. "But we can sure as hell, each one of us, make them fucking earn it."

As if on cue, the door near Petra's bed slid open and in came four aliens.

"Speak of the devil," she muttered.

Petra leveled a glare at their captors that cut through even Michelle's paralyzing fear. *If looks could kill,* she thought hysterically, *we'd be free to go now.*

The four hummed amongst themselves, then moved in sync past Petra, past Michelle, past the wall that separated her from Anna and Kate, until she lost sight of them. She shivered, and it had nothing to do with feeling cold.

A scream pierced the air; Michelle startled, nearly falling off her bed. She caught herself in time to keep from crashing to the floor as the sounds of struggle filled the room. Rapid-fire sensory impressions assaulted her: shouts, screams, the ever-present terrible white glare, crying, grunting, until finally, there was silence.

Michelle's chin trembled as she held her breath. A soft mechanical hum broke the quiet, and there was more crying. Protests rose on the other side of the wall, muffled cries of dismay from quivering voices, and one weepy name.

"Clara. No, Clara."

The four came back into view, and between them hovered a cot carrying the unconscious form of a woman Michelle knew only by sight, having passed her once or twice in the colony meeting hall. Except for another shudder that tore through her, Michelle remained frozen in place.

Petra did not. She leaped off her bed and pressed herself against the transparent wall that held her in, railing on it with the sides of her fists. "What's happening?! What are you doing?!"

She was entirely ignored. The aliens and the woman Michelle assumed was Clara went through the door to the outside; it swished shut behind them.

Petra paced like a lioness in the narrow space at the side of her bed. "What the fuck?" she mumbled, running an agitated hand through her hair. "What the *fuck*?"

It took all Michelle's courage to make herself move, to make herself ask the question. "Was... was she dead?"

Petra banged on the wall at the head of her bed, before turning around to continue her pacing. "I don't know. If she was when they took her out, she wasn't when they first came in." She ran her hand through her hair again. "What the shitflaming *fuck*?!"

The sounds of weeping from deeper within the room made it impossible for Michelle not to cry. The tears ran down her face and choked her voice. "What's happening?" She hated how tiny, how defeated, she sounded.

Petra just shook her head.

The doors opened again.

Michelle hugged her knees to her chest.

Again, four aliens. Again, the humming and the glide past Petra, past her, past the wall until she couldn't see them anymore. And again, the sounds of struggle, the screaming, the crying, and the awful silence. The mechanical hum ushered in the sight of the four aliens hauling a different woman on the hovering mattress this time, someone Michelle didn't recognize. Nobody called out a name.

A stillness born of despair settled on them all. Even Petra watched in silence as the four kidnappers took the lone, motionless woman out of the room.

Michelle's stomach threatened to vomit up her chicken-gel.

A funereal solemnity filled the room. No one, it seemed, was willing to move, to talk, to break the silence with anything other than a hushed whimpering or muffled weeping. The minutes ticked by as each of the women sat with her own fear.

Then the doors opened once more.

Oh dear God in heaven.

The four. The humming. The synchronized march.

Only this time, when they stopped, Michelle could still see them.

Anna.

"NO!" Kate screamed. "No! Let go of her! Leave her alone! *Leave her alone!*"

Anna murmured something, and Kate began sobbing. Another minute or so, and in between Kate's gasping sobs, the low mechanical hum started up for the third time.

And Michelle watched, horrorbound, as they took an unmoving Anna from the room.

Time passed, who knew how much, and the thick, heavy silence smothered everyone in the room.

Kate's broken, muffled wailing eventually subsided. Michelle knew she should be irate, or indignant, or terrified, or something, but she wasn't. She just wasn't. She couldn't feel anything. She was going to be picked off, exterminated, executed, by nobody knew who for nobody knew what reason, and there was nothing she could do about it.

She was never getting out of here. Just like Anna, and Clara, and the other woman, Michelle would be taken out of this horrific white room, still and silent on a stretcher.

Petra continued to pace. Michelle noticed the bruises that were forming on the older woman's midsection, on her legs and arms, from where the aliens held her down earlier. The lithe purple bastards were stronger than they looked. "Petra."

The woman stopped her movement. Dark circles had taken up residence under her eyes. "What?"

Even Petra's fire was subdued. Her fury had burned itself out into a smoldering resentment.

It took Michelle a moment to gather the right words. "I'm not making it out of here."

Petra turned away. "Shut up, Arensen."

"But if you do," Michelle continued, determined to have her say, "and you see Dave and Phil again, will you tell them —"

"Shut up!" Petra whirled on her, stabbing a finger in her direction. "I'm not telling anyone shit."

" — I loved them. I loved them more than anything. Not even death will change that. And tell Phil —" Michelle choked on a sob. "Tell Phil I'm sorry. I didn't want to leave."

The accusatory finger slowly drifted down to its owner's side. All the anger drained out of Petra's face, leaving only a sorrow that aged her a decade. "I'm not telling anyone shit," she repeated, but the whisper held none of the vigor of her earlier vow.

Michelle rested her face on her forearms and was grateful for the curtain of dark hair that fell forward and hid her from this harsh new world.

5

The light in the narrow white room never dimmed, so Michelle had no idea how many days had passed. Body hair grew and the odor in the room was becoming increasingly pungent. Michelle watched Petra's hair grow greasy and dank.

Sleeping for any extended period of time was next to impossible. A perpetual, raw exhaustion dogged her every waking moment. She was tired of chicken-gel but too hungry not to eat it when it too infrequently arrived.

She'd eaten it eleven times now.

The boredom was a form of torture in and of itself. Michelle spent most of her time thinking about her family. Were they safe? Had they been taken? Were they still on Mars? She liked to imagine they were still at home, going about their day-to-day. Were they worried? Were they sleeping well? Taking care of themselves? She knew that Dave would take care of Phil, as much as Phil would let him. But the man she had married, the man who had been her rock, her anchor, who had been there for her in all the good and bad since they were teenagers… he would be worried sick. Heartbroken. He would take care of Phil, but would he take care of himself? Would he be all right?

And Phil. God, it tore her up to think of Phil by himself, the last of the Arensens. Would he be able to move past this? He'd already overcome so much. She was the last remaining tie he'd had to his history, his last living blood relative. Now she would be the last in a line of tragedies he'd have to endure. She hoped he could.

She hoped they both would.

Then she would inevitably wonder if she, herself, would endure. Of course she wouldn't, her reason told her. She didn't expect to live through this, yet at the same time, no matter how she tried, she couldn't let go of the hope of seeing Phil and Dave again. Clinging to them, to the thought of them, both gave her strength and tortured her. She wondered if the other women felt the same conflict.

There were only four of them left. Kate was the only one on the other side of Michelle's wall, but Kate said there was another wall beside the empty bed where Susan originally lay. On the other side of it was a woman named Ingrid, who had worked in waste recycling.

The three of them sometimes passed the time playing stupid car-trip style games. 'I Spy' had been a bust, since every-fucking-thing was white, so they moved onto a storytelling game. One of them would start a story, and they'd take turns saying one sentence each. The next person had to build on what had happened before.

No matter how they started, their stories always ended with four women killing a group of faceless kidnappers with varying degrees of cunning or violence. It was predictable, but marginally satisfying.

Petra never played. She never even spoke. Petra sat quietly on her bed, staring at nothing. She ate when they brought gel, drank when they brought water, relieved herself once in a while, then went right back to her statue-like sitting. Occasionally, she showed a little more life and, in the skinny space between the edge of her mattress and the invisible wall, did push-ups, sit-ups, and lunges.

But mostly, Petra sat.

"Kate?" Ingrid's voice was soft, in case Kate was asleep, or just wanted to be left alone. The invisible force that confined them all ended at the foot of their beds, so between the invisible walls and the visible ones, they could talk to each other, but they couldn't see any part of anyone not within their own enclosure.

"Hm?"

"What was your favorite dessert?"

This was another game they played: What Was Your Favorite? At first, thinking of things they enjoyed was painful, the contrast between the familiarity and happiness of Before versus the humiliation and desperation of Now was too new. Recently, though, it had changed from something hurtful to something comforting.

Michelle didn't like to think about what that meant.

"Ice cream. Chocolate ice cream." Kate heaved a long sigh. "What was yours?"

"Dark chocolate layer cake with fluffy whipped cream icing." Michelle could hear the dreamy smile on Ingrid's face as she spoke.

"Michelle? What was yours?" Kate looped her into the game.

"Boston Cream Pie. Every time. Anytime."

Boston Cream Pie: better than chicken-gel. She almost snorted at herself. Clearly, there were reasons she hadn't gone into advertising.

"Apple crisp."

Michelle turned her head toward the croaking voice she hadn't heard in days. Petra blinked and met her gaze.

Michelle smiled softly. "Petra's a fan of apple crisp," she called to the others.

A ghost of a smile touched the corners of Petra's mouth.

When the aliens came back, Michelle knew instantly that something bad was about to happen. She wasn't hungry yet, and they never came with the chicken-gel before she was well into hunger.

She forgot to breathe as they huddled and hummed. There were four of them. It only took three to distribute food and water.

Four aliens signaled a death march.

They turned and began walking. Past Petra. Past her.

Past Kate.

Ingrid began to scream. Kate shouted her name.

The sounds of the scuffle broke through Petra's ennui. She exploded off her bed, pounding her fists into the clear wall. "Give 'em hell, Ingrid! Fight them! Fight, goddamn it!"

The horror of it made Michelle squeeze her eyes shut and clamp her hands over her ears, and none of it helped at all.

Another few moments of the sounds of struggle tortured her before the god-awful silence returned, save for a low mechanical whirring. Then Kate moaned, "Oh, Ingrid, no…"

The aliens took Ingrid away, past Michelle, past Petra, and through the door.

The loss was different this time. They'd had so much time together, had conversations, told stories, shared a ridiculous and abominable experience. Ingrid had become more than 'the woman who worked down the road' and had become her sister in tragedy.

Michelle would never hear Ingrid's voice again. The loss was more than frightening, more than appalling. This time, it was gutting.

Then she heard the swish of the door again.

With her heart in her throat, she was helpless to look away as the same damn four did their huddle and hum routine. She couldn't look away as they walked past Petra.

Past her.

Kate's name burst from Michelle's mouth unwillingly, desperately.

Kate did not scream. "Tell George he was the love of my life! Tell my girls that I loved them and they —" Her voice trailed off on a soft groan.

"Kate!"

Silence.

After a few eternal moments, Kate's body went by and, like the others before her, left the room on the hovering stretcher.

The silence stretched on as Michelle and Petra waited for the aliens to come back. Michelle stayed awake, waiting, waiting for them to return, waiting for her turn to die, for what seemed like days. When she finally couldn't keep her eyes open any longer, she curled into the fetal position, covered her head with her blanket, and willed her consciousness to slide into oblivion, the only refuge available to her.

When the swish of the door woke her with a start, Michelle's entire body locked up. She was lying on her side, facing away from the door. Her ears strained to pick up clues. They never made any noise when they walked, so she listened for the hum of their conversation.

Nothing.

There was a slight movement at the foot of her bed and she jumped away from it, cowering against the wall behind her, pulling her blanket tightly to her.

Three aliens glided away without a pause, leaving the room as quietly as they'd entered it.

The usual food and water cubes sat at the foot of her bed.

Michelle was ravenous but found that she couldn't eat. Revulsion filled her. She didn't want to touch it, to scoop out the goop with her fingers and suck it off like a child with some perverted kind of caramel all over her hands. She didn't want to taste the not-chicken, didn't want to swallow another mouthful of whatever they'd been eating for the past... weeks? A month? Petra's hair was visibly longer than it had been when Kate had been taken away. It *had* to have been at least a month now, with just Michelle and Petra and their faceless humming abductors.

"Shit." Petra, who was still lying down, sat up and reached for her food cube. The lid popped open like usual, and she sat there, just looking at it. "Do you remember," she finally said, "when it was kind of funny that this tasted like chicken?"

Michelle did.

Petra shook her head. "Shit," she said again, and with a resigned sigh, dug her first two fingers in.

Michelle did not.

"You have to eat, Arensen." She paused as she sucked her fingers clean. "You have to keep your strength up."

"Why?"

Petra raised an eyebrow at her. "What?"

"Why?" she repeated, though with no less listlessness than the first time. "Why should I keep my strength up? They're going to do what they want with us, no matter what we do in the meantime. Why should I make it harder on myself by fighting the inevitable?"

The scientist shrugged. "Fine. Whatever. Give up."

Frustrated, Michelle pushed herself up to sitting. "There is no shame, Petra, *none*, in quitting when you have good reason." She pointed to the rest of the room, where there had been other women, just like them. "There are seven reasons to give up, right there."

"Are you fucking kidding me?" Petra threw her chicken cube aside. "Those are seven reasons to keep trying to screw these bastards. If we give up, just throw our lives away, how does that honor them? How does that respect their memories? Seriously, Arensen," she ranted, beginning to pace, "do you think any *one* of them wouldn't have given anything she could've to still be here? To have had one more day, or week, or decade, or however fucking long we've been here, just the two of us? And you want to throw it away? Well, fuck those faceless bastards, and fuck you, too."

"Honor their memories?" Michelle was incredulous. "Who the hell knows whether we're honoring them or not? What does it matter?"

Petra regarded her with almost palpable disdain. "It matters because it's the right thing to do, whether 'anyone knows' about it or not." She shook her head and turned away. "Grow a spine already. You have two more reasons to fight than I do, and you're the one who's ready to stop swinging."

Petra's accusation knocked the wind out of her. What did Phil and Dave have to do with this? What did they have to do with her now? If they knew what she was going through, they would understand her willingness to give up, to let it end. *They **would** understand,* she insisted to herself.

Like you understood when Dad gave up? countered another voice within her. *Will Phil understand if you give up the same way? Will Dave?*

"Oh. Oh God," she whispered, then collapsed into broken weeping.

When they finally came for her, she was ready.

She knew it was futile. She knew that in the end, she was going out that door on a stretcher. But she also knew that not making them fight for it, succumbing to the exhaustion and the strain and the fear and the hopelessness and the torture of everything her abductors had subjected her to was not what Dave or Phil would want for her.

Michelle knew she was going to lose this battle, but she was going to show up for it, anyway.

When the doors swished open and Michelle counted four aliens and no food cubes, she knew. Out of the corner of her eye, she saw Petra tense.

For a moment that lasted for hours, nobody moved. Then the four hummed and began their walk.

Past Petra.

Michelle stood up on her bed and clenched her fists.

The aliens paused. After a quick hum session, they advanced again.

When the first of the lilac hands reached for her, she kicked. The being was fast, and strong, and grabbed her ankle on the first try, pulling her off balance. She stumbled into him, falling off the bed, breaking her fall on his surprisingly pillowy body. They rolled, and when they came to a halt, the alien was on top of her and her head hurt from where she hit it on Petra's bedframe.

They'd rolled into Petra's space.

The force field was down.

Petra jumped off the bed with a feral howl and pulled the alien off Michelle. Relieved of the weight, Michelle scrambled to her feet, only to find herself wobbly and dizzy from the blow to her head. More lavender hands came for her and she yelled, kicked, punched, clawed and scratched at whatever alien body part got close enough.

Amid the chaos, one of them squealed, a high-pitched sound that hurt Michelle's ears, a noise she'd never heard them make before.

"You hurt it!" Petra shouted from her own fight. "You goddamn hurt it!"

Michelle had no idea which one it was that she'd hurt, so she swung and kicked and did as much damage as she could to both of them. They had divided into two teams of two each, one team on her, the other on Petra.

Two on one wasn't terrible odds.

Michelle's heart clenched painfully in a feeling she would

have recognized in any other setting as hope.

She screamed and swung harder, kicked faster.

Then suddenly, the odds changed as the two beings trying to subdue her grew to four, then to six.

"No!" Petra shouted, her voice strained. "No! No!"

A sharp pinch bit the side of Michelle's neck, and the world went black.

6

Eighty years later

Samou had never discovered a new species before.

But as he continued to examine the two cylinders now standing in a cargo bay of the patrol cruiser Yukesi, kept in the cryogenic state in which they'd been found, he hoped that was about to change. The doctor with a lifetime of experience had never seen anything like the creatures frozen in the antiquated canisters in front of him.

There were two of the odd little things. And little they were, indeed: just over half his height and extremely petite. Unless their frame belied an unexpected strength, they must be quite fragile. They had the same basic bipedal, bilateral structure of his own people, though they were missing a pair of arms. The problem, if it was, in fact, a problem, was their faces.

They were hideous, at least by Vinyi standards. Their

hue was all wrong, lacking even a hint of gray. They had not a single facial tentacle. The creatures' protruding ears, if they were ears, were marked by giant flaps of skin on either side of their heads. Samou preferred the smooth profiles of his own species' heads, with simple, elegant membranes covering the ear canals. And their mouths... Samou pondered. *They could not use such small mouths to eat, could they? Then again, they themselves are quite small.* As for the bulge in the center of their face, he had not even a guess as to what *that* was supposed to be, but it was definitely not some kind of displaced tusk. These beings were so far beyond ugly they turned the corner to endearing, like a pet that couldn't help how homely it was.

Samou shook his head in wonder.

Captain Hegoh had ordered them brought aboard after the Chief Engineer's report. The Yukesi had discovered the derelict vessel floating harmlessly through the edges of their space. Its markings were unfamiliar, and with no pressing mission beyond their routine patrol run, Hegoh sent Suji over to investigate. Suji thought maybe they could glean some spare parts, or at a minimum, have a few moments of fun looking over old technology.

Instead of a bundle of spare nuts and bolts, though, *this* was what Suji had brought back with him. New creatures. Maybe dead creatures, but Samou's scans led him to believe that they were more likely in-stasis rather than irredeemably in the arms of the afterlife.

The door opened behind Samou, and a moment later, the Chief Engineer stood at the doctor's side. Suji was young, but brave and keen. Samou rather liked him.

"What are they, Sam?" Suji's question was eager, and his voice awed.

Samou raised two of his facial tentacles in a shrug. "I do not yet know." He tore his gaze away from the creatures and looked at his colleague. "But I hope the captain will allow me to find out."

Suji hummed low in his throat. "Do you think they're sentient?" He peered at the creatures through the glass of their containers. "They're very... unaesthetic."

Samou grunted in assent. "Yet their overall anatomical appearance presents sufficient similarities to our own that an attempt to determine at least their intelligence, if not sapience, would not be unreasonable."

"To a scientist."

Samou inclined his head in Suji's direction. "To a scientist."

"Which the captain is not."

"Neither is he uneducated nor crude," Samou reproached. "While science is more of an academic pursuit than an interest to him, Captain Hegoh is *not* ignorant."

"That is not what I was suggesting," rejoined Suji. "I was merely pointing out that sometimes, science requires more patience than the captain has the luxury of permitting us."

Samou grudgingly conceded the point.

"And what is it I will need patience for?"

Suji and Samou stood at attention and turned to salute their commanding officer as he and their chief research scientist, Rimoli, entered the room. Hegoh waved them off. "At ease." His eyes focused on the icy metal containers. "Well? What do you think?" he asked Samou.

"Initial exams indicate that the two subjects are in a sort of cryogenic stasis but are otherwise in good health. Scans have not revealed any injuries or illnesses that would have caused these two to have died or required time-suspended care."

Hegoh frowned. "What are you saying? They were frozen alive for no reason?"

Rimoli scoffed. "That makes no sense. Subzero preservation is a costly effort; it's hardly done at random, especially with equipment this old. There must be something you're missing, or more likely, misunderstanding," he sniped before turning his attention to the captain. "Let me and my team run our own examinations, Captain. We'll find the answers you seek."

"Your 'examinations' are nothing more than autopsies," spat Samou. "Nobody has seen anything like these creatures before! This is a tremendous discovery and should be handled with care and respect. These may be sentient being still capable of life. If they were frozen alive, they may yet be capable of returning to life. They should be given the opportunity to do so."

"And if they're criminals and you unleash them on the ship?"

Suji snorted. "My niece has dolls their size. Do you truly think that Lihku and his forces would not be able to subdue two mischievous marionettes?"

Hegoh lifted the tentacle under his left tusk in amusement. "Lihku would challenge you to an honor duel if he knew you even implied such a thing, Rimoli."

The scientist shifted his weight from foot to foot. "I did not."

"Doctor, ensure beyond doubt that they carry no pathogens, or anything else, that could harm the crew," ordered Hegoh. "If they are clean, you may proceed with your attempt to revive them." He turned to Rimoli. "If the doctor's reanimation attempts fail, the remains will be yours to do with as you please. Suji, with me."

The two Vinyi saluted the captain, and he and Suji left the cargo bay.

The research scientist looked the creatures over. "You know they are too fragile to survive a reanimation attempt."

Samou feared it was true. "Still, it is the ethical thing to make the attempt."

Rimoli rolled his middle two tentacles in disdain before turning and walking away. "Do what you will, I'll see them in my lab, doctor, sooner or later."

After the doors closed behind him, Samou leaned down to gaze into the pathetic, homely faces of the mysterious creatures and laid his lower right hand on the glass of the nearest one. "I will do my best for you, little ones, I give you my word."

"Mebeku," called Samou, "are the doors sealed?"

"Yes, doctor."

"Very well." Samou took a deep breath. "Let us begin."

Samou and his team were about to do what no Vinyi had done before: reanimate an undiscovered species. Reanimation wasn't unheard of in extreme medical cases, but it carried a high degree of risk and a low rate of success for his own species; performing the procedure on an unknown lifeform was barely better than gambling. The doctor knew he and his team could not possibly have thought of and mitigated all the risks involved, but they had been meticulous in their planning and zealous in their scans of the beings. Samou could not think of even a single other thing that needed to be done before they attempted to thaw this first of the two exotic creatures.

The plan was to bring it out of stasis and into a controlled unconscious state. This would allow Samou to conduct enough tests to determine how best to care for the creature's daily needs before bringing it to full consciousness.

Timing was everything. He had to balance the warming of the subject's environment with the reversal of the chemical agents that had preserved its cells against the tissue-destroying freeze of stasis. His analysis indicated that the preservative needed to be neutralized in stages, concurrently with a warming environment.

The creature was lying on an operating table, with Samou, his aide Mebeku, and two other support personnel, surrounding it. The temperature of the room had been lowered to the same -270 degrees *Enhkij* of the space in which the canisters had been found. Vinyi were tough, but that was far beyond what even they could withstand; the medical team was protected by environmental suits. The bulk of the gloves would make any delicate work slightly more challenging, but Samou had performed delicate work in them before.

He turned his attention to the monitor reporting the subject's vitals. Nothing.

"Warm the room one degree per second."

"Yes, doctor."

Five seconds passed. Ten. Twenty.

Samou checked the temperature. -250 degrees *E*.

"Syringe 1."

Mebeku handed him the first of seven prepared syringes. Every 37 seconds, Samou would inject a neutralizing solution as the air warmed. Once the room warmed up to 0 degrees, he would begin stimulating the subject's vital organs, bringing it back to a state of life. By the time the room got back to a normal 30 degrees, the subject would be fully alive, if unconscious. The entire procedure would take just less than five minutes.

If everything went according to plan.

Thirty-five seconds.

He pressed the syringe's pressure injectors to the subject's skin.

Two. One.

"Injecting first solution."

Samou remained focused on the vitals monitor.

"Chemical preservative reacting as expected," Mebeku informed him.

Samou's heart pounded. "Syringe 2."

Seventy-five seconds. -195 degrees.

Four. Three. Two. One.

"Injecting second solution."

Samou held his breath.

"The preservative is reacting as expected." Mebeku's tentacles lifted in excitement.

Samou exhaled.

The process repeated four more times. Then they got to the last syringe.

This part would be a little trickier. Samou would have to move quickly. The last syringe needed to be administered at 260 seconds, and the organ stimulant precisely ten seconds after that.

250 seconds. -20 degrees.

"Ready the last syringe and the organ stimulant."

"Ready and waiting for you, doctor."

Samou took the preservative-neutralizer in his upper

hands and the organ stimulant in his lower ones.

Three. Two. One.

He pressed the injectors to the now pliable skin of the creature.

A beat, then: "Preservative has been cleared from subject's system."

A thrill of hope beat its wings against Samou's ribcage.

The systemic organ stimulant was a combination of injection and external invigoration. The injection would make the system receptive to the signal from the external impulse generator. In a flurry of activity, the medical support staff removed the deep stasis and preservative monitors and set up the impulse machine over the creature's body. They attached the contact nodes and stepped back.

Samou readied the stimulant injection and queried Mebeku with his gaze.

Mebeku raised his inner four tentacles halfway in confirmation.

Samou pressed the injectors to the creature's neck while Mebeku operated the stimulus device.

A ping and a hum filled the room. Samou's eyes were glued to the vitals monitor.

Nothing.

"Again," he said.

Another ping and a hum.

280 seconds. 10 degrees.

Still nothing.

"Again." His every muscle was tense. He deliberately relaxed his grip on the now empty syringe.

290 seconds. 20 degrees.

A blip.

Samou froze, hyperfocused on the readout, as a murmur

arose among the staff.

They had brain activity.

"Again. We need more, and a heartbeat."

The ping-and-hum sounded once more, and there they were. More blips, more beautiful, wonderful, exhilarating blips. Brain waves. Heartbeat. Breathing.

Samou's thrill of hope faltered as the creature began to spasm and jerk.

300 seconds. 30 degrees.

Samou frantically checked his readouts. Breathing. It wasn't breathing. "Keep it still! Don't let it hurt itself!"

The spasms grew faster, more insistent. Many restraining hands gently stilled the small body, to keep the being safe from itself. A choking sound emerged from the tiny beast's throat.

"Choking? Why is it choking?!"

Confused voices shouted over each other as the team scrambled to figure out what was wrong. The airway was unobstructed but the lungs weren't working. There was no structural damage, no scar tissue. *Why won't it breathe?!*

The creature stopped fighting against the hands restraining it. It vitals readout was blank, except…

Brain waves. It still had brain activity.

"Again, Mebeku! Again!"

The machine pinged and hummed as Samou injected another dose of stimulant. *Come on, little one.*

No reaction from the small being. The vitals monitor went blank. Brain activity disappeared.

With all his might, Samou wanted to call for the stimulant again. But though his heart wished differently, the facts were staring him in the face.

This innocent being had come alive for a moment. Then

he had killed it.

"What happened?"

Rimoli handed his displeased captain his report. "The doctor and I have reached similar conclusions. The creature suffocated."

Suji looked sharply at the doctor. "Suffocated? In the medbay? How?"

Samou's tentacles drooped as he relayed the shared conclusion of both his study and Rimoli's autopsy. "The variations in atmospheric composition are well within tolerance. Within *Vinyi* tolerance," he corrected. "The creature's lungs are very similar to ours in structure; I had no reason to believe they would not be so in function, as well. It did not occur to me that they were incapable of simple environmental adaptation."

Suji held up a hand. "So, in layman's terms, doctor, it couldn't breathe our air?"

Samou lifted four tentacles halfway in assent. "The creatures require an atmosphere of mostly nitrogen, with some oxygen, and a touch of argon."

Hegoh huffed. "Those gases are in our air."

"They are," confirmed Rimoli, "but not in the right proportions. Also, our air contains significant amounts of other gases which are toxic to the creatures."

"Can we not compensate for that?" Suji was surprised and a little frustrated. He was excited about discovering a new species, particularly since he, himself, had been the one to find their canisters aboard the derelict vessel.

"Now that we know of their need," Samou said, "we can. I can inject stage 44 nanobots into the lung tissue of the remaining subject at the appropriate stage of reanimation to allow it to process our atmosphere as efficiently as though it were its own." The doctor hung his head. "This oversight, and the death of a creature that could have lived, are entirely my responsibility."

Hegoh grunted. "Was this the only error? If this is corrected, can you guarantee that the other one will survive reanimation?"

Rimoli, unseen by Hegoh, smirked as he curled a tentacle in the doctor's direction.

"No," Samou admitted. "There are no guarantees in this. But I am confident that, had these nanobots been injected at the proper time during Subject 1's procedure, it would almost certainly be alive now."

Suji looked at Hegoh. "That's as close to a guarantee as could be expected."

Hegoh hummed.

"And what is the alternative?" Suji continued. "Immediately assume the reanimation of Subject 2 will fail and go straight to autopsy in the research lab?" Suji shrugged. "Should the procedure fail again, Rimoli will end up with the creature's body, regardless."

"The reanimation procedure isn't cheap, Suji. The cost of resources is not insignificant." Hegoh turned to his first officer. "Lihku? You've been quiet. What are your thoughts on this?"

Lihku sighed heavily. "Captain, I am not a man of thick books and great learning, but it seems to me that, if the beast has a chance at surviving, we ought to try it. Samou, who's yet to steer me wrong managing my own wellbeing, knows what went wrong last time and is confident it'll work this time." He shrugged a mighty shoulder. "Sending the tiny thing off to be cut apart without giving it a chance to reclaim its life seems awfully similar to a summary execution without a fair trial."

Hegoh stroked his tentacles thoughtfully. "Indeed." After another few moments, he came to a decision. "All right, doctor. You get one more try."

7

Samou surveyed the frozen figure lying on the medtable through the clear mask of his environmental suit. After the first failed attempt, he was implementing some changes to the process for this little one, this last attempt to bring a new species back to life.

The crux of all the adjustments was, of course, the nanobots. Samou would introduce the microscopic technology into the creature's lungs at the four-minute mark, immediately following the sixth injection. At this stage, the cells would be sufficiently pliable for the bots to make the necessary changes to the small creature's lungs, enabling them to pull the gases they needed from the air. The bots would take roughly three minutes to do their work, so the temperature would have to be held steady and all progress temporarily suspended during until the bots' changes were complete.

Samou had spent much time in meditation the night before, centering himself in the focused mindset he would need to face this challenge today, but more than anything, seeking the forgiveness of the spirit he had unwittingly ushered into the After. The creature had been entirely dependent on him, and he had failed it. It had been *thisclose* to being alive, and his shortsightedness had cut off its chance.

He would not fail the second creature.

He took in the ugly face, the frail limbs, and he steeled himself for the next seven minutes.

A sense of *hisega* swept over him as he repeated the procedure from two days prior.

"Mebeku," called Samou, "are the doors sealed?"

"Yes, doctor."

"Very well." The doctor rolled his shoulders. "We begin. Confirm room temperature."

"Room temperature confirmed at -270 degrees." Mebeku's voice was as clear within Samou's suit as if the junior doctor were standing right beside him.

Samou hummed and viewed the vitals monitor. Nothing, just as expected. Just as before.

"Warm the room one degree per second."

"Yes, doctor."

The seconds ticked by as before, but the weight of each tick, the knowledge of what depended on it, echoed in Samou's head. Would this defenseless entity survive, or would he have two kills to his name in three days?

Mebeku's voice cut into his thoughts. "-250 degrees in five seconds."

"Syringe 1." Samou held out his top right hand.

Three. Two. One.

"Injecting first solution."

The vitals monitor remained still.

"Chemical preservative reacting as expected," Mebeku

said.

Samou forced himself to remain calm. "Syringe 2."

Seventy-five more seconds. -195 degrees.

Four. Three. Two. One.

"Injecting second solution."

Samou waited.

"The preservative is reacting as expected."

Fight for it, small one. Fight to have your life back.

The seconds continued to tick by, one by one.

"-150 degrees in five seconds."

The third syringe was injected without a problem, as were the fourth and fifth. As Samou pulled the fifth syringe away from the subject's neck, he ordered, "Prepare the bots."

"Yes, doctor."

Samou injected the sixth syringe of chemical preservative reversal agent and heard the sounds of shuffling as his team readied for the next phase of the procedure. A tray with the nanobot injectors stood ready at his lower left elbow.

"-30 degrees," announced Mebeku.

"Hold temperature," commanded Samou, reaching for the bot injectors with his left underhand.

"Temperature holding steady at -30 degrees."

Holding the first vial of bots in one hand, he trailed his fingers along his patient's right ribs from the bottom. At the gap above the seventh, Samou pressed the injector against the chilled skin, aiming slightly upward. A long, narrow implant skewer pierced the chest wall and stopped just short of the bronchial tubes. He released the bots.

Then he walked briskly around to the other side and repeated the process. With the implantation complete, he stood stock still, his eyes glued to the monitor they were using to track the bots' progress.

One minute elapsed. Samou could see the bots moving about in the small lungs, but couldn't yet see if any structural changes had been initiated or if the technology was still trying to gain its foothold.

Two minutes. If the bots couldn't make the changes they needed to make in three minutes, then his solution was a failure and the life of this innocent was, as was its companion's, on his conscience.

There! The first of the tracking trails changed on the monitor from green to blue in the right lung. Green was the bots' path; blue indicated physiological changes in progress. The blue paths in the right lung grew.

Samou watched the left lung anxiously.

It rewarded him with the appearance of some small blue streaks.

Samou exhaled heavily and made eye contact with Mebeku.

It was going to work.

It has to work.

Two minutes fifty seconds. Almost all blue. *Just a little more…*

Three minutes. There was a faint path of green left at the top of the left lung. Samou frowned. The tiny lungs were 95% blue. Would that be enough for the creature to survive? He let the bots carry on.

"Doctor, three minutes have elapsed."

"I am aware," he snapped. *Come on, just a little bit more!*

At three minutes, twelve seconds, all the paths glowed blue.

Samou let out a triumphant shout. "Resume temperature increase."

"Resuming."

Samou's heart raced.

"-10 degrees in five seconds."

"Mebeku, you beautiful beast, give me that last syringe."

The syringe appeared in his hand. Samou didn't even notice the sweat that was beginning to accumulate in his EV suit.

"Injecting last syringe." The skin on the creature's neck was pliable, giving way easily now.

Samou looked at his patient with a suspended sense of wonder.

"Preservative has been cleared from subject's system."

A tension swept over the medical party. This was the moment of truth. Here was where the sword would meet the shield.

"Organ stimulant."

Samou readied himself with the injection. He didn't even have to raise his gaze to his aide. "The machine is ready, doctor."

He pushed the stimulant into the being's system and waved a tentacle at Mebeku.

The familiar ping and hum echoed in the room.

Nothing happened on the vitals monitor.

"10 degrees."

"Again," ordered Samou roughly.

Ping. Hum.

Nothing.

"Again!"

Ping. Hum.

Blip.

Samou's eyes greedily consumed the readout on the vitals screen. Brain activity. They had brain activity, but nothing else.

"A —" The heart began to beat, cutting off Samou's order. To his utter delight, the little one's lungs inflated, deflated, and inflated again.

"20 degrees."

Samou's hope grew on pace with the vitals on screen, stronger by the second. He placed a device on the being's forehead, ensuring that the brain waves leading to full awareness would be suppressed while allowing the full functioning of all its other systems.

"30 degrees."

Room standard temperature. He studied his patient and reviewed all the data again. All its vitals were steady.

This one is going to make it.

Samou smiled at Mebeku. His aide appeared as stunned as he himself was elated.

"We did it, Mebeku." Samou looked proudly at his newest patient. "It's alive."

8

The sensations hit her gently, giving her time and space between each one.

Warmth.

Softness.

Comfort.

Peace.

She exhaled gently, not having been aware of inhaling, and the softest of smiles appeared on her lips. She inhaled deeply; the air smelled of vanilla.

Content, and relieved to her very soul, though she could not have explained why, Michelle rolled onto her side, snuggled her face into the cushy pillow, pulled the blanket up around her shoulders, and drifted back into a deep, restful sleep.

FOUND

When Michelle awoke, the first thing she noticed was how refreshed she felt. She couldn't remember the last time she'd awakened and not wished she'd had just a little longer to sleep. But this morning, she felt *good*.

She rolled to her left and reached out for Dave, wondering if they had time to take advantage of this energy she felt. Her searching hand found nothing but empty bed. A faint whisper from the back of her mind snaked through her sleep-induced fog.

Dave is gone.

Her pulse picked up as she tried to push away the last of the grogginess. Wait, what? Gone where? For how long? And why couldn't she remember?

Frowning, with some of this lovely energy beginning to twist into a panicky dread, Michelle opened her eyes.

A light from above illuminated a warm beige wall not far from the edge of the bed. She ran her hand over the sheet, not silk but smooth and cream-colored and smelling faintly of vanilla.

This wasn't their bed.

Where was she? Where was Dave? Michelle rolled from her side onto her back to go find her husband and instead found herself looking directly into the eyes of a monster.

She screamed and scrambled up to sitting, her back pressing into the wall and her scrabbling feet pushing the sheet down the bed as she tried to back away. Impressions flew through her mind.

Gray skin. Tentacles. Tusks. Black eyes. Huge.

Her hand landed on her pillow; she grabbed it and swung it at the beast with a primal shriek.

It dodged and silently continued to stare at her.

Michelle pulled the pillow into her chest and trembled, whimpering.

The monster took a step back and held up its hands, all four of them, palms facing her. Its fingers had no knuckles.

She eyed it warily, panting, her heart threatening to burst from her chest.

What the hell what the hell whatthehell…?

It took another silent step back, then sat down on a chair at the foot of her bed.

It stared at her in still silence for a long time.

The monster's bizarre appearance was arresting. It had the skin of a seal with the curved tusks of an elephant. Instead of a snout or whiskers in between its ivory protrusions, it had tentacles, at least eight of them. The ones in the middle were the longest; they grew progressively shorter as they approached the tusks. Its eyes were small black marbles in its head.

And it was huge. Its upper body alone was at least five times the size of her own.

Frantically, Michelle looked around. *Everything* was huge. Mahogany colored cabinets big enough for her to fit into if she crouched lined the walls. Shiny, light brown countertops underneath them rested at shoulder height. And the door leading from the room was at least twelve feet high.

When she cautiously peered over the edge of the mattress, keeping one eye on the monster, the bed she was in, and all the beds in the room just like it, was twice as high, twice as big, as anything Michelle had ever slept in. The beast's hands, even the smaller set, were nearly as large as her head. And its head, its torso, its muscles, its *everything* utterly dwarfed her.

An army of questions rampaged through her mind.

Where was her family? Where was *she*? Who and what was this thing at the end of her bed? But most importantly...

"What the hell is going on?!" she exploded, then winced at the sound of her own scratchy voice. Michelle pressed further back into the wall. Shouting a creature that could end her in an instant may not have been the smartest approach.

For its part, the monster merely lifted the two tentacles under its tusks until their curve paralleled that of its ivory. Michelle watched the beast a moment longer, then it raised its hands slightly higher.

A noise came from underneath the tentacles that sounded like gently rolling thunder, if thunder could speak.

"Nu hi qeki henu."

Michelle gaped. Were those words? Was it *talking* to her?

The giant lowered its hands. The rumble came from it again. *"Nu hi qeki henu."*

She stared unblinking and forgot to breathe. The thing was trying to *communicate* with her. *Oh my God. The first time extraterrestrial life — for that's what this beast had to be — makes contact with humans and somehow, it's **me** they're talking to. What the hell is going on?!*

What was she supposed to do? What was she supposed to say? What if she said or did the wrong thing? She was a fun-sized snack to this beast, and maybe it really did eat humans; she didn't know. It would make short work of her if she misstepped.

The thing laid its upper left hand on its chest. *"Juc Samou. Xaoin ikij?"* The thunder of its voice rolled over her gently rather than powerfully, and that defiance of her expectation cut through her terror.

Judging by the intonation, that last part sounded like a question. The linguist in her was unavoidably intrigued, despite her mind-numbing fear. A borderline-hysterical voice in Michelle's internal monologue suggested that it was asking whether she preferred to be roasted or deep-fried.

She shook her head to clear it and swallowed the lump that had formed in her throat. She tried to take a deep breath, and suddenly realized that she couldn't see for the tears welling in her eyes. Michelle blinked furiously and tried to gather her wits as effectively as she'd gathered the bedsheet in her fists. Now was *not* the time to panic.

The monster patted its chest with surprising gentleness. "*Samou,*" it said. When she just looked at it, it did it again, repeating itself, then it extended that same hand, fully open, in her direction, fingertips pointing at her.

Michelle inhaled shakily. Was it telling her what it was? Or who it was? Was it a Sumoo, or was that its name? Her mind grappled with the puzzle in front of her. If it was trying to make introductions, it was probably using its name.

She took a deep breath. OK, names it was. *Here goes nothing.* She made herself release the death grip she had on the sheets and brought her own left hand up to rest on her chest. Looking into the thing's shiny black eyes, she slowly, deliberately said, "Michelle."

The beast's tentacles quivered in a rapid horizontal motion. "*Mishel.*"

Dear God in heaven. She patted herself again and repeated it. "Michelle."

The creature bobbed its open hand at her. "*Mishel.*" Her name was a little garbled, but recognizable. It brought its hand back to itself. "*Samou.*"

Michelle swallowed as best she could. She extended her hand toward the thing the way it had toward her. "Samou," she said.

Its tentacles quivered again in the same motion as before.

She released a tremulous breath. Michelle wasn't sure if she was shaking from fear or elation. Or possibly both. "Whew," she said. "OK. So you're Samou."

"*Zoingi nohe, Mishel,*" the creature — Samou — replied.

She sagged against the wall, still staring at her bizarre companion. She'd just completed introductions with an honest-to-goodness alien. "So what the hell is happening right now, Samou?"

A low rumble issued from its chest. "*Mishel,*" it said again.

And even though she knew it was way too early to make assumptions of any kind, Michelle thought she recognized pride in the rumble of Samou's voice.

That tone, on the other hand, was undeniably scorn. And it was directed at Michelle.

Four other creatures like Samou had gathered to meet with him. They all shared many of the same features: tentacles, tusks, black eyes, smooth gray skin. But seeing them next to one another, Michelle noticed that the color of their skin varied, with some shades of gray warmer than others, some lighter or darker. And though they were all massive, some stood even taller and larger than others.

They now clustered in the room with her, where she still sat in the bed. She couldn't follow a word of the conversation happening in front of her, but the discussion was clearly animated, with much gesturing and debate. And nearly all of the gestures were directed at her.

Samou had provided her with clothes, of a sort. A coarsely woven top and pants, both slightly too large. The shirt had one too many pairs of sleeves (she tied the lower set together at her waist like a belt to keep them from flopping around), but it was close to her size. The clothes were neither very comfortable nor flattering, but she was surprised to see that they had anything at all to give her. She was glad for it; even ugly clothing was imminently preferable to traipsing around naked.

An unease poked at the edges of her memory. There was something disconcerting, something wrong, something about her being naked. It was important, but she couldn't remember. Something she needed to remember, to act on...

It wasn't until her palms stung that she realized she'd clenched her fists so tightly her nails had dug into her skin. She was grinding her teeth, and her body almost vibrated with the tension in her muscles.

Slowly, she released her fists, relaxed her jaw, and took a breath. *What I wouldn't give to recapture the first few peaceful, blissfully ignorant moments of this morning.*

Thoughts of Dave made it hard to focus, hard to concentrate on her strange new environment, of his not being here with her, of he and Phil not being anywhere near her. She knew they were nowhere near, but she couldn't remember why not. Her head started to ache as that fluttery not-quite-there memory tried to fight its way into her conscious mind. She gave it a moment, but when nothing was forthcoming beyond more vague discomfort, she rubbed her eyes and refocused her attention on the conversation unfolding in front of her.

Following the group dynamics was not always as hard

as Michelle thought it might be, even without understanding anything that was said beyond 'Samou' and 'Mishel'. Samou and another beast seemed to be in agreement, supporting each other's statements, while a third monster, the scornful one, appeared to be playing the role of devil's advocate. Or maybe it just didn't like her. They were all aiming the majority of their comments at a fourth alien, while the fifth, the largest of them all, stood silently watching the proceedings, only occasionally glancing in her direction.

She nearly smiled at the silent one when he made eye contact as a way to convey her amiable intent. Then she abruptly remembered that some wild animals took bared teeth to be a challenge, so instead, she kept her expression to a mildly friendly interest.

Keeping an ear out for a change in rhythm or tone, Michelle let her gaze travel around the room. Instruments of various sizes and shapes sat on the countertops. Sleek black screens hung on the walls above each of the four beds in the room. The open doorway at the foot of her bed led to another room that, from the little bit she could see, looked very much like this one, but without the countertops. It all seemed medical and scientific, and oversized by double.

She was in a land of giant aliens, surrounded by a language she couldn't speak, without a single soul she knew and no way to find Dave, or Phil, or anyone.

She was alone.

The panic began to twist her stomach. What was she going to do? What *could* she do? Where was her family? Where was *anyone*? What was going to become of her?

And why couldn't she remember anything?!

Her throat began to close and her breath came in short, tight gasps.

A sudden beeping from above her head got Samou's attention. He barked something at the rest of the group and moved quickly to her side.

"*Mishel,*" he rumbled as he leaned over her.

She shook her head, waving him off and pulling away from him. She closed her eyes and willed herself to relax. She hadn't been hurt. She had been clothed and treated well so far. There was nothing to fear right now, at this moment. *Breathe in, two, three, four and out, two, three, four.* She repeated the controlled breathing cycle a few times, lengthening it gradually, until her throat began to release and her shoulders slid down from their perch around her ears. She kept her eyes closed and tried to breathe normally for another few breaths.

The monsters will still be there when you open your eyes.

She dismissed the unhelpful contribution from her rogue mind and gradually opened her eyes. Samou was right there. He'd pulled the chair from the foot of the bed to beside it and was watching her intently.

She bit her lip and nodded, trying to look like she was totally in control. Her inner monologue cackled at the absurd lie.

His tentacles twitched. *"Ijhej zoin?"*

She bit her lip. Was he asking if she was all right? Or if she was ready to be executed? Or if she liked potato salad? Who knew? She almost giggled hysterically.

Samou rolled his top shoulders. He pointed at her with his entire hand, open-palmed, as he had earlier. *"Mishel. Zoin?"* He laid another hand on the center of his torso.

She had no idea what was going on, but what did she have to lose? Going with her gut, Michelle nodded again and rested her hand just under the center of her breasts.

"Michelle zo-inn."

The group simultaneously began rumbling together, tentacles waving. Samou sat up tall (which was really quite tall) and cast them a look before facing her again. He awkwardly jerked his head down and up in her direction, twice.

Samou was nodding back at her.

She forgot her no teeth rule when she smiled at him.

He lifted all his tentacles so that the half closest to his face was parallel to the ground, the other half bent 90 degrees, dangling toward the floor.

The effect was bizarre, but the gesture was still somehow oddly comforting.

Maybe she wouldn't be executed just yet, after all.

9

Suji was fascinated. Honestly, he'd been fascinated from the moment he'd seen the antiquated canisters in the derelict vessel, and he'd been sorely grieved when the first Little Being hadn't survived reanimation. That this one had made it was thrilling. Of course, he would get partial credit in the history books as having helped discover the Littles, but now he might actually get the chance to know one.

He'd expected them to behave much like *likkuj* or other small, domesticated animals that some Vinyi kept in their homes. Thoughtlessly displaying one of the many prejudices of his generally xenophobic species, he'd assumed their brain power to be, like the size of their bodies, significantly lesser than his.

But he'd just heard this one try to speak *Ijlenum,* mere moments after Sam had spoken to it. And while it was true that there were pets who could mimic speech, it looked like this one had just used it in the proper context, even.

That wasn't mimicry. That was understanding. And *that*

at least suggested intelligence.

He couldn't wait to tell Pekoe that he had discovered — *helped* discover — a new, intelligent species. But even more, he couldn't wait to learn more about this tiny Little that had been strong enough to fight its way back to life.

No time like the present.

He took a step toward the Little's bed.

The Little whipped its head around and stared at him with those strange white eyes. He stopped and held up his open hands toward it, hoping the gesture of peace looked enough like Sam's from earlier that it would put the small creature at ease. It didn't look very comfortable, but neither did it shy away from him.

Suji pointed at the Little with the usual open palmed gesture. "Mishel," he said. Then he brought his hand back and rested it on his chest. "Suji."

It watched him a moment longer, then proceeded to thrill him to the tips of his tusks. It pointed at him, and said, "Suzhi."

He tried again, just to see if the Little could do better. "Suji." He carefully enunciated the syllables.

Still pointing at him, Mishel said, "Suji."

This was incredible! He lifted his tentacles ecstatically and was rewarded even further when Mishel bared its teeth at him, just like it had done with Sam.

Does it really understand? Suji pointed to the doctor and waited.

Mishel shifted its gaze to Sam and clearly said, "Samou."

Suji turned excitedly to the others standing at the foot of the Little's bed. "Did you see that? It's intelligent! It already knows our names!"

Rimoli snorted.

"Don't remove the patch while you're still in the boat, Suji." Sam slowly stood, so as not to startle Mishel, and rejoined the group. "I agree, it would appear that Mishel is intelligent, but we'll need to determine exactly what and how much it can learn."

"Even if it is marginally intelligent, that doesn't speak to sapience," Rimoli objected. "Some species of *liyij* can recognize their owners. We still eat them." He cast a glance at Mishel from the corner of his eye.

An unexpected surge of protectiveness welled up in Suji's breast. "We are *not* going to eat it."

"Enough." Hegoh's command cut off any further commentary. Four pairs of Vinyi eyes focused on the captain. "Doctor, you will continue your examination of… what did you call it, Suji? A 'Little'?"

Suji lifted his tentacles in assent.

"Continue your examination of the Little and report your findings to me in three days, unless something arises that I ought to know sooner. Chief Researcher, you will prepare a proposal of what valuable information you believe you could glean from the Little, should sapience prove to be unlikely."

Both Vinyi acknowledged their orders.

"Captain," said Suji as Hegoh and Lihku turned to go, "I request permission to assist the doctor in his examinations of Mishel."

"Really?" The look the captain gave him was both amused and surprised. "Are you that interested?"

"Yes, sir, I am." Suji was beyond interested; he was spellbound.

Hegoh grunted. "If you can find the time without neglecting our engines, your request is granted, so long as the doctor approves."

Samou lifted in agreement.

Suji beamed. "Thank you, sir. Sirs," he corrected with a swift salute at both Hegoh and Samou.

As the captain and Lihku left, Suji took one last look at Mishel, then said to Sam, "I'll be back in three hours, maybe less."

Samou waved him off with a smile.

It was all Suji could do not to run back to the Engine Room. He had things to get done.

"Seriously, Pekoe, it's the most unusual, interesting, unique, fascinating thing I've seen since I've been out here!"

Pekoe smiled at him, reflecting his own excitement. She never gave Suji a hard time about being an absentee husband, like so many fleet wives did, but that was partly because he stuck to their bargain: at least three live visual transmissions per week. Some of the guys mocked Suji for being so tethered to his monitor, but he didn't mind. Pekoe was not only his wife, she was his best friend; he couldn't wait to talk with her.

She was also the mother of his first child, which was growing inside her at this very moment.

This was Suji's second tour aboard the Yukesi. He'd worked his way up, starting as a lowly engine tech aboard the Raikhi for a couple of tours, then serving aboard the Eaheb for three tours until he had risen to the rank of Senior Engineer. He'd come aboard Yukesi as Assistant Chief Engineer, and after the accidental death of the previous Chief a couple of years ago, he'd been promoted to the position.

And in all that time, finding Mishel had been the most exotic thing that had happened to him. Pekoe had been the best, no doubt, but Mishel was the most exotic.

"What does it look like?"

Suji's tentacles quivered. "It's about half our size and not nearly so visually pleasing. Only two arms, and —"

"Only two arms?" Pekoe interrupted. "How does it get anything done?"

"Right now, your guess is as good as mine," he admitted. "We don't know much of anything about it. It's got such a poor little ugly face," he added. "No tentacles at all, a strange lump in the middle, and its eyes - get this! - they're almost all white!"

"Ew," Pekoe said.

"I know! But I have to go. It took me a while to rearrange the duty roster to cover my time away from engineering, and Sam's going to start the next round of examinations in the next few minutes. I don't want to miss anything good!"

Pekoe smiled again. "All right. But call me back when you get back to your quarters. I want to say one of our 'special' good nights."

"Rabid *likkuj* couldn't keep me away," he promised fervently. This day couldn't get any better. "Love you, Peek."

"Love you, too."

They disconnected, and Suji fairly sprinted to the medbay.

When Suji walked back through the medbay doors exactly two hours and forty-seven minutes after he'd left, Sam was sitting with Mishel on the sofa in his office. "You started without me," he said as he ambled through Sam's office doors.

"Yes."

Suji had been expecting more of an explanation. He waited, then asked, "And? What have you been doing? What have you learned about it?"

Sam smiled slightly, a gentle lift of his tentacles, then turned back to Mishel. "*Xaoin ij?*" he asked it, pointing to Suji. *Who is that?*

The strangeness of its mostly white eyes unnerved Suji. Then Mishel said, clumsily but recognizably, "*Ij Suji.*" It lifted one of its tiny hands and wiggled its knobby fingers. "*Qume, Suji.*"

Suji's tentacles went slack. "Sam."

Sam grinned at him. "Yes."

"Sam, it…" Suji was elated. "You're teaching it to talk! It's speaking our language."

"Yes. It had shown an inclination toward spoken language already, so I decided to pursue that path. It's already learned quite a lot. I suspect that Mishel is really quite intelligent, very likely possessing its own spoken language." Sam peered at its doll-sized head. "Quite a feat, considering how little it has to work with."

"It's speaking our language," Suji repeated. The wonder of it made him almost giddy. Cautiously, Suji sat down on the sofa on the other side of Mishel. "*Qume, Mishel. Yupu ijhej?*"

It turned its head to look at Sam for guidance. He spoke slowly and clearly to it. "*Yupu ijhej? Ijhej zoin?*"

The light dusting of hair over its eyes moved closer together. "*Zoin,*" it murmured. "*Zoin…* Oh!" It aimed its words at Suji. *"Jo... ijhej... zoin?" Yes, you are well.*

Suji was enraptured, so much so that he didn't correct its mistake.

"Suji."

Sam's voice cut through his stupefaction and he tore his eyes away from Mishel. "Hm?"

"You have to instruct it," Sam said. "We have to demonstrate beyond doubt that it's smart enough to learn not just the words, but the proper meanings and uses of them."

"Right." He pointed to himself and repeated his question. *"Ijhej zoin?"* Then he pointed at Mishel. *"Ijhuc zoin."* He tried to emphasize the change in the verb between 'you are' and 'I am'.

Mishel tilted its head to the side, and Suji thought it adorable. It faced Sam again. *"Ijhej zoin?"*

Sam replied, *"Ijhuc zoin. Cha?"* He bobbed his head down and up twice. He caught the odd look Suji was giving him and explained, "It's a gesture Mishel makes."

"Ah."

"Jo, ijhuc zoin, Suji, cha?" Mishel said, looking at him expectantly. *Yes, I am well, Suji, and you?*

Suji exhaled. "May the gods of honor bless us."

Sam laughed. "Isn't it amazing?"

The younger man waved his tentacles back and forth, and Mishel's curious gaze focused on them. "There are no words for this... this feeling. This discovery!"

"Indeed." Sam's expression was as delighted as Suji's, though his gestures and tone remained calm and measured. "But don't leave the poor thing hanging, Suji. It asked you a question."

"Right." He looked back to the Little with a smile. *"Ijhuc zoin, Mishel.*" And for good measure, he tilted his head up, then down, like Sam had.

Mishel bared its teeth at him and leaned back into the sofa, looking back and forth between them.

"*Zainu, Mishel,*" the doctor told her. Then he said to Suji, "Let's see what else it can do."

Far more than they'd dared to hope, as it turned out.

By the middle of that evening, Mishel had learned at least 50 different words and was using them correctly in sentences. Short, childlike sentences, but it was speaking, really speaking, after only one day. And it wasn't simple mimicry, either. Mishel had started telling them things about itself and trying to ask questions. It had asked for food and water at one point, a request that Sam had been ready for. He provided Mishel with a mild grain fortified with some of the nutrients that his analyses indicated would be beneficial. Suji had been oddly fascinated to find that Mishel's manner of eating wasn't all that different from his own, though its mouth was so very tiny it had to take many more bites than he did to consume far less.

When Mishel managed to tell them that she was female, Sam was as proud as if her revelation had been the birth announcement of his own daughter.

She kept asking about some males, though, and that puzzled them both. "The anatomical structure of the first Little was identical to Mishel's, which suggests that both of our Littles were female," Samou said. "Did you see any other Littles on the derelict?"

Suji waved his tentacles from side to side. "No, it was just the two of them. The other cylinders were empty."

Sam frowned. "I wonder why they were there, and who these males are she asked after."

"Not to mention who the other Little female was. Well, I guess we'll ask once Mishel speaks well enough to explain." As though the Little wasn't already endlessly fascinating, now it — no, *she* — had grown yet more mysterious.

"*Cu juc Mishel,*" cut in the Little. "*Pej... pej qezmek.*" I am Mishel. More talk.

Suji barked a laugh, making Mishel jump. "That's exactly what Pekoe will be saying if I don't get back to my quarters and call her as we agreed."

The unmarried doctor rolled his shoulders. "Go on, then. I'll stay here with her."

Suji agreed and turned to the object of his fascination. "See you later, Mishel."

She tried to imitate the new word, stumbling over it and looking to Sam for guidance.

The medbay doors closed behind him on Samou sitting fixedly, contentedly, on his office sofa whilst repeatedly bidding Mishel goodbye and waiting for her echo.

10

Michelle watched Samou walk away until he turned the corner into the main medbay from the smaller, more private section that housed what she was already starting to think of as "her" bed. Once he was out of sight, she heaved a sigh that came from the bottom of her toes before falling back onto her pillow. After Suji had gone, Samou continued to work with her. He taught her more vocabulary, probably based on the things she would most likely need to know, words like 'food', 'sleep', and 'water'. He had taught her the word for 'cold', but given the temperature of every room she had been in so far, Michelle didn't expect to have to use it unless she were asking for cold food or drink. She was a little concerned that 'fight' was considered essential vocabulary, but she'd cross that bridge if she ever came to it. The important thing was to learn the words, to make them see her as *real*. She was so small and powerless in comparison to her hosts; she had to find a way to make them see her as equal, regardless of her size.

All that concentrating had taken its toll. Michelle couldn't remember the last time she'd felt this tired. And all she'd done was learn basic words and grammar. Well, that after waking up in a completely unfamiliar, *literally* alien environment. She felt sluggish, heavy, and awkward. Maybe it was the heat. Or maybe gravity was different and she was heavier than she was used to being.

Or maybe this day had simply been too much to deal with gracefully.

The aliens had been kind, speaking and acting with gentleness and patience. They fed her, clothed her, taught her. She wished she could remember how she'd gotten here, but, all things considered, that could wait. Right now, she had to figure out how to get them to listen to her, to take her seriously. She was going to need their help to find Dave and Phil, and, kind though they were, they wouldn't go out of their way to track down Mars for her if she were little more than a novelty hobby or exotic pet to them.

As she lay there, the warmth of the room settled on her more, bit by bit, making it hard to keep her eyes open. What wouldn't she give to feel Dave's arms around her right now? Her lower lip trembled. She missed his smile, his voice, the sound of his laugh, the passion in his kiss, the security of his presence.

And when was the last time she'd gone more than a couple of days without a good night hug from her brother? They'd been through so much, and he was becoming such a wonderful young man, clever and thoughtful and kind, a long way from the mischievous child-pest he used to be. She thought of the last time they had all been together, on Halloween. Forging new traditions, growing into their new family unit. The harsh blank made by their absence now gnawed a hole in her heart that made her physically ache.

She *had* to find them.

Michelle rolled onto her side and let the silent tears come.

Samou's footsteps abruptly intruded on her misery. Michelle didn't move. The sound of the giant's approach got close, then stopped, and Michelle knew he was, if not in the room with her, then waiting in the doorway. She pretended to be asleep, hoping he would go away. She didn't have any more in her right now.

After a few moments, Samou's footsteps started up again, fading this time. She lay still until she couldn't hear them anymore. Then she opened her eyes and stared at the warm beige wall, thinking of home, until her eyes drifted shut and she slept.

She dreamt of Mars.

Michelle had no idea how long she had been asleep when she was awakened by the growling of her empty stomach. She rubbed her eyes and gradually pushed herself up to sitting. Even more than she needed food, however, she needed a bathroom.

Easing herself down onto the stepping stool Samou had set up for her the day before, she padded on bare feet over to the small enclosure he showed her yesterday. It was oversized, like everything else in this ridiculous place. She had to use another stepstool to climb up to the bowl, which was situated at just under Vinyi shoulder height. Michelle didn't want to think about that too hard. She perched herself carefully on the edge, and did her business, taking care not to fall in. The bowl suctioned the contents to who-knew-where the moment she finished using it. She climbed down, and at the door, waved her hand vigorously above her head to activate the motion sensor that would open it. At least she didn't need a stepstool for that, too.

When Michelle emerged from the room, someone was waiting for her at the foot of her bed.

At first she thought it was Samou, but then realized that the skin was too dark a shade of gray to be his. Also, this being's head was slightly less round than that of her tutor. "*Qume,*" she said, slowing her walk to a cautious approach. *Hello.*

The two tentacles under its tusks hugged the bottom curve of the ivory. "*Qume, Mishel,*" it said, garbling her name the same way Samou and Suji had. Its voice was a little higher, a little smoother than Samou's. It laid a left hand on its chest and said, "*Mebeku.*"

"*Yupu ijhej, Mebeku?*" She was sure that was at least close to *How are you?*

Mebeku froze for a moment, then his tentacles raised at her in the half-lifted, half-relaxed gesture she was beginning to understand was a smile. "*Ijhuc zoin, cha?*"

"*Ijhuc zoin.*"

Then he (were they all male here? She'd only seen pictures of females yesterday during Samou's tutelage, and the only difference she could see between the two was that the females had smaller, bluer tusks) threw a string of unfamiliar words at her that had her shaking her head. "Sorry," she said. "Um… *nu zainu.*" *No good.*

Mebeku barked, making a sound very much like the one Suji had made yesterday that startled her so. "*Gin yunpovu,*" he said slowly, taking care with each syllable.

Michelle recognized the first syllable as *come*. Samou had

said that to her more than once yesterday. She slowly made her way toward the bed, her legs wobbling with the effort. Either she was really weak, or gravity really *was* stronger here.

The big beast seemed to notice and knelt in front of her. She was now just barely taller than he, though he was still built like a tank. Mebeku held out his two left hands. *"Hi ecaheki."*

She shrugged and shook her head. *"Nu zainu."*

"Ecahe," he said, then pointed to himself with a right hand, then to her, then mimed lifting something with his left hands.

He was offering to carry her to wherever it was he wanted them to go.

Well, sure, he could easily do that. Michelle thought of herself trusting this massive beast to pick her up without crushing or confining her.

Wait. Her breath began to come in short gasps. Confining her. *No. No, not again.*

A rush of images flooded her, unbidden. A white room. Her arms over her head, cuffed, confined. Prodding fingers, cold metal against her naked skin. Writhing. Kicking, punching. Screaming.

Michelle's knees buckled and she collapsed onto the floor. She squeezed her eyes shut, trying to block out the panic, the bile rising in her throat, the sudden, desperate need to fight back that made no sense. She wasn't captive here. She wasn't naked. She curled into herself as tightly as she could, burying her face in the space between her chest and her knees as she rocked back and forth, trying to sort it out, to make some kind of sense of it.

The sound of approaching footsteps had her scrambling

away, shrieking.

"Don't touch me! Don't touch me!"

She was in a full-on panic now, her breath harsh and jagged, tears pressing against her eyes. The hands, the strange purple hands. She wanted the hands to go away, she wanted the captivity to end, she wanted to go back home, back to Dave and Phil and home and Mars and the greenhouse and —

Michelle's screams hitched in her throat as memories exploded in her mind's eye. She remembered the Marsquake, the helplessness of the confinement in the all-white room, the red chicken-gel, the Faceless coming for them one by one, coming for her, the last desperate fight, the two of them against far too many of the devils to possibly win but they had to fight anyway.

They did. The two of them. Two of them. Who was the other? Michelle searched the memory. Straw-colored hair. Intimidating. Fierce.

Petra.

Where was Petra? Petra was there with her, the two of them fought the Faceless together, Petra should be here somewhere.

"Mishel."

The familiarity of the low rumble broke through her careening thoughts. She peered up slowly, cautiously. "Samou?" Where had he come from?

The doctor was kneeling on the floor in front of her. Two of his tentacles were twitching mildly. "Mishel, *xai leje?*"

Her mind was stuck. She couldn't get it to work, to reply, to be here now. All she could think of was the terror, the desperation, the punching and kicking and falling and —

"Nu hinvej poihu, Mishel," Samou said, and the gentle

rolling thunder of his words flowed over her like a healing balm. Her panting began to slow. *"Ijhej zoin, nu hinvej poihu."*

Gradually, her racing heart calmed. She took a deep breath and focused on Samou's shiny eyes and gently undulating tentacles. He was still kneeling before her. "Samou?"

He grunted.

Michelle wiped the tears from her face as she cast about for the words she needed. "Um… *Cu pej…*" She shook her head and swallowed. *"Cipej quipoke? Cu cipej quipoke?"* It was clumsy and she could only hope Samou would understand what she meant by 'another female and me'. Those were the only words she had right now.

His shoulders sagged and, after a beat, he lowered himself to sitting on the floor in front of her. *"Jo."*

Yes. Yes! There *had* been another female with her. Petra was with her, here. But where was she now? Michelle looked around foolishly, as though perhaps she had somehow missed seeing her.

"Mishel."

Something in Samou's tone got her attention and tied her stomach in a knot. *"Xai?"* What?

His tentacles gently, deliberately waved side to side. *"Nu,"* he said gently.

No.

No? "But you just said yes! You just said she was here! What do you mean, no?! Where is… Pet…" She trailed off as his meaning hit her.

"Mu joinhu." Samou's voice was soft, regretful.

Petra had been here, but she wasn't here now. Samou's people had found Petra, like they had found her, but Petra wasn't here with her anywhere. Not now. Petra must not have survived whatever it was the Faceless had done to them. Petra was gone.

Dave was nowhere.

Phil was nowhere.

Michelle was alone.

Grief consumed her in an unstoppable wave. Wrenching sobs tore at her, and she let herself drown in the overwhelming sorrow.

She was so lost in her anguish that she didn't even feel Samou's strong arms envelop her, lift her, and gently carry her back to her bed.

She had to get back to Mars.

After the grief finished ravaging her, leaving her wrung out and sore, Michelle wallowed listlessly in the hopelessness left behind. What was she going to do now? She'd always relied on her family for guidance and support. Hell, when the chips were down, even she and Petra Morgan, of all people, had come together to give one another strength. But now, Michelle was alone. She couldn't do this alone; it was too much.

So she had to get back to Mars. She needed Phil. Needed Dave. Needed safety and reassurance and to see that they were all right and to be with them. She needed not to be alone, not to be the only one.

She needed *home*.

But how? Michelle didn't know where she was. She didn't know who Samou and his people were, or where they were from, or what they called Mars, or if they even knew

Mars and her home solar system existed.

She didn't know anything. She didn't have anyone. When the backs of her eyes ached with more tears, Michelle made herself swallow and breathe.

Solve the problem, Michelle.

To get back home, she had to be able to tell Samou and the others where home was, and she didn't know how to do that. Therefore, she needed to learn more of the language, including reading and writing it, for she was going to have to be able to read maps and write out directions and descriptions and the like. And in order to learn, she was going to have to take care of herself. Eat enough food, drink enough water, get enough rest, and exercise enough to keep her body healthy and stimulate her brain.

It would take time, and a hell of a lot of luck.

Her shoulders sagged. She'd not had a lot of luck over the past few years. Maybe that meant that it was about time the tide turned for her. She closed her eyes and pictured Dave and Phil. *I'm on my way. I'm coming home. Don't give up on me.*

Michelle opened her eyes to find Samou sitting at a countertop console on the far wall, scratching into a tablet with a stylus. When she cleared her throat, he glanced over his shoulder at her. *"Qume,"* she said quietly.

Samou turned to face her, though he stayed seated. *"Qume, Mishel."*

He said nothing else, simply watching her instead. Had she offended him? Or was he concerned that she might meltdown again if he approached her? Or was everything fine? Probably that last. *"Evae?"* she said as politely as possible, asking for the water her parched throat demanded.

"Jo." Samou stood and walked to a recessed console in an adjacent wall. He pressed a few lights on a flat display and a

cup slid out from the side of the recess into the center of it. A clear liquid poured from above, filling the cup. He brought it to her. She reached for it, having to take the drinking vessel in both hands. Samou did not release it.

Michelle raised her gaze from the large cup to his face. She really wanted that water. *"Xai?"* she asked. *What?*

"Keyoej," he said.

She frowned.

He repeated the word, pushing the water toward her but still not releasing it. Seeing that she still wasn't getting it, Samou pointed at her. *"Evae."*

She nodded.

He pointed to the cup. *"Evae."*

She nodded again. So far, so good. She wanted water and there it was.

He pointed at her, then at his own mouth, then at hers. *"Keyoej."*

What was he doing? She repeated the new word. *"Keyoej."*

Samou released the cup into her possession. *"Hinehe,"* he said.

Then she understood. Michelle smiled tiredly up at him. Lifting the cup, she said, *"Keyoej."* *Thank you.*

Samou smiled back. *"Hinehe."*

The water was warm but felt wonderful on her throat nonetheless. Michelle and Samou watched each other as she drank. He had done a lot for her. She had clothes, food and water, a place to sleep, and instruction, and he had been nothing but kind and patient.

Maybe her luck really was turning. She said his name, set the nearly empty cup down on the bed, and gestured around the room, to the water, to her clothes. *"Keyoej."*

Samou grunted (he did that a lot, she noticed) and flapped his tentacles at her once. *"Hinehe, Mishel. Hinehe."*

11

Over the next weeks, Michelle, Samou, Mebeku, and Suji established a sort of routine. From the time she rose until the time she went back to bed in the medbay, one of them was nearly always with her, talking, listening, or simply keeping her company.

It was an experience entirely unlike being held captive by the Faceless, but somehow a sharp sense of isolation, a knot just under her breastbone that never really let her take a full breath, persisted. Her caretakers, the Vinyi, as she'd learned their species was called, had gone out of their way to care for her and tend to her needs. They fed her food that was of increasingly varied textures and tastes. They had provided her with multiple outfits. They asked her about herself, about her planet, her family. She was only too glad to tell them, and Samou and Suji were, after only these few weeks, trying to find her galaxy and help her get back home.

For her part, she had learned more of their words, and was beginning to figure out aspects of her situation, such as where she was (sort of), who her hosts were, and how to behave — and not behave — in public.

She was on board an interstellar vessel called the Yukesi. The Yukesi was a Vinyi vessel, and from what she had gathered, the Vinyi were a race of contradictions. They prided themselves on both their prowess in battle and the social structures that cared for their vulnerable. They were relentless in their pursuit of knowledge, yet stubbornly superstitious. They lived their lives according to a complex code of honor that, when not adhered to, resulted in vicious shame being heaped upon the violator.

Her meltdown when she first remembered her captivity with the Faceless could have been, for a Vinyi, an appallingly shameful act. A public display of weakness, especially panic, was thoroughly disgraceful. Thankfully, Samou and Mebeku considered her both a wonder of scientific discovery *and* a vulnerable outsider; they kept her shame to themselves. The case could also be made that they, as her tutors and two-thirds of her only Vinyi contact, weren't exactly "public", either.

She was going to need to toughen up, regardless. Not only to get along on the Yukesi, but to deal with the continued assault on her psyche from the Faceless.

Michelle resented it when the Faceless invaded her dreams, as they did more nights than not. She relived her captivity, over and over again, sometimes with Petra at her side, sometimes not. Sometimes she again watched helplessly as Kate was taken away. Other times, Bonnie's ghost stood there watching her and Petra mount their last and only rebellion before being overcome. The worst was when she dreamt of the Faceless dragging Dave and Phil away from her. She tried to get to them, tried to rescue them, but she could never make it past the invisible wall. She was made to watch, helpless, as they were dragged out of her sight. Those nightmares were the worst, and they made it impossible to get back to sleep, and so some days were harder than others.

As her understanding of Vinyi language and culture grew, so too did her understanding of her tutors. Samou was as her first impressions told her: calm, kind, patient, and steady. She suspected he was older than the other two. Mebeku, who also worked in the medbay, was every bit as patient and pleasant, though more inclined to teach her through stories or jokes rather than through rote lessons. Everything Suji did, on the other hand, carried an air of enthusiasm and energy. Michelle had a feeling that Suji would be the life of the party, if there were such things as parties here.

But until she discovered whether or not parties happened here, she had her routine. Upon waking, she would breakfast with one of them as they walked her through new words for their food and drink. They would try to teach her about a holiday or a cultural mannerism she hadn't been exposed to yet. They would introduce the rare stranger who entered the medbay and have Michelle practice her greetings before handling whatever business had brought their visitor there in the first place. Then they would move the lesson to either Samou's office or a private observation room with a view of the endless starscape outside.

It was there, in that privacy, where they would try to teach one another. Michelle focused on telling them her history, about Mars, and Earth, and Dave and Phil and humanity in general. Every day she was able to tell them more, and she hoped that, one day soon, she'd be able to tell them enough for them to pinpoint Mars' location in space and take her home.

Conversation would continue until the mid-morning

meal, a word that translated to "little lunch", after which they would move on to reading and writing for a couple of hours. At that point, they took a break for the regular-sized lunch. Michelle's meals often had samples of the same foods as those on her teachers' plates (Vinyi food used a bit more spice than she preferred, but it wasn't bad), and she also always had a helping of thin-sliced, crunchy sky-blue circles. They were there to supply her with the vitamins and minerals she wasn't getting from Vinyi food. She thought of them as her vitamin crisps. They needed a little salt, but they weren't bad.

After regular-lunch, whoever had been with her in the morning would switch off with another of the teaching team. Michelle and her fresh companion would then perform their own set of cultural exchange stories and, when that failed, charades until dinner, after which there were more reading and writing lessons. Finally, the day would end when she said good night, after a light snack.

This morning, Mebeku joined her for breakfast and morning lessons. By the time they got to regular-lunch, Bek had adopted the role of Hans Cristian Andersen and started telling her *yainhuj hiqehej*, the Vinyi version of fairy tales. Like Andersen's original fairy tales, the stories the Vinyi told their children seemed designed to shatter rather than protect their innocence.

This particular story was about evil flying merpeople and children who lied to their parents.

"Wait." Michelle held up a hand as Bek took a breath between sentences. Her *Ijlenum* was coming along, but there were far more words that she didn't understand than ones she did. "They ate the raw *what* of the children?"

Bek barked and wiggled his tentacles, then wrapped two of his hands completely around her head while tapping on the top of her skull with the pointer finger of a third.

She gasped and grimaced. "Their brains?! The sea monsters eat the children's brains, while the children are still alive, and this is a bedtime story? That's terrible!"

He released her head and sat back. "But Vinyi children do not lie."

Now Michelle laughed. "After *that* story, I'm sure they don't. What a brutal ending."

Bek smiled. "Lying is one of the Five Shameful Acts. We teach our young from early on not to engage in it."

"What are the others?" She leaned forward.

"Stealing, laziness, selfishness, and causing physical harm without reason."

Michelle thought for a moment. "All of those things are about valuing yourself more than you value others."

"Yes. The highest value is accorded to your family and your *yejorep*."

Suji had explained this concept to her at length a few days ago. It was a subject close to his heart, as his wife was pregnant with their first child. The closest parallel to *yejorep* that Michelle could think of was "godparent", but even that didn't really fit.

Children were prized and diligently cared for. Once a child grew up and reached sexual maturity, an elaborate celebration was thrown in the new young adult's honor. He or she was also taken to the doctor for a temporary sterilization procedure. Once the young adult grew into full adulthood and carved a place for itself in society, they could petition to have the sterilization reversed. A voting council of medical professionals and societal managers reviewed the adult's ability to provide family and support for any children, and if the council approved, the sterilization was easily and readily reversed. A child was almost always born within three years.

The Vinyi were both fertile and enthusiastic about the act that led to the children they valued so highly.

Children were not allowed to be subjected to the chance of instability or any dearth of essential care. Every Vinyi child had their parents to care for them, as well as a number of legally committed *yejorep*, citizens outside of their immediate family but within their parents' social circle, who would see to the child's various needs should those needs not be met by the parents for some reason. This arrangement lasted for the entire lives of the parties involved. To not be *yejorep* to anyone was selfish and deeply shameful, as was taking advantage of your *yejorep*.

Bek continued explaining the hierarchy of loyalty. "Then to your friends and colleagues. After them, strangers."

"But only Vinyi strangers." Michelle had begun to notice a strain of xenophobia in the Vinyi.

Mebeku confirmed it when he looked at her askance, appalled at the idea of universal compassion. "Of course." Then he grinned. "Except for you, Mishel."

She gave an exaggerated sigh of relief, which secretly wasn't exaggerated in the least. "Thank the gods of honor."

The doors of the observation room opened as Bek was chuckling.

"Hi, Suji."

"Mishel, Bek," he greeted them in turn. Suji's gray skin had a warm, almost pink tinge to it, unlike Bek's, whose deep blue undertones differed still from Samou's neutral gray. "How are things going today?"

Bek waggled the tentacles under his tusks. "I just told her *The Tale of the Merpeople of Ozobe*."

"Ah! A classic," Suji said approvingly.

Bek hummed and sat back in his chair, giving Michelle a look that said, *I told you so.*

"Mishel," Suji said, taking on the air of someone making an important announcement, "we are going to vary the routine today. Come with me."

"Oh?" Michelle rose. "What will we do?"

"I have a surprise for you. This way." And with one pair of arms behind his back and the other making a sweeping gesture toward the door, Suji escorted her out of the observation room and into the main corridor.

Mebeku had to return to his duties, so it was Suji and Michelle who walked down the main corridor of deck 7. He kept his pace slower than normal so she could keep up. In the twenty-five days that she'd been here, her muscles had grown stronger and now she could move without difficulty against the extra gravity of the Yukesi. However, his legs were still far longer than hers; her shoulder was at the same height as his waist.

The Yukesi was a well-populated ship, and they passed a number of other Vinyi on their way to the lift. Michelle alternately tried making and avoiding eye contact, uncomfortable with the piercing stares. They were huge. The corridor was huge. The ship was huge.

The vulnerability she felt nearly overwhelmed her.

"They have heard of you," Suji said, "but most of them have not seen you before now. They are curious, but they will not hurt you."

A green-tinged Vinyi walked in the opposite direction, his eyes boring into her as they passed.

Michelle made a sound in her throat that was both a hum and a moan.

Suji laid a reassuring hand on her shoulder. "I am with you."

She took a deep breath and patted his hand with her own. *Suji's here. I'll be fine.*

They stopped in front of the lift. "So where are we going?" she asked as they stepped inside.

Suji used the touchpad to order the lift down to deck 10. "Somewhere you haven't been before."

The lift doors opened and Suji led her to the first intersection, where he turned left, then right at the next one. He stopped in front of the third door on the right. Michelle craned her neck to take in the high ceiling; the top of the door itself was a head above Suji. He tapped in a code on a console to the side of the doorframe and the door slid open.

The room was lit, though the lights were soft rather than sharp, the way they were in the medbay. The floor was plush and plum colored, while the walls were a soothing grayish-blue. There was a variety of furniture arranged throughout the room, but Michelle's eyes focused on the Vinyi sitting at a table in the corner.

It was an almost laughable sight. The table and the chairs were, she saw now, lower than everything else on the ship. They were her height, and the Vinyi sitting there was clearly less than comfortable with his knees pulled up close to his upper shoulders.

Why was the chair so small?

She turned to survey the rest of the room and found that all of the furniture, which consisted of a sofa, a bed, and a dressing table, had been lowered to her height, though they were still as broad as normal Vinyi furniture would be. She looked up at Suji. "What is this?"

The new Vinyi answered her. "This, Mishel, is where you will live."

Suji smiled down at her. "Mishel, I present Captain Hegoh. You have seen him before, but I doubt you remember."

She didn't. "Well met, Captain."

He raised his center tentacles in greeting. "My doctor claims to be tired of having you underfoot in the medbay, though I suspect other motives. My engineer," he gestured to Suji, "redesigned this supply closet into a livable area."

Michelle blinked and looked around the room again. "You're... you're giving me my own living quarters?"

"Yes."

Her breathing began to pick up its pace. "But..."

Living quarters suggested a more-than-temporary arrangement, they suggested a home. But Michelle already had a home.

Suji tensed beside her. He knew her well enough now to know when she was about to become emotional, and she knew him well enough to know that her tendency toward panic made him desperately uncomfortable. Feeling fear should lead to a display of self-control: acknowledging but controlling one's panic was a sign of courage. A person was free to feel whatever they felt, but what one could decently *show* was a different matter entirely.

If she gave in right now, she would bring shame upon herself and, by extension, upon her tutors, one of whom was standing right here. In front of his commanding officer.

She lifted her chin and cleared her throat. "But this is... I don't know the word." Suji regarded her patiently while she forced herself to remain calm and found other words to describe the one she wanted. "Something that will be the same for a long time, that won't change."

"*Likpehninhi,*" Suji supplied.

Permanent.

"Yes," she confirmed. *I don't want this to be permanent. I want to go home.*

Hegoh stood. "That is what I am here to discuss." He gestured to the sofa. "Please."

Reluctantly, Michelle took a seat.

"Suji and Samou have kept you isolated and protected from the upheaval —" At her confused glance to Suji, Hegoh tried again. "The excitement you have caused on my ship. Indeed, among our people," he said.

"I have?"

At a wave from Hegoh, Suji explained. "We have never seen anyone like you before, Mishel. You are a new discovery, a new species. We are proud and honored to have been the ones to have found you. It is something to celebrate."

"It is also a problem that requires a solution. Our scientists have reviewed all the data in all the archives on Hoikke," said Hegoh, referring to the Vinyi homeworld, "and nobody has ever seen anything remotely like you. We searched the data archives of allied planets and found nothing. Nobody has any idea where you come from. As far as we can determine, you are the only Little in existence."

"But... but I'm not!" Michelle looked desperately at Suji. "You know I'm not. I told you my story, about where I'm from, about Mars and my family and... everything." She was still trying to fight the panic and losing.

"Yes," he replied gently. "But we cannot find any planet

that fits the description you gave us. We cannot find any *galaxy* that fits the description you gave us."

"But…" How was that possible? She shook her head in nonplussed silence.

"Mishel, you must listen." Hegoh's voice, though not harsh, was firm. "The Yukesi has a mission to complete. We have suspended it, with permission from the Council, since we found you. But now we must resume our patrol and reconnaissance duties." He exchanged a glance with Suji. "We cannot exert a concentrated effort to look for your planet Mars any longer."

Michelle couldn't breathe. Spots danced before her eyes.

"We will continue to search when we can," interjected Suji. "But we cannot continue to make you and the search for your homeworld our priority."

"But…" she whispered. *I have to go home.*

"The manner of your discovery is a complicating factor." Hegoh shifted from one foot to the other. "I do not wish to distress you further, but you need to know."

Michelle couldn't think, couldn't breathe.

"I am still here, Mishel," said Suji softly.

The weight of his hand on her shoulder anchored her back to the present moment. She raised her gaze and focused on his shiny black eyes until she could inhale again. Then she turned back to Hegoh. "What is it?"

Hegoh's posture relaxed slightly, as though he had been braced for her dishonor and was relieved to have avoided it. "The vessel in which you were found was a derelict. Do you know this word?"

"No."

"It was so old," explained Hegoh, "that not only was it not functioning well any longer, the technology in it has not been used in a long time."

A 'long time' among the Vinyi was not the same as for humans. The average Vinyi lifespan was roughly 250 years.

"The radiation on the hull, along with the antiqu - old technology, suggests that you were in space for between 75 and 90 years."

Everything in Michelle froze.

Finding Mars suddenly became a moot point. At least 75 years had passed since the Faceless kidnapped her, stole her away from her life, her family. She had been floating in space for an entire human lifetime. Even if the Vinyi somehow found the red planet, there would be nobody there waiting for her after all this time.

Michelle forgot to breathe.

Dave and Phil were dead.

12

No. The word bubbled up in her, stubborn and insistent. *No, that can't be right.*

Michelle didn't feel as though she'd been asleep for 65 years. Then again, she *had* felt refreshed when she first woke up, her perverse memory reminded her.

No. It wasn't possible. Was it? And... and even if it were, she needed to get ahold of her runaway mind. Dave and Phil would be old, yes, but not dead. There was still a chance that she could get back to them.

There had to be.

Now that the odds were stacked against her again, she had to figure out the best way of making it work. She had to get back to her family.

"Given these facts, we must find a solution to the problem of what to do with you."

Michelle focused sharply on Hegoh. "What to do with me?" *Like I'm a piece of luggage.* She looked from him to Suji and back again. "What are the options?"

"There are two paths forward in this matter. The first is that, as you have demonstrated not only intelligence but sapience, inasmuch as any being can demonstrate it, you must be treated as a sapient being, and considered the only one of your kind. As far as we can prove, this is indeed so. If a sufficiently strong case can be made, the Council may be petitioned to grant you asylum."

There were a lot of words that Michelle didn't catch, but she picked up the gist of it. "The Vinyi might give me a home?"

Suji confirmed it with his tentacles. "If we can convince the Council that it would be beneficial to both you and the Vinyi culture as a whole."

"Can we do that?" She knew nothing about this Council or how difficult it would be to sway them.

Hegoh grunted. "If you wish it, we will make our best effort."

Michelle tried to kick her brain into gear; her thoughts were sluggish, like they were moving underwater. "What is the other path?"

"Because you are not Vinyi, you are not and never shall be equally sapient and the people would not benefit from your inclusion in society. Therefore, you should be considered an animal, treated as such, and kept for our purposes."

Her gut burned lowly. She thought of the Faceless. "What purposes?"

"Whatever purposes the Council decrees," said Suji. "As a pet, an exhibit…"

"Or a research subject," finished Hegoh.

The burning in her gut erupted into a full flame. "Like hell."

The Vinyi glanced at one another and Michelle realized she had spoken English. "No," she said in Ijlenum, crossing her arms over her chest to emphasize her point.

Hegoh's voice was stern. "If the Council decides on that path, we have no choice but to honor it."

I can't convince anyone to help me get home if I'm only a lab rat. "Then we have to convince the Council to decide on the path of... what did you call it?"

"*Ejomu*," said Hegoh. *Asylum.*

It was her only viable option. "What do I need to do?"

"The Little has chosen to apply for asylum."

Lezmu's face betrayed his surprise for only a moment before settling into schooled neutrality. "I see. And has it been informed of what this will require?"

Hegoh lifted his tentacles respectfully. "She has."

Lezmu contemplated him silently for a moment, then templed the fingers of his two underhands. "You get yourself into the most unusual situations, Hegoh. It was just a simple patrol run."

The captain of the Yukesi grunted. "Yes, sir. It was not intentional."

"It never is with you. Apparently, you have a natural talent for finding complications."

There wasn't much to say to that, so Hegoh said nothing.

"Tell me plainly, Hegoh. What do you think of this being, this - what have you called it? - Little."

He had to choose his words carefully now. He and Lezmu had a solid working relationship; Lezmu had been his superior officer for a dozen years now and the mutual respect between them was solid. But Lezmu had a keen strategic mind and would not support Hegoh's radical proposal without at least a fair probability of success. "I believe the Little is sentient, and the behaviors we have observed to date support the conclusion that she is also sapient. She is intelligent; she has learned much of our language and is learning our customs. She is frail, but that appears to be a trait of her species and not to be held against her specifically. Her courage in this situation has been... acceptable."

"Explain."

"She briefly exhibited panic."

Lezmu's growl sounded low in his throat.

Hegoh was quick with his next statements. "She has since learned of the dishonor in such behavior and has made noticeable improvements in her comportment."

"But dishonor is her tendency."

"Which she has been quick to show can be controlled." Hegoh leaned toward his monitor. "She only needs to be taught properly. She is adapting."

"And her frailty? What of her ability to participate in important ceremonies?"

"She can begin training. We will see what she is capable of and then make accommodations."

Lezmu scoffed. "Why would we make accommodations?"

"Do we not make accommodations for our own children and elderly when it comes to ceremonial combat?"

"The Little is not our own."

A whisper of inspiration came to life in Hegoh's mind. "If she has *yejorep*, she would be our own."

The heavy silence told Hegoh everything he needed to know. "She has *yejorep?*"

"She does not yet understand the concept," he admitted, "but she will."

The admiral hummed. "It would be a significant point in her favor." Hegoh noted that Lezmu was now using *she* and *her* to describe Mishel instead of *it*. "But alone, that would not be enough."

"Agreed."

Lezmu waved one of his overhands. "What could she possibly do to contribute to society?"

"She has learned our language quite quickly. Surely that speaks to a useful ability. Samou and I will find something."

In the pause that followed, Hegoh took a chance and pushed one final appeal. "She is unique, Lezmu. My people have discovered a new unique, sapient species. Give us a chance to show you, the Council, all the people of Hoikke, what she can do, and what she may become if given the opportunity and guidance."

Hegoh held his breath as Admiral Lezmu considered. Finally, he assented. "I will speak with Chief Councilman Sijaj and put a petition before the Council to hear arguments granting asylum to the Little."

"Thank you, Admiral." Hegoh's sense of relief was fleeting. Now the hard work began: it was on him and his men to make a persuasive case for Mishel's value in front of a cohort of Vinyi who would be as inclined to see her as an insect as anything.

"Don't thank me yet," said Lezmu darkly. "If your arguments fail, this folly will plague all of us for years. Do not fail, Hegoh."

"No, sir, Admiral."

Lezmu huffed, and the screen went dark.

The Vinyi had the most onerous definition of asylum Michelle had ever heard. There was no difference that she could see between asylum and immigration. She had no interest in becoming a permanent resident, she just needed a safe place to live until she could go home. For a society that prided itself on its compassion, it became increasingly clear to Michelle that their government spent its mercy on their own; everyone else had to merit basic decency.

Thankfully, she didn't have to go it alone. "There are four main subjects in which you will need to prove competence: language, culture, government, and contribution. The first three can be taught, and you are already on your way to basic language ability," said Samou. "The last one may be difficult, but it is, at its most basic, nothing more than finding you a job, though the more uniquely the job is suited to you the better.

"I will focus on your language lessons," he continued. "Suji will teach you about our government, and we will all seek a contribution opportunity for you."

"What about cultural awareness?"

The chime signaling that someone was at her door sounded. She stood and walked to see who it was.

Not long after Hegoh left a few hours ago, two new Vinyi had come to her door and carried in two regular-Vinyi-sized chairs. They arranged her visitor chairs in one corner and left, all the while eyeing her suspiciously but chatting comfortably with Suji. Suji had left not long after that with an amiable squeeze to her shoulder, and Michelle had laid down on her new bed and stared out her window at the stars.

She hadn't had too much time to dwell on the recent development before her door chime sounded. Suji hadn't explained how to open the door before he left, so Samou had called instructions through the door until she was able to let him in.

Opening the door now, she looked up at yet another new Vinyi. "Ah, Lihku," said Samou. "We were just about to talk about you."

"We were?" Michelle turned back to the doctor.

"We were," he confirmed.

She turned back to her new visitor. "Please come in."

Lihku grunted and stepped into the room. His skin was paler than the other Vinyis', reminding her of the gray of Earth's sky just before a winter snow.

"How are you, Lihku?" Michelle was mindful of extending the tradition greeting to the one who was going to teach her of their culture.

"Well, thank you, and you?" he replied, not waiting for an answer before he asked Samou, "Is she ready?"

"Remedially."

Lihku grunted.

"Ready for what?" Michelle sat in one of her chairs and faced them.

"Training, Little," said Lihku.

"What kind of training?"

He lifted one under-tusk tentacle in her direction. "You are applying to join a culture of warriors." He surveyed her from head to toe. "You are not strong. Can you fight?"

Michelle knew it was true, but she bristled anyway.

"What do you mean, I'm not strong? How do you know I'm not strong?"

Lihku blinked. "Are you strong?"

She grimaced and tilted her head. "Not compared to you," she muttered.

"Can you fight?"

She sighed and rolled her eyes. "Not compared to you." The truth was that she couldn't fight at all, but he didn't need to know that.

By the time they walked out of Michelle's quarters, however, Lihku had figured that out. They had just left her chambers and were en route to the lift when he said, "You are no warrior. If you had merely lost your strength, you would still move like a warrior." He peered down his tentacles at her. "You do not move like a warrior."

She shrugged. *The jig is up.* "I'm not a warrior. I'm a kind of scientist."

"What do you know?"

An interesting way to put it. "I know languages. I study how languages work."

Lihku grunted. *As common as that sound is, it really ought to count as its own word.* "This is why you are able to learn *Ijlenum* so quickly."

"Yes."

The huge warrior said nothing for a few moments as they stepped into the lift, then, once it got underway, "What else do you know?"

Michelle thought of Mars and a pang of longing so sharp

struck her that she almost winced. "I know a little bit about plants."

"Food plants or pretty plants?"

She laughed. "On my world, some food plants *are* pretty, but I understand. Food plants."

He grunted again. "Tell Samou of this. It may be your contribution."

"It was on Mars," she said. "I would be happy to make it so here."

The lift doors opened. "Come."

He strode out and, unlike Samou and Suji, Lihku made no effort to slow his step or shorten his stride to accommodate her. She had to lightly jog to keep up. Given how her muscles had strengthened over the past weeks in the stronger gravity, Michelle thought this would be easier.

By the time they reached a set of brown doors set into the beige walls, she was panting a bit and had broken a light sweat. Lihku opened the doors and marched in, clearly expecting her to follow.

She did.

He made for a large black mat in the far corner of the room. The rest of the room was filled with all kinds of machines Michelle didn't recognize, and one wall was lined entirely with what appeared to be weapons. Angry, vicious weapons. "Today we will - "

Lihku stopped abruptly and stared at her.

"What?"

"What is this?" he asked, pointing to her forehead. "Your skin is wet."

Oh. "Ah, that's... I don't know the *Ijlenum* word for it. We call it sweat. It means that my body is working harder than it is used to and is too warm, so it sweats to cool back down."

"Swayt." Lihku tried the strange word. "Ssssswayt."

Michelle nodded. *Close enough.* "Sweat."

"If you are too warm, you may remove any clothing necessary. Many Vinyi train without clothes."

Her face grew warm at the thought. "What?"

Lihku removed his uniform jacket.

"Wait!" Her face now felt uncomfortably hot. "Are you… you're not going to…"

"To what?"

She cleared her throat but couldn't meet his eyes. "Are you going to train without clothes?"

Lihku barked. "I do not think, Little, that training with you will require such measures."

Thank God. "Yes," she heartily agreed. "Yes, you're absolutely right."

He hung his jacket on a large hook on the wall and turned back to her. "Now, Little, we begin."

Her stomach fluttered with nerves. Gym had never been her best subject in school.

"Do what I do, as well as you can." And Lihku struck a pose that reminded Michelle of the yoga classes she would take from time to time when she lived on Earth.

Following his example, Michelle lifted her right foot and brought the bottom of it to the inside of her left calf. Then she extended her arms straight out at her sides, parallel to the floor.

They stood there.

This isn't so bad.

Two minutes later, they were still standing there. Her left ankle was trembling, making her wobble, and her shoulders were beginning to burn like a hot iron.

Lihku stood there like a statue.

A bead of sweat rolled into her eyes. "Lihku..?"

"I am still standing, Little. Do what I do."

"Yes, I understand the instructions, but - "

"I am not talking. Only standing. Do what I do."

Michelle's ankle was talking, though, and it was saying that she had approximately three seconds left in this position. Sure enough, her left ankle gave a great shudder and she stumbled, flailing a bit as she fell hard onto her butt.

Lihku hummed. "I see." He bent over and extended a hand to help her up; Michelle's arm objected to being lifted to take it. He straightened, and that's when Michelle realized he was still standing in the damn pose. Slowly, he lowered his foot to the ground and assessed her.

She stood up straight and met his gaze.

"Now the other side," he said.

Michelle wisely kept her groan to herself.

Training with Lihku for 90 minutes felt like... well, she had no frame of reference to compare. She had *colonized Mars*, for crying out loud, and she had never - *never* - felt this bone-deep tired before. After taking her through a series of poses that left her muscles burning and weak, she then did some calisthenics, some resistance training, and the very beginning of a sequence that would teach her how to avoid an assailant grabbing at her.

She could barely move her legs.

Lihku walked her back to the hall that led to her quarters. At first, as they'd left the training hall, he'd walked along at his normal speed. Michelle had been literally incapable of jogging alongside him, an absence Lihku had noticed after only a few strides. To his credit, he slowed his stride on the return trip.

When they arrived at her corridor, Lihku stopped. "Have a brave heart, Little. Your body will become strong." His tentacles shimmied. "Stronger," he corrected himself.

She gave him an ironic half-smile. "Thanks."

Then Lihku did something he had not done before. He smiled at her. It wasn't big, just a small lift with the familiar bend, but he did it. "You will improve."

The irony faded from her expression. "Thanks," she repeated, this time sincere.

He grunted, which was pretty much what she expected him to do, and walked away.

Michelle turned, walked three doors down, and went into her quarters. She ordered a glass of water from the wall unit. Standing there, unwilling to shuffle even another step, she chugged it all. She drained the last drop, then set the glass down and stared at her bed.

It was only a few meters away, but it may as well have been a hundred.

It's only a few steps. Only a few more steps. Baby steps. Comfort is only a few more baby steps away.

With a deep breath, she gave the last of her energy to the objective of reaching her bed. When she finally reached it, she fell on top of the covers and was out cold before the mattress stopped bouncing from the sudden impact of her grateful collapse.

13

Michelle noticed the change in her routine right away. Now that the Yukesi was back to performing its normal duties, patrolling its assigned sector of Vinyi space, Suji, Samou, and Mebeku had a bit less time to spend with her. The schedule had become precise, and when her time was up with one of them, it was abruptly up. This ended up working in her favor, however, because it gave her time to study in between sessions with her tutors, accelerating the effectiveness of her lessons over the week after Hegoh's Council announcement.

Suji started her government lessons with the area of the government she had the most exposure to: the military. The Yukesi was a government-commissioned battle cruiser, a standard patrol ship equipped with enough firepower to defend Vinyi territory if needed, but not nearly as much armament as a warship. Its orders came to Captain Hegoh through the Council.

The Council was a 13-member group of representatives, one from each of the occupied continents on Hoikke, a planet that was more than 85% water. The Council ran the government, including the military, in peacetime, but in the event of war, that power ceded to the King. The King could, at any time, override the decisions of the Council, but was very selective about doing so, as nullifying a Council decision eroded the authority of the Council, which in turn decreased its effectiveness. The King hadn't overruled the Council in 1,700 years.

Michelle didn't know what, exactly, the King did in times of peace, or what his name was, for that matter. She made a note to ask Suji.

She read another page of Suji's lesson on the purpose of the Vinyi military and holidays associated with it or its mission, but she found her gaze drifting lazily to the small viewport in her room rather than on the scrolling text of the monitor. After the third time she caught herself daydreaming, Michelle rolled her eyes and sighed in frustration.

The room they had given her was nice, all the more so because they had made it especially for her. It wouldn't be mistaken for a luxury hotel, but it had everything she needed plus privacy to boot. But sometimes, privacy was overrated.

Like now, when it felt more like loneliness.

Her thoughts drifted, as they often did, to Dave and Phil. Where were they now? Were they still on Mars? Or had they returned to Earth after she was taken? Was Phil all right? She worried for Dave, of course, but she knew her husband would recover; he had a strength of character she could only envy. But Phil… he'd lost Katherine, then their dad, and then Michelle herself, too. The sharp sting of regret made her wince even now. She'd promised him she wouldn't leave, then within days, she was gone.

She shook her head to clear it. Going too far down that thought path would reduce her to helpless tears, and that wasn't going to help her get back to them. She needed to study.

Michelle tried to focus, but a persistent restlessness foiled her. She looked around the already familiar room. All she had seen of the ship was this room, her hallway, the medbay, a couple of private observation rooms, and the training hall. There had to be other places she could go, other things to see. Where did the crew go when they were off duty?

A cafeteria. There had to be a cafeteria on board.

Michelle pulled up the Yukesi's schematics the way Suji had shown her. There it was! *Group Eating Room* surely meant cafeteria, didn't it? She examined the schematics until she had memorized the way. And if she got lost, what was the worst that could happen? Suji and Samou both had confirmed that everyone knew she was here, and lots of Vinyi had seen her walking the halls with one of her three regular escorts plenty of times. She spoke the language now and could easily ask for directions if she needed them.

She stood. She was going to go to the cafeteria.

The corners of her mouth lifted as she exited her quarters with a rising sense of morale. Who knew that a simple quasi-exploration would be so exciting?

She only passed one Vinyi on the way to the lift. It concerned her a little that he stopped in his tracks and stared at her as she went by, but she tried to shrug it off and kept walking as though she belonged there. She got onto the lift, which was empty, and programmed in her destination. When the lift doors closed and the machine began moving smoothly in the desired direction, Michelle stood a little straighter. *I'm doing it. I'm making my way on my own.*

When the lift doors opened, she navigated the corridors with increasing confidence. The Vinyi she passed still stared, some of them slowing their stride to do so, but nobody stopped her. She took a right, then a left, then another left.

There it was. The door to the cafeteria loomed large at the end of the hall.

Michelle came to a slow halt. Suddenly, this didn't seem like the great idea she thought it was in the safety of her quarters. She would be the only human in an enclosed room probably chock full of Vinyi. She was used to being the only human by now, but her exposure to groups of the hulking aliens had been controlled, never more than three at a time, and she always knew all three. Who knew how many would be in there, eating? She knew the capacity of the room was about 80. What if it were full? That would be a lot of strangers to navigate even if they were all human, and this was a much greater challenge. What if she made some grievous misstep and offended everyone, with nobody there to assist her?

She swallowed and wiped her suddenly sweaty palms on her pants, still yards from the door. She had proven that she could find her way around, she didn't need to ruin that triumph by making a fool of herself in front of everyone. Maybe it would be best if she just went back to her quarters.

Michelle turned around and ran smack into a solid Vinyi body. It was like walking into a wall. She lost her balance and tumbled to the floor, scrambling up quickly with her face aflame. "I'm so sorry! Please excuse me." She kept her gaze down, and counted four feet in addition to her own.

One of the Vinyi hummed, an elongated sound that had her looking up at the being making it. He was somehow slenderer than most of his kind, but that made him no less intimidating. His skin had an amethyst undertone; she'd seen that color somewhere before but couldn't quite place it.

The Vinyi beside him had a yellow cast. He bent down at the waist to better peer at her. "What do we have here, Rim?"

Rim's tentacles curled in a sneer. "Obviously, that's Samou's new pet. Even if I hadn't already seen it, you could tell simply by how ugly it is."

Yellow barked. "I've never seen anything like it." He reached out a finger and poked Michelle in the shoulder.

She tried to think over the sound of her heart pounding in her ears. "I'm very sorry. Excuse me, I'm just going back to my quarters," she managed as she sidled to the space between Rim and the wall.

He smoothly moved and blocked her way.

She looked up. Rim smiled at her, but there was no kindness in it.

Yellow moved to her other side, penning her in. He poked her again, this time in her breast. "It's small and soft. How disgusting." But he was smiling as he poked her in the belly.

"Please don't," Michelle said, trying to breathe and avoid the next finger that was coming her way.

Yellow barked again. "Did you hear that? It mewls like a newborn *vehohu*." He bent a little further and before Michelle could do anything about it, two of his great hands encircled her hips and lifted her off the ground.

She yelped and squirmed. "Stop it!" She pushed fruitlessly against his grip. "Put me down!"

He brought her closer to his face. A tentacle reached out and caressed her cheek and neck. It was cold, damp, and slightly sticky, and she shuddered in revulsion.

"Put her down, Vaomi," said a voice Michelle knew.

"Ah! It's the great doctor himself," Rim said. Vaomi still held her tight, his tentacle snaking its way under her shirt and creeping around her waist.

"I'm surprised you would condone behavior like this, Rimoli." Samou broadened his shoulders as he faced them.

Rimoli huffed. "Please. Nothing dishonorable is occurring here. Vaomi is just curious about the Little, aren't you?"

The yellow one hummed. "For being so puny, it's rather tasty." Vaomi's tentacle was exploring her ear now.

"Please," Michelle whispered, wincing and pulling away. "Please stop."

"I won't say it again. Put her down." And the membrane that covered a third of Samou's tusks slid back to reveal the entirety of their deadly curve.

Rimoli sighed. "You're upsetting Samou, Vaomi. Best let his pet go."

"I'm sure I'll see you again soon," the yellowish one said as he lowered her back to the floor. The moment Michelle's feet set down, she dashed for the safety behind Samou.

"She is a sapient being," Samou growled. "Treating *any* sapient being in that manner calls one's honor into question."

Rimoli smirked. "Your flair for the dramatic doesn't disappoint. We do not know of the sapience, or lack thereof, of your little pet."

Samou ignored Rimoli, putting his face very close to Vaomi's. "Ensure that this disgraceful behavior remains an isolated incident."

Vaomi's tusks bared slightly. "I was doing nothing dishonorable. I'll do what I want, old one."

Samou glared at him a moment longer, then turned, pushed Michelle ahead of him, and stormed down the corridor toward the lift. Michelle ran at his side through every turn.

She was shaking inside. She still felt Vaomi's slobber all over her skin as she and Samou entered the lift. When the doors closed, she said, "Samou - "

He cut her off with a brusque wave of his hand and a low growl that raised the hairs on the back of her neck.

She stood next to her rescuer in silence, waiting for the lift doors to open.

When they did, she had to full-on run once more to keep up with Samou's rapid stride. When they arrived at her door, he merely said, "Open it."

She did, and they both stepped inside.

The moment the door closed behind them, Samou exploded. "That was *stupid*, Mishel!"

The tears filled her eyes unbidden.

"Why would you do that? *Why?!* Walking through the halls on your own like that. You... you..." He waved all four of his hands in spastic movements before he turned on her. "Do you truly think that one of us is always with you in public because we have nothing better to do?! Not everyone on board shares our opinion of you, Little One. Far too many of them will see you as *they* did, as nothing more than a plaything, a non-entity here for their small-minded amusement. How *dare* you venture out on your own and put all of our hard work, put *yourself*, at risk?! Is your respect for us and for yourself as small as your stature?!"

He took a breath and sat down in one of her visitor chairs, head in hands. "Mishel, you are not ready to be out there on your own. What were you thinking?"

She was trying to honor him, really she was, but she couldn't stop the tears from rolling down her cheeks. Nonetheless, Michelle fought to keep the quaver out of her voice. "I wasn't thinking. I only wanted to see more of the ship, to get out of this room, to… to do something, accomplish something, on my own," she admitted.

Samou lifted his face to regard her. "Do you think you have accomplished nothing?"

She shrugged, her palms facing the ceiling. "I can't do *anything* without one of you."

"Mishel." His voice was softer now. "You speak a language you knew nothing of four weeks ago, and you speak it well. You are shouldering the burdens of your circumstances and adapting. You are striving now to climb a steep hill and petition the Council for asylum. But most of all, Mishel," he paused and shook his tentacles at her, "you survived. When no one else did, you survived. That is not nothing, child."

She hung her head. The sorrow in his tone lowered her spirits even more than Vaomi's unwelcome exploration. "I'm sorry, Samou."

"Sam. Just Sam. And until Lihku says you're ready, do not leave your quarters without one of us."

And he stood and left without another word.

Michelle sank to the ground where she stood. Silently, she trembled, a crumpled heap too weary even to cry.

Sam all but burst into the medbay, blew past Mebeku and the others, and stormed into his office, closing the door behind him. *How could she have been so stupid?!*

The heat of combat-lust pulsed through his veins. He couldn't believe she had wandered out alone, making herself vulnerable, presenting herself a tempting prize for low-minded *yezkunij* like Vaomi. Sam pounded on his desk at the thought of the two bullies arrogantly lording themselves over her. How *dare* Vaomi lay his hands on her? Scare her? *Taste* her, by Qunuk! He again banged a meaty fist on his desk so hard the equipment sitting on it jumped. He had seen Mishel there, squirming helplessly in Vaomi's grasp as (Sam's tusks bared themselves again) he tasted her, with Rimoli looking on, and he'd wanted to pound both of them into dust and blow them out the nearest hatch. His need to get Mishel to safety was all that had spared the wastes of skin from a fierce beating.

Then, through the rage, the shame began to creep its way into his thoughts. *How could I have been so stupid?*

Of *course* she would grow restless, cooped up in her quarters all the time. Sam had turned her living space into a glorified cage and Mishel was not a being who should be caged. He should have seen that coming. And he had been a blind old fool to think his connection with her, his reputation, would be enough to protect her should she ever need it.

He had heard the gossip about her, about his so-called obsession with her, had noticed the whispers that cut off abruptly when he entered the room. No, there were too many with minds and hearts too small for Sam to be able to rely on common decency and the reputation of a war-hero-turned-doctor. Lihku could not bring Mishel to a point of basic self-defense competence soon enough.

The door to his office chimed and he wondered who would have the audacity to interrupt him *now*. "Sam?" called a voice from the other side of the door.

He opened the door and invited Suji in. "How did you know?"

"The only thing that travels faster than the Yukesi is gossip aboard the Yukesi," Suji said, sitting on the edge of his desk. "Tell me."

Sam relayed his version of the events in the mess hall corridor. Suji's fists clenched as his tusks bared a little. "Vaomi is a bottom-feeder," he said, "but Rimoli? I don't like him, but I expected better of him."

Sam huffed, sitting down in the chair behind his desk. He felt a bit calmer now that Suji had come to join him. He wasn't the only one fond of Mishel, a fact he had to remember. "Rimoli is no better than Vaomi. He's just smarter and so hides it more effectively."

Suji swayed his tentacles from side to side. "What do we do about it, Sam? Lihku can only do so much, we can't be with her all the time, but can we really expect her to cower in her gilded cage?"

Sam didn't know the answer, but one thing had become clear to him since he'd come back to his office. "We have erred in this, Suji. We have tried to encourage Mishel, but in doing so, we have isolated and overprotected her. She felt comfortable leaving her quarters today because she assumed the entire crew complement would be like us, that they would hold our same attitude toward her."

"Many do."

"But not enough, or today would not have happened. Do you think nobody else knew what was happening in that hallway? That I was the only one who saw? No," Sam sighed heavily. "I was merely the only one who stood to stop it."

"Then my question stands," Suji said, frustrated. "What do we do?"

Right then, Sam's communications console pinged and Suji's mobile communicator buzzed. They looked at one another, then opened the message they had just received. It was from Hegoh. The Council had agreed to hear arguments petitioning for Mishel's asylum, date to be determined.

Sam looked back up at Suji. "We convince the Council to see her the way we do. That will be her best protection."

14

She was supposed to have afternoon lessons and dinner with Samou that night, but he did not return after issuing his edict for her to stay put. Michelle had wallowed in her misery for a while, then reluctantly got to her feet and pulled herself together. She had bathed until not even a hint of stickiness remained on her skin, and then made up her mind to keep studying. Even if Samou wasn't going to guide her this afternoon, she could certainly read aloud on her own.

It beat doing nothing. Doing nothing led back to wallowing, to dwelling in the emptiness in her heart, drowning in the increasing pain from missing Phil and Dave so much. She longed to turn the clock back a few years, before her mom had died, and find a way to keep this all from happening. Unfortunately, she didn't have that kind of power. All she had the power to do now was study *Ijlenum*.

As the hours passed, Michelle read and spoke and wrote. She was reading *The Tale of Two Axes* over a small dinner of *kizunehe hilen*, a dish that reminded her of a cross between croûtons and spaghetti, when her door chime went off.

It was Suji.

He entered when bidden and waited until the door closed behind him to speak. "Sam is beside himself."

She nodded. "Yes." That had been pretty clear when he left.

He sat and regarded her regretfully. "What happened today is our fault, Mishel, far more than yours."

"What?" Michelle blinked at him. "What are you talking about? Samou saved me from my own stupidity, getting myself into a situation I wasn't ready for. It was my fault."

Suji firmly shook his tentacles from side to side. "No, we erred in our judgment. We made a decision, Sam and I, to mostly shield you from the rest of the ship while we tried to teach you about our world. I can see now that we should have given you a more complete picture of our people. I was going to get to it in our lessons soon, but it wasn't soon enough."

Michelle sat. "So tell me now."

"Yes," Suji agreed. "I will.

"Vinyi, on the whole, do not trust outsiders. We are stronger, smarter, faster, and, in many ways, simply better than other species we meet." He shrugged. "It is perhaps arrogant to say it, and more so to believe it, but it is true. Vinyi are *proud* of being Vinyi, and we look down on anyone who is not our own.

"This is as true for me as anyone else," he said, "except when it comes to you."

"Why me?"

He smiled shamefacedly. "Because I found you. You are my discovery. I have an interest in you that extends beyond my curiosity. If you are found to be more than an animal, you are the most important discovery, the most important contribution I will ever make to history, to science, to my people. Sam is the same. Discovering a new intelligent species is a highly uncommon event. Together, we decided that we would examine you, gage your abilities, see what you were."

He shook his tentacles again. "Then you surprised us by speaking. At first, we thought perhaps it was advanced mimicry; there are both birds and fish who can do that."

The image of a talking fish out of Dr. Seuss ran through Michelle's mind.

"But no, you understood. You began speaking, not just the words, but the content you chose, communicating your own message, listening to ours. When you told us of Mars, of your family, of your mistreatment at the hands of those you call the Faceless, Sam and I realized that we had far more responsibility than we had anticipated when it came to you. But then we could not find your planet, and we still cannot find any others of your kind, so now we must resolve the problem of what do with you, and convince the Council accordingly."

"The problem of what to do with me."

Her flat affect had no impact on the engineer. "Yes. If you are sapient, you are not merely an animal. But you are obviously not Vinyi, so by custom, you do not merit better treatment than an animal. Not unless the Council acknowledges your sapience as equal and grants you asylum."

Michelle's stomach rolled. "Suji, this Council... it's made up of Vinyi who faithfully represent the people of the 13 continents?"

Suji lifted his tentacles in his version of a nod.

"And has the Council *ever* acknowledged an alien as

having equal sapience and granting it asylum?"

"No," he replied, making her heart sink. He quickly followed it with, "but there has never been a need before. We have never made contact with a species of which there existed only one member. We have never met a species that *needed* asylum."

"Until me."

He nodded again.

She sighed and ran a hand through her hair. "Great."

Suji stayed with her into the evening, spelling out his and Sam's strategy. The current plan was subject to change by the day depending on her progress. Because she had consistently made the most progress in the area of language, Sam was going to start training her on more official documents and language, specifically the format of official ship's records. If Michelle could become sufficiently fluent, she could begin to compare reports of the same incident from various crew members and begin to find discrepancies that needed to be followed up. If she could achieve that by the day of her Council hearing, she may be able to demonstrate an ability to contribute to society as a ship archivist.

Lihku had declared that Michelle's physical abilities were so remedial, he was not going to be able to bring her up to speed on his own. Lihku would train her in self-defense, mostly how to avoid being caught or, if caught, how to free herself. Kalik, one of Lihku's officers, would function as her personal trainer, improving her cardiovascular and muscular fitness so that Lihku's lessons didn't injure her.

Suji would continue to teach her how the military was organized; the better she understood how and why the Yukesi ran the way it did, the better she would be able to perform her contribution. He was also going to teach her about their holidays and the history behind them. An important one, *Negoheh*, was coming up at the end of the next Vinyi month, which was about 38 days long.

They didn't know when Michelle's Council hearing would be held, and they would receive only 30 hours notice before it was due to begin. But one thing was certain: the Council would reach a decision before *Negoheh*. The two weeks leading up to the day itself were full of celebration and feasting, day and night, with two weeks of rest and recovery following. Only essential duties got done during this time. The Councilmembers would not want to have outstanding business hanging over their heads during their two weeks' holiday, especially not business of such an unusual nature.

Once Suji bid her good night, Michelle walked over to her desk and began to write. The words poured out of her, driven by her dread. If the Council decided against her, what would become of her? Would anyone even remember her in five years' time? Would everything she had experienced simply vanish into the vastness of forgotten history?

Someone should know. *Someone* should remember.

So she wrote. She wrote letters that she knew would never be delivered, and she wrote ones that needed to be. She wrote a letter to Dave, pouring out her heart; and one to Phil, exhorting him to be strong. Then she wrote one each to Sam and Suji; without them, she would have been dead from the moment she left the possession of the Faceless. She wrote a letter to herself, the version of her that existed five years ago, telling her of everything that was going to happen to her and how insane it would all be. She wrote a letter to herself ten years from now, wishing for the foreknowledge and experience that version of her would have, if she lived through this.

She wrote until she fell asleep at her desk.

The next days passed in a blur of studying, exercising, fighting, and deeply, blissfully sleeping. Sam's unfiltered comments in the midst of his frustration with her had struck a nerve. Yes, she was the one in an extremely awkward, even dangerous, situation, but every one of her tutors had other things they could be doing with their time. Instead, they were giving her hours of their attention every day.

The least she could do in return was her best.

Her body grew stronger, her muscles taking on form and volume thanks to Kalik's relentless instruction. Her reaction time decreased the more she practiced with Lihku, and by the end of the next two weeks, she was eluding grabs that had stopped her cold at the start and beginning to mount a counter offense. Sam channeled his energies into eliminating her accent until it was almost nonexistent and her writing was easily legible. Suji taught her all about the chain of command and the structure of the spacefaring forces, and gleefully introduced her to the joys of *Negoheh*. It was a combination of excessive feasting, gift giving, combat displays, and costume wearing, the discussion of which transformed Suji from a fierce warrior engineer into an excited child.

Michelle was so busy she hardly had time to miss Phil and Dave during the days. The nights, though, were a different story. Each night, from the time her head hit the pillow until she fell into desperate, dreamless sleep, she longed with everything she was to be home with them.

"An asylum hearing?! For the creature?!" Vaomi was astonished.

Rimoli was equally appalled, though calmer about it. "I, too, am at a loss. We are *Vinyi*. We are the noble, courageous, strong, and victorious. This *Little* thinks it should be considered the same?" He spat.

"When?" Vaomi still sat there, slack-jawed, in Rimoli's guest chair.

"I do not know."

Vaomi stood and began pacing, his tentacles growing more rigid with every step. "It's insulting. It's absurd. The Little cannot be equal to us. It is…" He waved an underhand in the air. "*Inferior*. And the Council has agreed to hear its arguments? Why would they debase themselves this way?"

Rimoli lifted his glass in agreement. "Again, I do not know, but our proud culture has never been lower. Imagine it." He took a sip. "Next thing you know, we'll be holding hearings to determine if *liyij* are sapient and should no longer be menu items."

"It makes all of us look bad, especially those of us here, on Yukesi. We're the ones who discovered it, who brought it aboard, who reanimated it." Vaomi sat, shoulders sagging. "We brought about this shame on our own people."

"No." Rimoli's voice was hard. "Samou and that annoying engineer have done this. The *Little* itself has done this. The strangeness of the creature and the thrill of making a significant new discovery have swept our people up in a current of insanity. It will pass, but not before it does its damage to our dignity. You and I, and those like us, those of us who still have our right minds, who remember who we are, who are still mindful of what it means to be Vinyi... we are the ones who must save our own people from this mess."

"How?"

Rimoli ran a finger over the rim of his glass. He had been giving this some thought. "Some battles are waged and won far from the battlefield, if one only has the proper ammunition. Surely there are those on the Council who have not always upheld the highest of Vinyi standards, and even more surely, there are those who know about their indiscretions. If we can find those indiscretions, those secret holders, we can, perhaps..." He made a show of seeking the right word. "*Enlighten* those on the Council as to the errors of their ways."

Vaomi hummed. Rim had always been the cleverer of the two of them, using knowledge, leverage, and intimidation to turn situations to his advantage. But that was not Vaomi's way. No, let Rim manage the subtlety and manipulation. Vaomi himself preferred simple solutions.

There were simpler ways of removing obstacles and solving problems.

"We cannot do nothing," he agreed.

Sweat rolled down her forehead; she wiped it away before it got to her eyes. They didn't sweat, so no Vinyi had ever bothered to invent a sweatband. Maybe that could be her contribution.

Lihku stood there, sizing Michelle up as she waited, her weight in the balls of her feet. He growled and lowered himself into a half-crouch, lifting a tentacle at her. The action, which scared her shitless a month ago, instead now caused her to curl her lip at him in response.

He lunged, and she spun to the outside like Lihku had taught her, letting him go by. He was ready for that, though, and lost no time pushing back in her direction. Michelle ducked and rolled out of reach, springing back to her feet in time to see him turn toward her. He growled again, and she simply watched him, waiting.

Lihku jumped toward her, his arms outstretched. Michelle took advantage of the extra height he gained with the jump to duck and roll under his legs, coming to her feet behind him. He was fast, though. He pivoted before she could fully gain her balance. His hand shot out and grabbed the back of her shirt.

She stuck her arms straight up overhead and dropped into a squat, letting him have the shirt. She pushed off from her squat into a forward roll then stood and made to sprint away.

After two steps, her head snapped back and her scalp stung.

Lihku had her by the ponytail.

The past weeks of training kicked in. Where before she would have whimpered and helplessly grasped at his grip on her hair, now she curled into his arm and jabbed the inside of his wrist with all her fingers, first stabbing then scratching with her fingernails. It was one of two vulnerable spots in the Vinyi's tough hide; the other was where the base of a human's sternum would be, an area usually well covered and unreachable.

Lihku yelped and released his grip.

She ran for the corner of the room.

When Michelle got there, she turned back, panting, to see where her attacker was, only to find him still standing on the mat where she'd left him.

Lihku stood straight and tall, his chest puffed out and a big grin across his face. "You did it."

She relaxed. With an increasing sense of pride, she began to grin back at him. "I did, didn't I?" She'd finally done it. After a month of conditioning and training and trying and failing so very hard, she'd finally gotten away from him.

He nodded once. "Well done, Little."

Michelle felt ten feet tall. "Though she be but a Little," she joked, "she is fierce."

15

The day of *Negoheh* itself wouldn't officially be for two more weeks, but the festivities began tonight, according to Suji. He'd had Michelle read a history of the holiday herself, and he was so excited about the impending revelry he couldn't restrain himself and told it to her again.

Eons ago, when history was ill-kept and murky, Hoikke was ruled by two primitive tribes, the Pemiha and the Nuzmi, each of which sought to take control of the other's territory. The Pemiha were rude, slovenly, barbaric louts, while the Nuzmi were brave, noble, and courageous.

And clearly the ones writing the history books.

The tribal wars had lasted for centuries, and things were looking bad for the Nuzmi. The most elite of the Pemiha fighters had taken control of Pehkoh, the cultural and governmental center of Nuzmi territory. They destroyed art and books, executed the men, raped and enslaved the women and children. In the meantime, other Pemiha fighters were tracking down and executing the Nuzmi in the surrounding area, slowly but surely, bringing the Nuzmi to the brink of surrender.

Then arose a great Nuzmi warrior named Vaikkiku. He was of such noble bearing in life and unfailing victory in battle that when he petitioned the gods for aid in defeating the Pemiha, Qunuk, the god of honor, and his honorable pantheon heard him and granted his prayer. They sent a battalion of angels to fight alongside the remaining Nuzmi soldiers. Though the Nuzmi were half-starved and failing fast, the sight of the angelic battalion spurred them to war with renewed vigor in their bodies and spirits. The Nuzmi charged the gates that the Pemiha had erected around Pehkoh and, at Vaikkiku's direction, the angels swung their flaming swords as one and felled the walls. The Nuzmi stormed into Pehkoh, killing all the Pemiha and rescuing their people, their families, and their culture.

Michelle lost count of the tribal feasts that followed. There was one honoring Vaikkiku, one for the gods, one for the battle angels, one in celebration of the overall victory, one for the recovered art, one for the rescued books, one for the freed captives... the list went on. The day of *Negoheh* was the supposed anniversary of Vaikkiku's victory, but the celebration began now.

Clearly, nightly feasts were a key feature of *Negoheh* season. So too was costuming. It had begun with many Vinyi dressing up as either Vaikkiku, angels, or Nuzmi warriors, or even the enemy Pemiha fighters. Nowadays, though, it was accepted, even encouraged, to masquerade as anything at all.

To that end, Suji had altered a costume of Vaikkiku to fit her. It had taken her a fair while to get into it, and, looking into the mirror now, Michelle wasn't sure if she looked more like a Viking or a hedgehog. No matter. Suji had gotten this for her, and she would wear it proudly.

Well, she would wear it, at least.

Her door chimed and Michelle went to answer it. It would be Sam and Suji, there to escort her to the party. The sight that met her eyes when she opened the door made her brain lock up.

Sam (she could tell it was him by the color of his hide) was an angelic warrior. He wore silver armor from head to foot, topped with a silver helm of intricate design that finished in a wicked spike. He bore a shield as big as the side of a bus and a sword that, through some kind of special effect, glowed and flickered in shades of red and orange, giving the impression of flaming. Michelle stared. He was jaw-dropping.

A shuffling movement at his side caught her attention and she looked at Suji. Then she tilted her head and goggled at Suji some more. He wasn't Vaikkiku, nor an angel, and if the mess standing in front of her was what either side's fighters had looked like, she would eat her fake fur-lined boot.

He had a raggedy brown nest on his head, a snarl that was a cross between a mop and a tangle of yarn. His face was completely covered by a stretchy orange mask with oversized, glowing white eyes and a small red slit for a mouth. His shirt and pants were simple, functional clothes with no special characteristics that would give her a clue about -

Wait. His shirt had only two sleeves. His two lower arms were snugged up against his sides inside it.

Michelle's mouth began to twitch. *Oh. Oh, no.*

Brown hair, white eyes, small mouth, two arms.

"I'm YOU!" Suji announced, throwing his two free arms wide. "I'm a Little!"

For the first time since before she was taken from Mars, Michelle belly laughed.

Michelle had been nervous going to the feast, milling about in a room full of giants, some of whom had no desire to have her there. Even accompanied by Sam and Suji, she was keenly aware of the pressure of every set of eyes that stared at her too long, or with too much heat or chill. To her surprise, there were far fewer of those than she had expected. Instead, she was greeted with open joviality.

"Hearty Feasting, Samou! Suji! Little!" toasted someone Michelle hadn't met as they walked by. Judging by the fact that all four of his hands held drinks rather than food, she'd bet that he'd done more imbibing than feasting.

"Hearty Feasting, Daikor!" replied Sam. A burst of raucous laughter had Michelle's head whipping to the other side of the room. Suji was proudly parading his costume in front of a group of six Vinyi sitting at a table. Their tentacles were quivering with mirth, and more than one was either holding his belly or pounding a fist on the table.

Suji flipped his hair and sashayed away to enthusiastic applause.

Michelle and Sam followed him to a table at the edge of the room. They sat down, while she climbed up into her seat and knelt on it in order to reach the table comfortably. The cafeteria, which she now knew was more correctly called the mess hall, had been festooned with glittery decorations from top to bottom. Stars, swords, shields, and figures of the angelic battalion adorned every surface, catching the light and glimmering merrily. Round tables with chairs set up around them dotted the room; long rectangular tables were filled to their edges with plate after plate of different foods. The air smelled of vanilla and cinnamon and mango and cloves and maybe even a trace of a wood fire. The noise level in the room was a little louder than a dull roar, but the joy and camaraderie in it made it exhilarating rather than intimidating.

Sam stood. "I will bring back food for us," he said to Michelle. He grinned at Suji. "You can get your own after I return."

Suji grinned back and leaned down toward Michelle as Sam walked away. "You see those three over there?" He pointed below the surface of the table where only she could see.

"Yes."

"They write plays for the crew to enjoy when we're off duty. They've done it for years, and they've gotten to be pretty good. And those two - " Suji gestured to two Vinyi dressed as Nuzmi fighters who were making their way along one of the many buffet tables, "they're a couple, but they're trying to be quiet about it, so even though everyone knows, nobody lets on. Oh! And that one - " He pointed to someone wearing an explosion of shimmering colors that reminded Michelle of oil floating on water. "He got so drunk at last year's *Negoheh* that he woke up the next day naked and sprawled out on the main map display in Stellar Cartography."

She laughed at Suji's chortle. "What is he dressed as?"

"The Gods' Painting." At her puzzled expression, he explained. "In the southern hemisphere of Hoikke, on the western coast of the southernmost continent, the night sky lights up every night as the gods cast colors of all tones and brightnesses among the stars." He shrugged. "We know, of course, that's it just a gaseous reaction, but the sheer beauty of it takes you aback. Just because we have explanations for things doesn't mean those things aren't sacred or wondrous."

She regarded her friend thoughtfully. Apparently there was a poetic aspect of Vinyi culture that she had yet to uncover.

Sam returned with a heaping plate for himself and a snack-sized one for her. Her stomach growled in anticipation, but nobody heard it over the din of the party.

The food smelled incredible and tested better. Michelle wasn't sure what she was eating at least half the time, but Sam was her doctor, after all, so if he'd brought it to her, she would take it on faith that it wouldn't kill her.

"Are *Negoheh* celebrations like this everywhere?"

Sam shook his tentacles. "They are like this here because we are confined to this vessel and away from our families. We act as family for each other during the holiday. Typically, there is neighborhood feasting, then there is at-home feasting."

"That's a lot of eating."

Sam laughed. "Yes, but there is also a lot of fighting. Battle contests are nearly as constant as the feasts, and the combatants are usually very grateful for the abundance of fuel."

Battle contests. "Will there be contests held aboard the Yukesi?"

"They are already in progress."

"Really? Can we see one after we eat?" After so much intense training with Lihku and Kalik to achieve the bare minimum, Michelle wanted to see how it was done by people who truly knew what they were doing.

"Of course."

Michelle took a bite, rolled her eyes in happiness, and asked, "What is your family doing right now? Are there special times for the neighborhood party versus eating at home?"

Sam paused mid-air, his bite halfway to his mouth. "My sister, her family, and our *yejorep* will pass the first part of the season together. There are no prescribed times for eating, as it is expected to be in progress the entire two weeks."

Suji rarely went a day without mentioning Pekoe and their soon to be born child, but Michelle had never heard Sam mention a love back home. "You're not joined?"

Suji's hand clapped down on Sam's shoulder as the gigantic pseudo-Little returned to the table. "Sam has always had too many suitors to choose just one."

She dropped her fork in surprise. "Sam? Really?"

Sam stared impassively at her for a heartbeat, then smiled sheepishly and shrugged. "The ladies like a Fleet doctor."

For the second time in an hour, Michelle laughed until her sides hurt.

Throughout her time at the feast, there were those Vinyi who studiously avoided greeting her, choosing instead to glare or stare at a distance. But there were far more who came up to her as easily as they came up to Sam and Suji, full of well wishes and exuberance.

Eventually, the three of them cleared their table and made their way out of the mess hall and toward the training arena. Michelle's heart felt lighter than it had since she first woke up as a captive of the Faceless. The cheer, the food, and the drink all combined to buoy her spirits, and the only lack in the joy she felt was that she wasn't sharing it with Dave and Phil.

"Lihku is ship's champion, of course," Suji was saying. "He's not undefeated, but he's only been bested a handful of times."

"Three of those times by Captain Hegoh," Sam said. "I wonder if Hegoh will be competing. I didn't give him a clearance physical this year."

"As Captain, I declare myself fit for competition," said a deep rolling voice from behind them.

Sam and Suji stopped and saluted. Michelle stood tall and still. The captain saluted back and everyone went back to their casual postures. "I know you prefer to do all the examinations prior to the start of the tournament, but..." he interrupted himself and turned to Suji. "I can't concentrate without knowing. What *are* you?"

Suji smiled and looked pointedly at Michelle. Hegoh followed his gaze, blinked, and let out a hefty sigh. "Oh, for merciful..." Then he looked back at Suji and guffawed. "I... that's... you..." Hegoh waved at hand at the hot mess that was his engineer and sighed again before turning back to Sam. "I will come to you tomorrow morning. My duties prevented me from making time for it over the past couple of days."

Sam nodded. "I will see you, Captain, when your schedule permits."

Hegoh hummed. "Actually, scheduling is why I came

looking for you both... you three," he corrected, including Michelle. "The Council has decided. Your hearing will be day after tomorrow."

Her stomach dropped into her feet.

"Yes, sir," said Sam and Suji in unison.

"Are you ready?"

Well, that was the question, wasn't it? Michelle was still inhaling when Suji replied, "Yes, sir. Mishel knows more than enough about the government, and in particular the military, to satisfy the Council's questioning."

"And she is reading and writing at an advanced level, while speaking more than adequately."

Hegoh frowned and did her the courtesy of turning to her. "You are not yet fluent?"

She cleared her throat. "No, sir. There are too many figures of speech I do not yet understand for me to claim fluency."

"Ah. But if I speak plainly to you, you will understand?"

"Yes, sir." *I hope so.*

He grunted. "Lihku says you have a long way to go, but also that you have come a long way. To fight like a Vinyi requires years of training; the Council will not expect that. And your contribution?"

Sam answered. "Mishel has been practicing reading mission logs and looking for discrepancies."

Hegoh tilted his head. "You settled on mission audits, then."

"Yes, sir." Sam looked down at her. "Mishel is a keen linguist."

"And her *yejorep*?"

Sam and Suji looked at one another. Sam spoke first. "I will see to her educational and medical needs."

Then Suji said, "Pekoe and I have agreed to accept responsibility for her physical needs of food and shelter."

"What?" Michelle's voice came out as a whisper. She swallowed thickly. "You... you what?"

"Mishel." Sam knelt so that he was almost level with her. "If the Council grants asylum, you will need *yejorep* to support you until you have established yourself. They will not grant asylum without it. Suji and I would like to be your *yejorep*."

"But..." She almost couldn't get the words out. "But that's... family."

"Yes!" Suji's enthusiasm rang through that one word and went straight to her heart.

Her chin trembled and she made herself put it away until she was alone. Crying in public was *not* the Vinyi way. "I don't know what to say."

"Technically," Sam said in a low voice, "you have to accept our offers for them to be valid."

"Of course," she blurted. "Of course I accept, I accept both of you! I..." She shook her head. "Thank you."

Suji looked like he was fit to burst. Sam stood and gently placed a hand on her shoulder.

Hegoh bobbed his tentacles in an efficient nod. "All right. Day after tomorrow, starboard conference room, 0930."

16

"Again, Mishel!"

Michelle groaned. Kalik was a taskmaster. He'd heard about the hearing tomorrow morning and was determined to have her physique in top form. She'd run 1000 meters, done a series of squats and lunges, run another 1000 meters, and now she was doing push-ups. She usually did push-ups, having worked up to two sets of 25, but Kalik was singleminded in his pursuit of her physical perfection this morning, and had just ordered her to start on the third.

Her arms were burning at 5, burning and shaking by 8, but she kept at it. Sweat stung her eyes, but she tightened her core and pressed the floor away again. Ten down, dear god there were fifteen to go.

The communications unit on the wall chirped and Kalik went to answer it. "Don't stop, Mishel! I'm still watching."

Jerk. She barely topped out 11 and wasn't at all sure she could lower slowly to the ground even one more time.

"Yes, sir," Kalik said then the comm unit chirped again,

closing the channel. "On your feet!"

Michelle tried her best to hop up to standing, but it ended up being more of a lurch.

"Lihku has called me to the armory. I'll be back in the time it takes you to run 3000 meters."

At least it isn't push-ups. "Yes, sir."

"Get going, Little!"

The name's Arensen, she thought, but dutifully turned and began her third run as Kalik left the room.

After a minute, she let her mind relax into the beat of her feet hitting the floor. Her arms swung freely at her sides and her heart and lungs settled into a sustainable rhythm. This time tomorrow, she'd be standing in front of a holographic Council, pleading her case to be acknowledged as a person.

Now that the shock of it all had passed, Michelle was able to see the wonder in her situation. She was living not on Mars Colony, which sounded exotic enough, but on a starship. She was the only human to have made contact with an alien species! And boy, had she made contact. She spoke their language, ate their food, celebrated their holidays. She even had two alien brothers. She was, by default, humanity's foremost expert on the Vinyi.

For all the good that did her. If tomorrow went against her, she may be consigned to spend the rest of her life in a cage or a lab or worse.

But if tomorrow went in her favor, she would be able to become part of the crew, become part of Suji's and Sam's families, and maybe, one day, if she kept trying, she'd make it back to Mars.

When the door opened, she was expecting to see Kalik coming back in, ready to berate her for not having finished the distance he assigned her. But it wasn't Kalik who walked through the door.

It was Vaomi.

And he closed and locked the door behind him.

She slowed her pace until she stood still, watching him purposefully close the too-small distance between them.

He flexed all four of his hands into fists and shook them loose again. "All I hear on this ship anymore is talk of the Little. The Little this, the Little that." His tusk membranes began to roll back, baring more of them. "And now I hear that the Council is deigning to consider granting you personhood?" He spat through his tentacle onto the floor. "You are not Vinyi. You are not worthy. You are not *real*. This hearing tomorrow is nothing more than a circus, lowering my people from proud dignity to ridicule." He snorted. "Considering granting equal status to such an inferior creature."

He stopped, far too close for Michelle's comfort, and glared at her. "You have done this." His voice lowered to a growl and Michelle broke out in a cold sweat. "But with no Little, there will be no debasement because there will be no hearing."

Vaomi lunged at her.

Michelle dodged, spinning to his left and sprinting toward the door. She hadn't gotten far enough, not nearly far enough, when his thundering footsteps behind her grew too close to ignore. She dove to the side, rolling into a ball and springing to her feet. She dashed for the other side of the room. All she wanted was to put distance between the two of them. Maybe it would buy her some time to think.

Vaomi roared in frustration and came after her again. He was huge, strong, and fast for his size, but with her shorter, lighter body, Michelle was the nimbler of the two. When he got close, she dove and tried to roll again, but he caught the back of her shirt when she stood up.

She stuck her arms up and slid out of it just as his other hand closed around the clothes she left behind with a loud smack. She jumped to her feet and sprinted again, toward the furthest wall.

The weapons wall.

She put on a burst of speed. She had to reach those ceremonial shortswords on the end. They were the only weapons on the wall small enough for her to handle, and they would be none too short in her hands.

"*I will crush you!*" The angered warrior's bellow struck fear into her very bones, causing her to stumble. She pinwheeled her arms and managed not to fall. Michelle put all her focus into running forward, running for those swords.

He was close, his footsteps pounding right behind her.

She sprinted harder.

A rush of air cooled her back where Vaomi's grab barely missed her.

The swords were there, they were right there.

Michelle dove, reaching for the swords.

She landed belly first on the floor, sending a sharp pain through her cheekbone and knocking the wind out of herself. But she was only on the floor for a moment and Vaomi's hands scooped her up in a vise grip, his vast palms around her hips, fingers digging into her ribcage.

He held her up to his face. She twisted in his painful grasp so that she was looking over her shoulder at him. He sneered and extended a tentacle, licking her skin from waist all the way up to her cheek. "I will kill you, then I will eat you."

Michelle swung the sword that she held in her far hand

as hard as she could, cutting off the ends of three of his middle tentacles.

He dropped her, screaming and pressing his hands to his face. Silver fluid spurted from his wounds. Michelle, gripping the sword for dear life, ran for the door. She wouldn't be able to reach the lockout controls without climbing onto something. She looked around frantically for something, anything to climb on.

Vaomi's shrieks grew louder; he was chasing her. Every footfall rang like a death knell in her ears.

Nothing. There was nothing to climb onto.

She was going to have to face him.

Michelle pivoted and held the sword up in front of her. If she was going to die, she was going to go out like Petra had taught her, using what Lihku had taught her, and take as much of Vaomi with her as she could.

A blast of air hit her in the back as the hall doors opened and a freight train roared past.

Kalik barreled into Vaomi's chest, knocking him off his feet. The two behemoths sailed through the air for what seemed like miles until they finally crashed to the floor. Kalik landed on the bottom, but wasted no time kicking Vaomi up and over his head and flipping on top of him. All four of his mighty fists slammed into Vaomi's face and body again and again, until at last Vaomi lay motionless underneath him.

Michelle hissed.

"Sorry," Bek apologized, placing a small adhesive electronic device on her ribs. "It may ache a bit while the bones knit."

She gave him a tired smile. "No problem."

Vaomi had broken five of her ribs when he'd grabbed her. That was the worst of it, though. She had some bruises and contusions, but all in all, she'd come out of it on top. *She wasn't the one in surgery right now, after all.*

When Kalik had reported to Lihku after his summons, Lihku had been surprised and confused; he hadn't called for Kalik at all. The security officer had instantly gotten a bad feeling and raced back to the training hall, only to find the door locked. That's when he knew something was going on inside, so he was ready for action the instant his security override unlocked the door. Lihku and a few more of his team had arrived moments after Kalik had subdued Vaomi, and had carted both Michelle and her unconscious attacker to the medbay.

When Samou saw them, he was furious. Despite his personal desire to disembowel Vaomi, his medical ethics demanded that Sam to try to save his patient's face. While the medical team prepped Vaomi for surgery, Sam came over to check on her.

His large hands were gentle as he examined her. "Vaomi did this?"

"Yes."

"You were alone? Where was Kalik?"

"He got called away."

Sam glowered; Kalik would be getting a talking-to later. "And did *you* do that to *him*?"

"Yes."

Sam grunted, a sound of approval. "I will thank Lihku later." He laid a hand on her shoulder. "You did well. I'm glad your wounds are not worse."

She gripped his hand and smiled grimly at him. They both knew it could have been much worse. Had it lasted another few seconds, it would have been.

A medical attendant called for Sam; Vaomi was ready. "Mebeku will attend you," Sam said gently before he walked away to try to save Vaomi's face.

And now she was lying on the bed where her journey with the Vinyi had started for her, where she had woken up reaching for Dave, where she had first remembered all that had come before her arrival on the Yukesi. Had that really been less than two months ago?

"Mishel!" Suji's shout broke into her thoughts. He marched in determinedly, scanning the room. When he spotted her, he made a beeline for her bedside.

"I'm fine," she said before he could speak.

"No, you're not," he rejoined, his bulky fingers caressing her cheek carefully so as not to aggravate the bruise blooming on it. He studied the side monitor. "He broke you," he said with surprise, noting the injury report.

"Only my ribs. They'll heal soon enough."

His tentacles quivered in rage. "I will kill him."

Michelle laid a hand on top of the one he still had at her face. "Only if you must because of a social construct I don't understand yet. Because I kind of broke him, too."

"What?" Suji's face shuddering came to such an abrupt halt it was almost funny enough to make Michelle forget the pain in her side. Almost.

"He's in surgery right now. I cut off some of his face."

"He is?" Suji looked back toward the surgical arena. "You did?"

She smiled at him wearily. The pain, and the pain killers Bek had given her, were beginning to set in. "You really shouldn't leave all those swords out in the open. Somebody's gonna get hurt." Her last few words came out slurred.

Michelle blinked, but her eyelids were so heavy it wasn't worth the effort of opening them again. Suji's astonishment was the image she passed out to.

Suji blinked. Mishel had cut off part Vaomi's face? *Mishel* had? A warm glow filled his chest as he looked at the sleeping Little. Lihku had said that her training was coming along well; he'd even taken to calling her *Rikubohe*, Fierce Little One, in his reports. Suji had thought it a term of growing endearment from the ferocious battle commander. Now he realized it may actually be more of a character assessment.

Rikubohe. He liked it.

Suji's blood boiled as he looked at her face, the angry discoloration marring its abnormally smooth surface. He reviewed the injury report Bek had prepared. Vaomi had broken some of the protective cage around Mishel's most important internal organs, undoubtedly intending to do more than that. Suji, like everyone else, had heard the disgruntled mutterings of Vaomi and his ilk, their smug superiority threatened by the possibility that a creature half their size and only a fraction of their strength might have every bit as much heart and soul, every bit as much right to exist and thrive as any Vinyi. It was a small-minded, closed-minded, fragile superiority that could neither stand on its own merits nor extend itself to others who were deserving. But while it was tempting to dismiss the mutterings of the small-minded as infantile, it was foolish to disregard them entirely.

Children were known to throw tantrums when they didn't get their way. Vaomi had tried to crush Mishel with an adult warrior version of a tantrum, and Mishel had, against all odds, thwarted him. The thing about children, though, was that they needed an adult to guide them, to show them the way.

It was obvious who had encouraged Vaomi to commit this heinous act. Suji stood and, with one last look at Mishel, left the medbay, all four fists flexing.

Every step that he took on his way to Rimoli's lab gave Suji's fury time to burn hotter. Other crew that he passed on the way took one look at him and gave him the widest possible berth. By the time Suji arrived at the lab doors, he was ready to tear Rimoli's head off his shoulders. He made his way through the maze of cages, three-walled rooms, and experimentation zones until he stood in front of the closed door of the chief research scientist's office.

He raised a fist and pounded on the wall. "Rimoli! Face me!"

Suji pounded until the door slid open, an irritated Rimoli standing on the other side. "If you upset any of the experiments we are conducting here, I will -"

Suji's fist flew out and smashed into Rimoli's face, right between his eyes. "You'll what? Get another of your henchmen to take care of me?"

Rimoli's tusks bared, long, sharp, and threatening, matching Suji's. "Check yourself. If you strike me again, I will take you down myself."

Suji was the larger of the two and he used that size to his advantage now, pressing his physique into Rimoli's, his tusks lowering onto the smaller man's, putting an uncomfortable pressure on his face.

Rimoli refused to flinch.

"I know you were behind it."

"Behind what?" the scientist sneered.

"Vaomi's attack on Mishel."

Suji was startled to see the surprise flash across Rimoli's face. *He didn't know.* Rimoli's surprise was quickly replaced by a sneer. "I had no idea. When is the funeral?"

Almost faster than he himself was aware of, Suji's right overhand gripped Rimoli around the throat and squeezed. "There will be no funeral. Vaomi will come out of surgery just fine, unfortunately."

Now confusion filled the struggling Vinyi's expression. Suji squeezed tighter, enjoying the panic in Rimoli's desperately grasping hands on his arm. "That's right. Mishel sliced your lackey so badly he requires surgery to be put back together."

He waited until Rimoli turned a decidedly unhealthy shade of gray before releasing him, shoving him back against the far wall of his office. "Now, unless you are even stupider than I believe you to be, you'll all leave her alone." He glared at the gasping Rimoli, who had used the wall to regain his feet and was slowly regaining his color. "If any of your kind accosts her again, Dr. Samou is going to be a very busy surgeon, indeed."

Then he turned his back on his enemy, a grave insult, and walked away without a backwards glance.

Michelle opened her eyes and saw the white and beige

medbay walls instead of the blue-gray of her room, and her momentary confusion added to her disorientation. She started to sit up and her side protested, pointedly reminding her of why she was here.

Would she ever wake up in this room and *not* feel off-center?

"How are you feeling?" Sam's voice rolled over her, comforting her in a way she hadn't realized she needed.

She sat slowly, one of his hands helping her up. "All right, I suppose. A little sore still."

He squeezed her shoulder lightly, then sat in a chair beside her. "You will feel that way for a couple more days yet, I'm afraid. Mebeku did good work, but you do not heal quickly."

Michelle chuckled, then inhaled sharply at the pain that caused, then involuntarily tried to inhale again at that pain the inhalation had caused. "Oof," she said. "To me, healing broken ribs in a few days *is* quick."

"Oof?" Sam rolled the word around in his mouth. "Oof. Oooooffff." His tentacles flapped with the extended 'f' sound, causing a minor ruckus on his face.

She tried not to laugh again. "How is Vaomi?"

The Vinyi doctor glowered at the mention of her assailant's name. "I saved his face, except for one tentacle that could not be saved."

Great. Now her enemy had a permanent, prominent disfigurement that would remind him of her every time he saw himself. "So he's thrilled, then?"

Sam only tilted his head at her.

"Mm-hmm." She worried the edge of the bedsheet. "How long was I out?"

"The hearing is in ten hours." Sam rested a hand on top

of hers. "You should get more sleep. It is too late to acquire any new skills with any level of competence, and with recent events, you need rest more than anything."

Tension and disquiet provoked a wave of nausea. "Sam?"

He waited.

"Do you think it will go well?"

The length of his pause made her even more nervous. "I cannot tell, Mishel," he finally said. "Nothing like this has ever been tried before. But," he said, patting her hand, "we have prepared as much as possible, and you have made exceptional progress. I do not know what the outcome will be, but I do know, beyond doubt, that you are ready for the attempt."

Michelle hoped his belief in her was strong enough for the both of them.

17

With only a couple more hours to prepare for the hearing, Sam had Bek take Mishel back to her quarters so she could ready herself. Now alone in his office, Sam washed and dried his face, wishing he'd gotten more sleep the night before, but after an attack that resulted in an emergency surgical procedure, there was far too much paperwork to be filed for him to relax.

He was proud of Mishel, but also more worried for her now than ever.

The door chime sounded and Sam bristled. *If this isn't an emergency, I'll eat whoever that is for breakfast.* When he answered the door, however, he found Captain Hegoh standing there.

"Sir," he greeted the captain, saluting.

Hegoh saluted back and entered the room. "I read your report, Sam, but I want to hear it directly from you. What happened?" He sat in the visitor's chair directly across from Sam's chair behind his desk.

Sam sighed and took his seat. "Mishel was training with

Kalik when he was called away, on false pretenses as it would turn out. While she was alone, Vaomi entered the training hall, locked the door, and cornered her, intending to do her, at a minimum, lasting harm."

Hegoh held up a hand. "How do you know this?"

"Mishel told Mebeku that Vaomi threatened to, quote, kill her then eat her."

Hegoh grunted, gesturing the doctor to continue with his report.

"Lihku has been combat training Mishel. She had no background in it at all, so Lihku started with self-defense. Due to her size, Lihku focused on evasion as her primary strategy." Sam ran a hand over his face. "There was a chase, during which Vaomi caught her, but not before Mishel was able to get her hands on one of the *ijlehohej* hanging on the weapons wall. When he would not release her, Mishel swung the *ijlehohe* in her hand and severed three of his tentacles."

Hegoh hissed. Every Vinyi would wince at the pain of that image.

"Indeed," Sam agreed. "At that point, we think Vaomi dropped her and she ran for the door but, again because of her size, she couldn't reach the unlocking mechanism. When Kalik, who had realized the subterfuge as soon as reasonably possible, overrode the lock and reentered the training hall, Mishel was facing a charging Vaomi with the *ijlehohe* in her hands."

Hegoh hummed, sat back, and templed the fingers of his underhands.

Sam stayed quiet, letting him think.

Finally, the captain said, "This will be the linchpin, Sam."

Sam nodded. He'd reached the same conclusion.

"We have to be absolutely certain this incident is presented to the Council the way we want it to be."

Sam nodded again, putting away the cold fear in his stomach. "Everything rests upon this now."

"Yes," Hegoh agreed. "Her actions against Vaomi will either secure her status as equal or condemn her beyond redemption. The question is how and when to relate this event to the Council."

Sam grunted in agreement. Timing would be everything.

Michelle smoothed her hair down. She needed a trim, but a braid secured with an improvised tie would have to do as long as she was living among a completely hairless species. She only had two outfits, and the shirt of one had been lost somewhere between Vaomi taking it from her in the training hall and her return to her quarters. She wasn't sure the top she wore now was meant to be worn with the trousers, but she didn't have any other option.

She took as deep a breath as she could, and tried to calm her nerves. Her hearing would start in an hour, and if she got any more on edge than she already was, she'd surely forget everything she'd learned and bomb in the most spectacular way imaginable.

Her door chimed.

Michelle sagged with relief to see Suji and Sam. "Please, *please*, come in." As they entered her quarters, she said, "I have no idea what I'm doing. What do I do? What do I do?!"

Sam grabbed her upper arms. "First, Mishel, you breathe."

She nodded. "Right. Got that."

"Next," he continued, releasing her shoulders and sitting down, "you receive your *Negoheh* gifts."

She nodded. "Right. I -" She blinked and looked up at him. "Wait, my what?"

The two men smiled at each other before Suji pulled a box from behind his back. "It is part of *Negoheh*: feasting, fighting, gifting, and resting." He set the box down on the small table in the center of the room. "You've done the feasting, and, unfortunately, the fighting. Now..." Suji gestured to the box, "the gifting."

"Now?" she blurted. "I mean... I don't have anything for you two, and the hearing is in less than an hour now, and you want to... do a gift exchange?"

"Nobody expects you to have anything for us," Sam assured her. "And yes, now is the precise time we want to gift you items representing our well-wishes for you." He took a small box out of his pocket and placed it on the table beside Suji's.

"Oh." Wasn't it just like Sam to put her in her place with his steadfast kindness? She felt even smaller than she actually was. "Then, thank you."

Suji rolled his tentacles. "You have to open them first, Mishel."

"So many rules," she muttered, only half-joking. She reached for Suji's box. "Is this one all right to open first?"

They nodded.

Michelle sat, the smooth plastic box on her lap. She ran her hands over it until she found the lip of the lid. Tucking her fingers in the gap, she gently pried the top off the box.

Inside sat a folded pile of fabric. It appeared to be dove gray in color, but when she lifted it out of the box, the fabric caught the light in a rainbow of undertones. It felt soft and strong at the same time. When Michelle finally had it all the way out of the box, she realized it was a pullover shirt, but far nicer than any other she'd owned here.

"Suji, this is beautiful."

He smiled and gestured to the box again.

A pair of trousers joined the top, made in the same fabric and design. "Going before the Council requires formal wear."

"Which I didn't have."

"And now you do!" Suji grinned at her. "Pekoe chose the color. She thought that shade would present you formally without being excessive."

Michelle's throat tightened at the thoughtfulness of a woman she'd never met. "Thank her for me, will you?"

Suji shrugged. "Once the hearing is over and you're a citizen, you can do it yourself."

Goosebumps covered her arms. *Here's hoping.* "Thank you, *penejhku*," she said, using the Vinyi term for a *yejorep* brother.

His reply was soft. "I am happy to provide for you, *penejhke*."

She reached for Sam's box next, but he stopped her. "Put on the formal wear first, *penejhke*."

Michelle took Suji's gift with her around the corner into her bathroom and changed. *Sister.* Sam and Suji both called her sister. Michelle was glad for it, glad for the connection, the sense of belonging. An ache in her chest haunted her that had nothing to do with her fight with Vaomi and everything to do with missing her husband and brother. On the one hand, she would give anything to have them here with her, supporting her, helping her to rally against whatever challenges she was going face. But on the other, she was glad that they were far away, that they would never be ridiculed, shamed, or assaulted by any of Vaomi's kind, never be put on trial simply for being different from everyone else. She needed them with her, and she needed them to be safe, far away from her, at the same time.

She stepped out of the small bathroom and in front of the mirror. The fabric clung softly to her, the light reflecting opalescent shimmers as she moved. It fit her well, though the high collar was missing a button and kept flopping open just a touch. It was a world of improvement from what she'd just had on.

Michelle turned to where Suji and Sam sat. They grunted, and Sam turned to Suji. "Pekoe made a very good choice."

Suji beamed. "She did."

"Sit now, Mishel, and open my gift."

Michelle sat and reached for the much smaller box from Sam. As with the first one, it took her a moment to find the lip that she could slide her finger under to open it. When the box slid open, she gasped. There, sparkling in the light, sat a brooch. She picked it up to examine it more closely.

It was a sword.

It was made of a variety of metals, gleaming gold, silver, and a shade of rose, alternately, in different places. There must have been crushed gemstones in it, as well, for it glittered and shimmered along the edges of the blade.

The piece of jewelry was just the right size to close the high neck of her new formal wear.

"Sam." Michelle couldn't find the words for a moment. "Sam, it's beautiful."

"It is the Sword of Mercy," he said. "It is the symbol of my field. I selected it for you days ago, long before you displayed your own prowess with just such a weapon."

"Prowess?" she looked at him askance, remembering the desperate swing that she had hoped against hope would do something, *anything*, effective against her assailant, only to find a teasing twinkle in Sam's eye. She chuckled and smiled. "Thank you, *penejhku.*"

He bowed slightly. "It is, and ever shall be, my pleasure, *penejhke.*"

"Excuse me while I go put this on." Michelle stood and retreated to her dressing area, where she could see herself in the mirror.

Once she arranged the brooch, she stepped back and surveyed her reflection critically. Still, the hair needed help, there was no denying it. She just hoped that a hairless species wouldn't know any better. But as for the rest of her... She looked good. Ready.

Michelle wished she felt as ready as she looked, but it was too late to do anything about it now. She took as deep a breath as she could, due to the still-bruised state of her ribs, and squared her shoulders. Walking back into the main room, she faced her stalwart supporters.

Her new brothers. Her new family.

Michelle's heart yearned for her *old* family.

"Are you ready?" asked Suji.

Michelle nodded.

He and Sam stood. "Then let us go," Sam said, placing a bracing hand on her shoulder. "Remember, Mishel, we are with you."

Michelle laid a hand on top of Sam's, reached for Suji's with her other, and squeezed them both. "Thank you," she said, tears standing in her eyes.

But she did not let them fall.

18

The corridors of the Yukesi were surprisingly quiet. The three of them didn't pass a single other Vinyi on the way to the starboard conference room. "Where is everyone?" Michelle asked.

"Either working or viewing, certainly," answered Sam.

"Viewing?"

"The hearing."

His answer surprised her. "Do you think there's that much interest in the proceedings?"

The two Vinyi glanced at one another. After a brief pause, Sam simply said, "Yes." There was, in fact, no doubt that every off duty crewman, and as many on duty ones as could get away with it, would be tuning their displays to the hearing's video feed this morning.

The three of them turned the last corner and approached the room where her fate would be decided. Two fully armed and armored Vinyi stood guard, one on either side of the door. "Is that really necessary?" Michelle asked in a barely audible voice meant only for her Vinyi brothers.

Again, the two Vinyi shared a glance. This time, it was Suji who said, "Yes."

A pit of misgiving began to form in Michelle's stomach, weighing down the butterflies that were already there. The guards nodded their recognition but still made Sam and Suji show their credentials before allowing them entry to the conference room. The guards allowed Michelle through without a question; she supposed it was obvious that she was who she claimed to be. Besides, she didn't have credentials to prove otherwise.

She wouldn't be able to obtain any until after the successful outcome of this hearing.

When Michelle entered the room, the shock of what she saw would have stopped her dead in her tracks had Sam and Suji not been ushering her forward. The room was huge, easily the size of a football stadium, and it was packed to the gills with Vinyi observers. Just inside the door stood a semicircular table with a row of chairs; Hegoh sat in the largest chair, at the far end of the table, furthest from the door. She noticed that he, too, was adorned in formal wear, like the three of them; they four were the only Yukesi crewmembers in the room. Suji entered the row, indicating that Michelle should follow behind him with Sam bringing up the rear. They sat, Suji helping Michelle up into her seat, onto which a booster cushion had been placed.

She felt like a toddler at a restaurant, but at least she could see what was going on.

Maybe ten yards away, directly across from them, was another semicircular table, larger and more ornate than their own. There were thirteen chairs at it, all of them occupied by Vinyi in excessively decorated formal dress. That could only be the Council. Going by the blue tint of their tusks, four of the thirteen Councilmembers were female. In between Michelle's table and that of the thirteen Councilmembers, precisely situated in the middle, was a large chair under a spotlight, with a small set of stairs off to the side.

The stairs must be for me.

A low murmur filled the room, the excited speculation of thousands of Vinyi spectators buzzing around her head. Michelle leaned into Suji. "How is this possible? The room isn't this large. The *ship* isn't this large."

"Holographic technology," he answered. "The only people physically in this room are the ones aboard Yukesi. Everyone else is a projection." He titled his head at her. "How do your people have meetings?"

"Later," rumbled Sam from her other side.

Suji hummed, lifting his tentacles in agreement.

Hegoh called Michelle's name from Suji's other side. "Yes, Captain?"

"We have done, and will do, our best by you, Mishel. May you receive the optimal outcome and find the desire of your heart."

She tried to smile but it felt more like a grimace. Michelle felt both comforted and annoyed. It was a lovely sentiment, but did he not know how close to tears she was already, simply due to nerves? She swallowed and nodded. "Thank you, Captain. I will do my best to honor your efforts."

He hummed in approval.

A horn blew, startling Michelle with its volume. Had she expected a trumpet to herald the start of the hearing, she would have been disappointed. This sound was much more akin to a herd of stampeding elephants charging a lion pack. She could feel the table vibrating beneath her hands.

The most ornately decorated Vinyi sitting in the middle of the thirteen stood and the horn's blast ceased as abruptly as it had begun, taking all other noise with it. "This hearing, opening on the eighth day of Hoyo, will come to order. Senior Chairman Sijaj presiding. This hearing regards the petition of Mishel the Little Being, sponsored by Captain Hegoh of Yukesi and Admiral Lezmu of Mejihi, requesting formal asylum among the Vinyi people."

Regally, he resumed his seat among the reverent silence, then looked at Hegoh. "Captain, you may begin."

Hegoh stood. "Thank you Senior Chairman, Members of the Council." He moved out from behind the table to stand in front of it, right in front of his chair. "As we are conducting proceedings of an unprecedented nature, I beg the patience of the wise and just Council in beginning by reviewing the requirements for successful petition as they have been provided to us.

"First, it is incumbent upon us, certain personnel aboard the patrol cruiser Yukesi, to demonstrate that Mishel the Little is sapient. We who have worked with her since the day she was found believe this to be the case. We are confident that we shall demonstrate Mishel's sapience at a level equal to any of our own."

A restrained murmur ran through the crowd, quieting down almost instantly.

"Second, we must demonstrate that Mishel the Little is capable of acquiring sufficient knowledge of our customs and culture that she will be capable of full assimilation into our society." Hegoh turned toward her slightly and gestured gallantly. "We will demonstrate that Mishel's ability to learn has far exceeded even our own early medical assessments."

Michelle gave Sam a little side eye. He shrugged almost

imperceptibly.

"Third, we must demonstrate that Mishel the Little will be able to add value to our society, that she will be able to contribute as any other citizen is required to do. Her surprising ability to learn and adapt will be key to proving this requirement.

"And last, we must demonstrate that Mishel the Little is in *need* of asylum, that without the generous compassion of the Vinyi people, she will be homeless, alone, and lost among the cosmos. We will demonstrate this clearly and with no room for refute.

"Thus, by the end of this hearing, ladies and gentlemen of the Council, we will have proven to each of you that Mishel the Little is everything we have reported her to be, that she will meet all the requirements as explained, and that she does, indeed, merit the merciful offer of asylum by the glorious Vinyi people." Captain Hegoh bowed at the waist and returned to his seat.

Michelle's heart threatened to pound right out of her chest. Her entire future depended on this hearing, but if Hegoh was truly as confident as he sounded, she might have a chance. She fervently hoped she wouldn't let him down.

Senior Chairman Sijaj waited until Hegoh was seated, then said, "The requirements as explained by Captain Hegoh are in agreement with the requirements as provided to Admiral Lezmu by this Council. Does the Council require any clarification at this time?"

Silence was his answer.

"Captain," said Sijaj, "you may proceed."

Hegoh stood once more. "Our first proof shall relate to Mishel's need for asylum. We will begin by relaying to the Council the Yukesi's discovery of the Little Beings."

The gallery of observers twittered in excitement before promptly resuming its hushed state.

Michelle leaned forward as Suji strode to the center chair.

After identifying himself and his role for the hearing's record, Suji explained his purpose in visiting the derelict. "It had been determined that the vessel was at least sixty-five years old, adrift, and, with no life signs on board, abandoned. Given its age, it would be a fascinating opportunity to examine the engines of a now obsolete propulsion system close up. We had no pressing issues in Engineering, so I was granted leave to board the derelict. The vessel's layout was unfamiliar to me, but I found the engine room after only a few minutes." He smiled charmingly. "That was convenient, as the ceilings of the vessel were so low that I had to crawl on all sixes to get through the hallways.

"When I entered the engine room, I found the canisters."

Canisters, plural. Michelle's gaze drifted inward while Suji described finding the bodies of two Littles frozen in a suspended state. *Petra.* Why had she, Michelle, been the one to survive? Petra Morgan, tough, gritty, foul-mouthed badass Dr. Morgan would have been by far the better choice to have awakened here.

And Michelle wouldn't have had to live with the near-constant hole in her heart where Dave and Phil used to be.

Suji concluded his narrative at the point where the canisters had been brought aboard Yukesi and was dismissed by Senior Councilmember Sijaj.

Then Sam stood and took the center chair in his place. As Suji had, he identified himself and his role before beginning his narrative. "After thorough examination of the canisters and the bodies, it was determined that reanimating the Littles was a possibility. In other words, they were confirmed to be in a state of suspension rather than death. Upon receiving the captain's approval, my team and I proceeded with a reanimation attempt on Little subject number one."

Michelle's breath hitched in her throat. *Petra.*

"My team and I took all conceivable precautions in a good faith attempt to mitigate the myriad risk factors, which included, but were not limited to, the standard risk of failure that comes with reanimation of any suspended living tissue; the advanced age of the suspension equipment, which could cause potentially unknown problems; and the entirely alien anatomy and physiology of the new species before us."

Sam paused and took a deep breath, and when he next spoke, Michelle could hear his regret. "Subject number one did not survive the reanimation attempt due to an unforeseen inability to breathe our air."

Michelle's mind was whirling. Sam had explained early on that Petra had died after the Yukesi found them, but he never told her specifics. Had Petra's lungs been damaged in her fight with the Faceless? Or with the passage of time in the vessel?

"Little pulmonary physiology appears, on its face, very similar to our own. Unfortunately, Little lungs are less advanced and are unable to adapt to extract the necessary gases from the environment; they must be given exactly the mixture they require or…" Sam cleared his throat. "Or they do not survive. Our air is not the combination of elements the Littles require; hence, subject number one's demise."

Michelle took as deep a breath as she could, because she could. *But how am I sitting here?*

"We were able to prevent this tragedy with subject number two, who we learned later was named Mishel." Sam gestured at her and an entire gallery of faces turned in her direction. She squirmed uncomfortably under the sudden increase in scrutiny. "An injection of nanotechnology into Mishel's pulmonary system provides her lungs with the adaptive ability ours have naturally."

She laid her fingertips on her ribcage as she inhaled another great lungful. She was able to breathe because of microscopic robots that Sam had put into her lungs?

Would Petra still be alive if Sam had known about this before trying to reanimate her?

Michelle felt lightheaded from all the excess breathing and forced herself to take long, slow breaths.

"Both the medical and the research teams scoured all available data for any references to Littles or to their homeworld and found nothing. After Mishel acquired a basic use of *Ijlenum*, she told us of her world and her galaxy; further research has revealed no matches to the descriptions she has given us. The official conclusion of the medical and scientific research teams is that Mishel the Little is the only one of her kind that we have encountered, or are likely to encounter. Thus, unless the compassionate and wise Councilmembers grant her asylum among us, Mishel the Little, the sole survivor of a species, will be fully alone and utterly vulnerable in the universe."

Under the table, Suji patted her knee.

"Thank you, Doctor. You may step down."

Sam stood and made his way back to her side, deliberately brushing her arm with his as he sat.

Senior Chairman Sijaj said, "The testimonies of Suji, Chief Engineer of Yukesi, and Samou, Chief Doctor of Yukesi, have been entered into the hearing record and accepted by this Council. Do the Councilmembers require any clarification at this time?"

"Yes," said a female sitting four seats down from Sijaj.

"I yield to Councilmember Epimoe."

"Doctor," she said with no ado, "you mentioned that the Little is able to speak basic *Ijlenum*?"

Sam stood. "Yes, Councilmember, that was true at the time covered by my testimony. At this time, however, Mishel is able to speak at quite an advanced level."

The bangles adorning her tusks jingled as she tilted her head. "Does it understand what I am saying now?"

Sam looked down at Michelle and nodded once. She started to climb down from her chair, then realized the disadvantage that would put her at and stood up in it instead. "Yes, Councilmember, I understand."

A rush of gasps and hurried whispers blew through the crowd.

Councilmember Epimoe hummed. "And do you have anything you would like to say in regards to the testimony that the doctor and the engineer have given?"

"Yes, Councilmember, I do." Michelle squared her shoulders and tried to project. "I am grateful to have been given the opportunity to live, to live again, by the efforts and skill of both Suji and Samou. I am honored to be standing before you here today. It would be a privilege to stand among your people, and I hope that these proceedings are considered successful by all involved." She started to sit down, but then stood up straight again. She had one last thing to say.

"Subject number one's name was Petra. She was strong and brave, and she should be remembered." Michelle herself would remember Petra's sacrifice with every breath. She nodded at Epimoe, then at Sijaj, unsure of the protocol. "Thank you."

And she resumed her seat.

When there were no further questions from the Council, Hegoh stood again. "A moment ago, Mishel demonstrated a number of behaviors that are presumed to be limited to sapient beings, the most objective among which is intelligence.

"But clearly, there is no objective test for sapience. There must be sentience, which we can define as consciousness, sensate capacity, and the ability to react to those perceived sensations. All of these characteristics have been clinically confirmed in Mishel."

Hegoh walked slowly around the end of the table as he spoke. "In addition to sentience, however, there must also be present higher levels of cognition, reasoning, intelligence. All of these traits culminate in a self-awareness that cannot be measured by any known test, but is nonetheless plainly known and understood when it is encountered.

"This Council has encountered Mishel's sapience in the form of her commentary given to Councilmember Epimoe. Her comments, unscripted and spontaneously given as the answer to a spontaneous question, reveal the following.

"First, Mishel is an intelligent being. Not only has she learned to speak *Ijlenum*, she has learned to communicate in it. There are many household pets who may mimic words; Mishel has understood their meaning and crafts that understanding into word sequences that communicate her own, individual thoughts to us.

"Second, Mishel uses reason." Hegoh turned to face her. "None of us was able to identify subject number one by name. None of us told Mishel who subject number one was or what she looked like. Yet Mishel has identified subject number one as her compatriot Petra, through the use of abstract thought and applied logic."

He turned back to face the Council. "Most telling, however, Mishel acts as one who is not only *self*-aware, but is also aware of others, including having the understanding that other individuals *are* individuals, and are, within themselves, self-aware, with separate identities, motivations, and desires.

"As I stated earlier, there is no definitive test for sapience. However, I am confident that, as we navigate the remainder of this hearing, you will come to understand, as we have, that Mishel is the sole representative, not just of a previously unknown species, but of a previously unknown sapient species. For a creature that is not sapient could neither contribute nor adapt to Vinyi society, and we are ready to show that Mishel can do both."

With a small bow at the waist, Hegoh thanked the Council for their attention and returned to his seat. Michelle's heart sank. It wasn't the most convincing argument, but how much could Hegoh - or anyone, really - do with a qualitative characteristic? Michelle much preferred simple, objective tests, something with no room for debate, when the stakes were as high as her freedom and her future.

Senior Chairman Sijaj performed his role. "The testimony of Hegoh, Captain of the Yukesi, has been entered into the hearing record and accepted by this Council. Do the Councilmembers require any clarification at this time?"

"Yes," said Epimoe.

"I yield to Councilmember Epimoe."

"Mishel the Little, how will you prove to us that you are sapient?"

Adrenaline jolted through her, and she could barely hear for the pounding of her heart in her ears. She stood, addressing the Councilmember. "Councilmember Epimoe," she said, then paused to find the right words. Finally, she spread her hands wide. "I cannot."

The gallery came to life, buzzing with surprised murmuring. This time, it lasted long enough that Sijaj reached for a long stick with a rounded head on the end and struck a gong with it. The ringing of the gong quieted the crowd, and when the echo of it died down, Michelle continued. "As Captain Hegoh correctly said, there is no definitive test for sapience. Without a definitive test, there is no proof that I can offer you. However, as sapience cannot be proven, I suggest that we all, in truth, walk around every day, not *knowing* that the others we encounter are as sapient as we are, but instead simply *believing* them to be so. We believe this about our friends and colleagues because the behaviors they exhibit are similar enough to ours that we see our own sapience reflected in them."

Michelle looked down the length of the Council table before returning her gaze to Epimoe. "It is my belief that you will see your sapience reflected in me, as I see mine now in you."

The Councilmember said nothing, merely tilting her head at Michelle in reply.

Michelle nodded. "Thank you," she said, and sat back

down.

    Sam's underhand nudged her happily under the table.

    Sijaj struck the gong again. "The Council calls for a brief recess. We will reconvene at 1100."

19

"Mishel!" Suji hissed at her as soon as the Council stood to adjourn and the noise was great enough that he wouldn't be heard. "You did great!"

"Did I?" Her knees were still weak and she was starting to tremble a bit as the rush wore off.

"Why, you were as eloquent as a Councilmember! I was most impressed."

"As was I, Mishel," commented Hegoh in his typical low rumble. He made his way down the table, stopping in front of her. "You made us proud to stand beside you today."

She sighed, though still not quite as deeply as she would have liked due to her ribs. "Thank you, Captain."

He lifted a tentacle in salute. "Excuse me. There is ship's business I would attend to during our respite." And he walked toward Lihku, who had just entered the room.

A comforting hand fell on Michelle's shoulder and she reached up to lay hers atop it. "Sam," she said, looking up at him. "It wasn't too much?"

He beamed at her, the very picture of pride. "No, *Rikubohe*, it was exactly right."

An image of Dave sprang unbidden to her mind. It was at her graduation from college, and he was beaming at her, his posture almost identical to Sam's now. Dave's warm smile, the happy gleam in his eyes, the protective way he enveloped her in a hug, the love and tenderness that words could never express that were conveyed in his kiss…

Michelle blinked furiously. *Put it away.* In the middle of the hearing where she was appealing to the Vinyi for permission to become one of them was not the time to weep like a child. She cleared her throat. "So, what now?"

"Now," Sam answered, "the captain will present the topics of your ability to contribute to society and your ability to adapt and take on the customs of a regular, compliant citizen."

She nodded. "And my contribution will be based on my ability with the language?"

"For now," Sam confirmed. "You will continue to grow and learn; with time, you may even be conscripted into the Covert Intelligence Division."

"The…?" Michelle puzzled the words out in her head. "A spy? I might become a spy?"

Suji hummed. "You are very small. You would be able to go places, hide in places, none of my species would ever even think of."

"And you are resilient. Even now, certain of your bones are still healing, yet you are defending your sapience as eloquently as if your speech had been planned." Sam suddenly sobered. "Speaking of your speeches… her name was Petra?"

Sam's testimony came back to her in a rush. "Yes." Her

voice was barely more than a whisper.

He gently rubbed her back. "I will amend our records to note it. To name her."

Michelle thought back to her initial impression when she first awoke in the medbay, convinced that Sam was a monster.

She had never been so wrong.

"Thank you," she said, squeezing his hand.

Beside her, Suji suddenly tensed and turned in his seat.

"What?" Michelle quickly scanned the room. "What is it?"

The growls of her brothers vibrated through her before reaching her ears. "Rimoli." Sam's and Suji's tusks were bared, not fully, but more so than they had been moments before. "Rimoli is here."

"Who? Why?" she asked. "What's wrong?"

Sam whispered, or as close to it as a Vinyi could do, in her ear. "Suji and I believe that Rimoli had something to do with Vaomi's attack on you."

"What?" Michelle followed Sam's gaze and saw the amethyst-toned gray Vinyi she'd run into the other day in the mess hall corridor with Vaomi. *Rim.*

"He did not know of Vaomi's attack on you until I told him," said Suji, "but he and Vaomi are *pujyej vopimej*."

Michelle shook her head. "I don't know what that means."

"They are..." Suji rolled his hand around his wrist.

"They are similar in values, morals, and, often, behavior," Sam clarified.

"Ah." *Birds of a feather.* "Yes, I understand."

Before she could get any further information, though, both Hegoh and the Councilmembers came filing back into the room. Everyone took a seat, and Sijaj announced that the hearing was back in session.

Michelle's neck prickled. She looked over to find Rimoli staring fixedly at her.

"This hearing, resuming after the first recess on the eighth day of *Hoyo*, will come to order. Senior Chairman Sijaj presiding. This hearing regards the petition of Mishel the Little Being, sponsored by Captain Hegoh of Yukesi and Admiral Lezmu of Mejihi, requesting formal asylum among the Vinyi people.

"Captain, the floor is once again yours."

Hegoh stood from his reclaimed seat at the end of the table. "Thank you Senior Chairman, Members of the Council.

"Mishel's ability to have and express complex original thought has, at this point, been well demonstrated. It is that ability, the ability to learn our language and use it effectively, expressing her own thoughts and understanding those of others, that will put her in good stead with the requirement to contribute to society."

Hegoh reached behind him and picked up a tablet off the table. A square of light that reminded Michelle of a projector screen began to glow in the middle of the room, above the chair. "I direct your attention to the exhibit currently on display."

The empty white space filled in with one of the writing exercises Sam had her working on a couple of days ago. "This," Hegoh said, "is only one of the many examples we have of Mishel's writing. As you can see, it is precise and accurate, easily legible."

He walked away from the projection, pacing in front of their table. "You may also notice that the content of the document is a review of a series of mission logs from an away mission undertaken by four of my crew members last week." Hegoh poked his tablet and a number of sections of her text began to glow green. "Mishel was reliably able to identify and describe discrepancies, producing a mission log audit that adheres to Fleet standards."

Hegoh turned off the display. "Admiral Lezmu and I have spoken about this and are in agreement. Should the Council, in its wisdom, grant Mishel asylum, I will provide her a restricted post aboard Yukesi conducting mission and report audits. Over time, her skills will grow and perhaps her contribution will increase in value, but the contribution she is capable of making immediately is more than enough to meet the requirements as decreed by the esteemed Council." He bowed to the Councilmembers. "Thank you."

Senior Chairman Sijaj accepted Hegoh's testimony into the record and called for questions from the Council. Like before, Epimoe spoke up. Unlike before, so did two others.

"I yield to Councilmember Jenqu."

"Senior Chairman, I request time to conduct a brief, but detailed, review of Hegoh's exhibit." He glanced uncertainly at Michelle. "If we do grant asylum, I would like to be assured of the Little Being's ability to contribute beyond the assurances of the captain." He turned his gaze to Hegoh. "I'm certain Hegoh's assessment has been arrived at in a reasonable fashion," he conceded, "but all the same, the responsibility to assuage my conscience and represent the will of the people of my continent rests on me; I would satisfy it to the best of my ability."

The other councilmember who had spoken up raised a red stone in his overhand. Upon being recognized by Jenqu, who had the floor, the second Vinyi said, "I, too, would make this same request."

Sijaj hummed. "The exhibit review requested by Councilmembers Jenqu and Sojai is granted."

The councilmembers picked up their own tablets and began reading, along with a half dozen others. Sijaj turned to Epimoe. "I yield to Councilmember Epimoe."

"In the event that your assessment is incorrect, Captain, how shall the Little Being be supported?"

Hegoh stood. "Mishel has *yejorep*, Councilmember."

Once again, a burst of low buzzing filled the room as the onlookers murmured their surprise. Sijaj struck the gong and the crowd fell silent.

Epimoe continued her questioning. "Who, Captain?"

Suji and Sam stood, flanking Michelle. "We are Michel's *yejorep*, Councilmember," Sam said.

"I see." Her shiny black eyes turned to Michelle. "And for whom shall the Little Being be *yejorep*?"

Oh, shit. She hadn't thought of that. *Yejorep* was a two-way street. It was dishonorable to accept the benefits without also accepting the responsibility, but she couldn't provide for herself yet. How could she commit to providing for someone else?

Suji's voice broke through her racing thoughts. "My wife, Pekoe, will birth our first child within the next month. My wife and I will ask Mishel to be *yejorep* to our child."

Michelle's heart melted as she looked at him. Suji and Pekoe must have seen this coming, talked about it already, and agreed to allow her to be an inextricabble part of their child's future. Suji glanced down and smiled at her, quickly returning his gaze to Epimoe. Michelle again blinked away the tears that tried to fill her eyes and swallowed thickly. When she looked back at the Council, she met Epimoe's gaze calmly and lifted her chin.

"I see," said the Councilmember again. Epimoe looked at Sijaj. "That is all."

"And have the other Councilmembers finished their review of the captain's exhibit?" Sijaj asked.

Jenqu answered. "We have. It is…" Michelle tensed, waiting for him to finish. "…of acceptable quality," he concluded.

She relaxed.

"Very well. Are there any further clarifications required?"

Silence.

"The matter of contribution has been entered into the hearing record. Captain," Sijaj gestured at Hegoh, "you may continue."

"Thank you, Senior Chairman," said Hegoh. "The question of Mishel's ability to adapt to Vinyi life, to assimilate as a citizen of our society, is the only remaining item. I would propose that, in some ways, this question is more akin to the question of sapience than the items of need and contribution. There are less definitive measures and more qualitative ones that must be employed to answer and discuss this requirement, so I beg the Council's patience as we explore this requirement accordingly.

"I present Chief Engineer Suji to give testimony."

Suji stood from beside Michelle and made his way to the center chair. "Adaptation and assimilation require familiarity," he began, and proceeded to summarize the content and progress of his lessons with Michelle. He explained how he and Bek had taught her the classic Vinyi fable, how she understood family structures and *yejorep*, her knowledge of government and the military, and her increasing awareness and appreciation of Vinyi holidays.

Considering that, so far, Michelle only really understood *one* holiday, perhaps Suji was overselling it a bit, but it wasn't as though she would never learn of any others. And it did seem fair to get recognition for all the bizarre fables she'd been made to read. Though when she thought about it, *Little Red Riding Hood* probably wouldn't make much sense to a Vinyi, either. She'd have to tell them the next time she had a chance.

Suji finished speaking and Sam took his place in the chair. He confirmed Suji's statement, reiterated some of the language lessons summary he'd already made, and then did an unexpected thing: he admitted how much there was left to teach her. "Mishel has learned nothing, as of now, about Vinyi biology and lifecycles, the geography and ecosystems of Hoikke, or anything substantial of our history beyond the legends and fables that have already been mentioned. All of these subjects are expected of our children at a young age; why would we not expect them of Mishel?"

Sam directed his gaze to the Councilmembers one by one as he spoke. "We ought to. And we will. Suji, Mebeku, and I will continue to educate Mishel beyond what she has already attained until she can hold her own on any scholastic evaluation. What we must remember, however, is this: Mishel has learned all that she has in less than three months. Is it reasonable to expect her to possess competence in all basic academia after so short a time when we give our own children forty years to accomplish the same?"

Forty years?! How long does Vinyi childhood last?! She realized she'd never asked. Listening to Sam, she was beginning to realize that there was a lot she'd never asked. She'd been too busy trying to return to her past to concern herself with her present beyond simply surviving it.

Perhaps, even as she searched for Phil and Dave, she should reconsider that mindset. After all, should she be so fortunate as to find them, and both alive, they would be elderly now. She would never be able to reclaim her past exactly as it was when it was ripped from her. Phil and Dave would not be waiting for her at the card table, Phil would never again leave his shoes strewn haphazardly about her living room, Dave would never take her in his arms and make love to her all night. It would never be the same.

She might one day go back to Mars, but she would never really go *home* again.

The nascent knowledge settled like a weight in her stomach.

Sam stood, snapping Michelle out of her reverie, and returned to his seat beside her.

"I present Battle Chief Likhu to give testimony," Hegoh announced.

Lihku stood from where he had been watching the proceedings and strode unhurriedly to the center chair, taking his seat.

Michelle discreetly cleared her throat and blinked until the pressure from unshed tears dissipated.

"We are a strong people, a victorious warrior people," boomed Lihku confidently, diving right in. "It is easy to see at a glance that the Little Beings, if Mishel is representative, are not."

A general hum of assent rose from the crowd, who then quieted hurriedly so as to hear what Lihku said next.

"That strength is inherent to who we are, and someone without it has no hope of ever truly belonging within the Vinyi." Lihku looked at Michelle. "I had little hope for Mishel when I began training her in the ways of combat." He looked back at the Council. "She had no previous experience."

The crowd stayed quiet this time, but some of the Councilmembers exchanged scandalized expressions.

"She is small. Her muscles are weak and she will never grow taller than she is at this moment. She is easily damaged, and could be easily killed."

Way to talk me up, friend.

"Anyone who looks at her will conclude instantly that she is no warrior." He paused. "Not yet. What Mishel lacks in physical prowess she makes up for in spirit. I have trained her hard, pushing her to her breaking point each day. And every next day, she was there again, willing to take on more. So I pushed further. And still she returned and fought as hard as the day before.

"If all of my soldiers possessed the same strength of spirit, our established combat superiority and military might would soar to heights previously unimagined outside of legend."

Goddammit, Lihku. She'd just gotten her tears under control and now she had to fight them again, although for an entirely different reason. Michelle hadn't known Lihku thought that highly of her. *I guess the way to a Vinyi's heart is through combat.*

Lihku shifted and grunted. "Now, a mighty spirit is well and good, but a spirit requires a strong body to live in; this is common knowledge even to our youngest children. Mishel's body has grown strong within the physical limitations of her species, and her ability to evade capture may now be rated competent. She has proven herself, in a variety of scenarios, able to evade effectively and, when caught, to reacquire her freedom as efficiently as possible. To the doctor's earlier point, after so short a time, this may be considered a remarkable accomplishment."

The great warrior turned his upper body to directly face the Council. "Mishel has faced a degree of unwarranted antagonism, simply due to her differences. There have been incidents, significant enough to be duly recorded in this vessel's logs, of violence perpetrated against her for no reason other than her status as *idehkelikjune*."

Suji leaned over and softly translated. "Not Vinyi."

"Recently, she was deliberately attacked, with a clear purpose of doing her bodily harm up to and including death, by a... shipmate..." Lihku reluctantly ground the word out through a clenched jaw. "Mishel had never done this Vinyi harm. He wished her existence to end because he did not like her and was far stronger than she, and therefore able to execute his wishes, by executing her, without resistance."

Low murmurs filled the room. Michelle couldn't tell if they were favorable or not.

"It is a small minded, weak hearted warrior who is filled with hatred for another simply because they *are* other." Lihku paused. The room was silent, waiting for his next statement, and Michelle saw, for the first time, how Lihku's ability to command troops extended also to his words. "Mishel the Little, against the odds, subdued her attacker."

He turned to look at her now. "The heart of a Vinyi beats within her diminutive frame. The spirit of a sister warrior lives within the body of a doll."

He turned his focus to her one last time. "I would be pleased to continue training Mishel during her posting aboard Yukesi."

Michelle sat straighter than she ever had and smiled through the tears that, despite her best efforts, stood in her eyes.

Councilmember Epimoe tapped something into her console. Chairman Sijaj briefly looked down to his own screen, then glanced over at Epimoe, who nodded subtly once.

Sijaj returned his attention to the center of the room. "Thank you, Battle Chief. You may step down."

Lihku left the center chair and went back to his seat on the sidelines. As Michelle followed him back with her eyes, she caught sight of Rimoli.

He was still staring right at her. Had he ever stopped? Michelle's stomach turned but she had no time to ponder it. Sijaj was moving on. He accepted all the testimony and asked, "Do the Councilmembers require any clarification at this time?"

Silence from the Councilmembers.

But as Michelle watched, Rimoli stood. "I would speak on this matter, if it pleases the Council."

The crowd murmured and the Councilmembers on either side of Sijaj leaned in for a conference. "Captain Hegoh," said Sijaj from within his huddle, "who is this?"

Hegoh stood. "The one who spoke is Head Research Science Officer Rimoli, Senior Chairman."

The murmuring grew louder and the conference continued. Michelle's palms began to sweat. If Rimoli was in league with Vaomi, it was certain he was not planning to say anything favorable. "Is that allowed?" she whispered to Suji.

"It may be; it's up to the Senior Chairman."

She held her breath as Sijaj's advisers pulled away. "Head Research Science Officer Rimoli, take the center chair," he ordered.

Michelle's heart sank as she watched him take his seat.

20

"Head Research Science Officer Rimoli," said Sijaj, "please begin your statement."

"Thank you, Senior Chairman." Rimoli, sitting ramrod straight, began. "We have all been treated to stories of this alien creature's courage, intelligence, and value. We have heard of its improvement in various subjects and aspects of daily life correctly deemed important by the Council.

"What we have not heard is how dangerous it is."

Silence reigned as he took in the room.

"We are teaching this creature all about our culture and our ways, equipping it with all the knowledge of our people, and we are congratulating ourselves and the alien on making such marvelous progress. But nobody is asking if imparting this knowledge to an alien species is a good idea." He shook his tentacles back and forth. "I submit to you that it is not."

Rimoli glared at Michelle. "This being has taken the glorious principles of Vinyi combat and perverted them into an attack on one of our own, an attack against our own people which is now being lauded in front of the most vaunted Council itself."

Suji tensed and his tusk membranes rolled back almost imperceptibly.

"True, it is not I who was attacked, but the one who was cannot be here today. He is still recovering from surgery after his encounter with the unnecessary violence exhibited by this 'Little'." He turned and delivered a poisonous look at Lihku. "An act extolled by some within our own ranks who are too enamored by the exotic nature of the creature to think clearly, as a proper warrior should."

The crowd erupted into a raucous uproar. Some of the Council appeared to be taken aback, casting suspicious glances at Lihku. For his part, the Battle Chief calmly met every eye trained on him with a steely resolve.

Michelle grabbed Sam's arm. "Vaomi was going to kill me!" she hissed.

Sam quickly but gently placed his large hand over her face, shushing her. After a few moments, Sijaj struck the gong, calling for silence. "You will explain further." It was not a request.

"My colleague, Vaomi, an Operations Analyst, noted that Kalik, a Battalion Leader, and the alien were exercising in the training hall when Kalik was abruptly called away. Vaomi entered the hall to aid Kalik and continue the creature's training. He approached it, telling it that he would spar with it while Kalik was away. It began to run from him, a beginner-level evasion technique, so Vaomi gave chase, thinking, understandably, that he was continuing the training already underway. When he finally caught the creature, it used a weapon it had secreted on itself to cut off three of his tentacles."

The crowd erupted again, and Michelle's heart pounded as a few of the Councilmembers began throwing dirty looks her way.

But... that isn't what happened. Not exactly.

Sijaj's face was a thundercloud. "Doctor."

Sam stood. "Yes, Senior Chairman?"

"Is this true? Is there a Vinyi recovering from surgery that was administered as a result of an encounter with the alien?"

"Yes."

"What was the nature of the surgery?"

"My team and I attempted to reattach the subject's tentacles."

"And the outcome?"

"Two of the three are fully functional."

A murmur of disquiet ran through the room. "And the third?"

Sam took a deep breath. "The third could not be saved."

The mood in the room had turned. Nausea threatened to overwhelm Michelle.

Sijaj looked down at his tablet and made a note, then looked back up. "Have you anything further to add?"

"Yes, Senior Chairman." Michelle tried to breathe. Sam would put it right. He was Sam; he always put it right.

Sijaj grunted. "Proceed."

"Thank you, Senior Chairman. The report of the injuries to the Vinyi is accurate. However, what has been omitted from Rimoli's statement is the extent of the injuries to Mishel. This encounter resulted in required medical attention to both parties, not only the Vinyi. Vaomi broke multiple of Mishel's bones, bruised some of her internal organs, and caused numerous contusions as well as the injury to her face." Sam gestured at Michelle's still colorful cheek.

"This is not its normal coloring?"

Sam's tentacles shook. "No, sir. Typical coloring is even; Mishel's entire face would, in a healthy state, be the same color as her other cheek."

Sijaj thought for a moment. "Does the Little often experience injuries after sparring bouts?"

"No, sir," Sam replied promptly. "Both Lihku and Kalik have sparred with her on numerous occasions with nothing more than slight bruising and sore muscles to her as a result."

Sijaj was silent again.

Michelle was bursting to testify in her own defense but knew better than to speak without being called on.

"Battle Chief."

Lihku stood. "Yes, Senior Chairman?"

"You did not mention these details in your statement. Why not?"

Lihku broadened his shoulders. "I did state, sir, that Mishel has proven herself able to evade and escape. She has done so many times, both in sparring with me and with Kalik, as well as in fending off an actual attacker in this incident. The extent to which she overcame her aggressor, and the extent to which she was injured in the process, were secondary to the fact that Mishel proved herself worthy of our respect in combat by earning victory."

Bless you, Lihku. He had made the distinction between sparring partners and an assailant.

Sijaj picked it up. "You are not of the opinion that this was a sparring bout, as stated by Rimoli?"

"No, sir. As Samou explained, Kalik and I have sparred with Mishel multiple times and have never caused her to leave a session broken. Her interaction with her attacker bears no resemblance to a bout, as evidenced by the wounds experienced by both parties. Also, when Kalik left the hall, he did so in response to a call he received stating that I required his presence. I made no such call. This timing is surely more than coincidence, suggesting an element of forethought, planning, and malice."

The Chairman looked back to Rimoli. "Researcher, what say you to this?"

"I know nothing about the call Kalik received," he replied almost dismissively. "Lihku and Kalik are trained combat professionals. Vaomi is an operations analyst." Rimoli lifted his hands and shrugged. "He is not as skilled at minimizing his own impact, controlling his own force, as the Battle Officers are. Vaomi may have shown poor judgment in offering his aid to the alien, but that should not have resulted in a ghastly permanent disfigurement."

A few of the Councilmembers nodded at one another in agreement.

Michelle tried not to hyperventilate. Apparently she really should have tried to stay away from Vaomi's tentacles. But she had just swung wildly; it was bad luck, or good luck, depending on your point of view, that she had sliced part of his face off.

Sijaj sat pensively, and everyone waited.

"Battle Chief, what was the weapon the alien used and where did it come from?"

"Mishel availed herself of the resources available by wielding one of the *ijlehohe* mounted on the wall of the training hall."

Sijaj hummed and fell silent yet again.

Michelle was ready to snap in two from the tension. She

could feel heat rolling off Suji in waves.

Finally, Sijaj sat back in his chair. "The testimonies of Rimoli, Head Research Science Officer of Yukesi, Suji, Chief Engineer of Yukesi, Lihku, Battle Chief of Yukesi, and Samou, Chief Doctor of Yukesi, have been entered into the record and accepted by this Council. Do the Councilmembers require any clarification at this time?"

Before Sijaj had finished speaking, Epimoe said, "Yes."

"I yield to Councilmember Epimoe."

"Little."

Michelle drew as steadying a breath as she could and got to her feet. "Yes, Councilmember?"

"I would hear your statement on this matter."

She sighed. "Thank you, Councilmember." She cleared her throat, buying a moment to try to choose her words carefully. "Shortly after Kalik was called away on what we later learned to be false pretenses, Vaomi entered the room - I mean, the hall." Michelle's rattled nerves were making her stumble over her still-foreign Vinyi vocabulary. "He told me that it was an insult to the dignity of the Vinyi that this esteemed Council was willing to hear my petition for asylum. He said that he would prevent the hearing from occurring and save the Council's self-respect by eliminating me before the hearing date arrived."

Suji was practically vibrating now, and Sam bared his tusks slightly more than was appropriate for the venue.

"He pursued and eventually caught me, breaking my ribs and doing much of the other damage already reported. He lifted me close to his face and said he was going to kill me, then eat me."

A murmur broke out among the crowd again, but Michelle couldn't discern its tone. The noise died down before

Sijaj could strike the gong.

"In the moment before Vaomi had captured me, I was able to grab one of the *ijlehohe* from the wall. After he threatened me with death, I swung the *ijlehohe* in the hope that Vaomi would let me go. I did not intend to disfigure him." *Not that I'm sorry about that.* "I only wanted my freedom.

"He dropped me," Michelle continued, "and I ran. I tried to open the door, which he had locked behind him, but I couldn't reach the unlocking mechanism. He was about to catch me for a second time when the door opened from the outside and Kalik stopped him."

Epimoe regarded her for some moments. Michelle stood there as calmly as possible, trying to rest in the assurance that she had told the truth and surely that would matter. Epimoe at last turned to Rimoli. "Researcher, have you anything to say in response to the Little's statement?"

"I was not there, Councilmember; none of us was except for the alien, so I must do my best to stand for my incapacitated colleague. The alien caused a great deal of supposedly unintentional damage. If the Little truly meant no harm, then that kind of recklessness could present a great danger. And the Little caused this terrible damage in response to a misunderstanding."

Michelle's jaw dropped. How could there have been any part of this that was a misunderstanding?

"Explain," Epimoe demanded.

"Vaomi told me that he told the alien that he was going to capture and conquer it. It was a taunt to a sparring opponent, nothing more."

Shit. The *Ijlenum* words for 'kill' and 'capture' were very similar. 'Eat' and 'conquer' were less so, but still not completely unrelated. Still, Michelle knew the difference.

"An easy mistake to make, I'm sure, for an alien with a small brain who is new to the language and was feeling panicked."

"That is NOT what he said!" Michelle shouted, unable to contain herself.

The crowd erupted.

"ORDER!" barked Sijaj, gonging loudly.

Suji's underhand came to rest on Michelle's foot, out of view of the Council.

"Does the Council require any further clarification?" Sijaj asked in a tone that made it clear what the answer should be.

None of the Councilmembers made a sound.

"Researcher, you are dismissed. Everyone may be seated." Sijaj struck the gong one more time. "This Council is adjourned for deliberation. We will reconvene to deliver our verdict."

And the hologram disappeared, taking everyone except the handful of Yukesi crew in the room with it.

Michelle looked around, but Rimoli was already gone.

Hours passed. Sam and Suji insisted on waiting in the mess hall, loathe to miss any of the *Negoheh* revelry. Sam didn't want any of them to wallow in their uncertainty, and Suji admitted that he probably shouldn't be left to himself if Rimoli was supposed to survive the night.

"Until Rimoli's statement, everything was going very well, Mishel," said Sam in an attempt to comfort her while also doing a little Monday-morning quarterbacking. "Hegoh was careful to present you in ways that were factual while emphasizing your accomplishments and courage. His order of the four points was logical; each one built off the previous one. It was quite well put together."

"So was that slug's statement," Suji grumbled. "He didn't say anything that could demonstrably be proven false, yet he did nothing but lie. The dishonorable *yikhu*."

"That was what was so terrible about it. He turned an assault motivated by prejudice into my word, an alien trying to gain official recognition as more sapient than a fish, against an injured Vinyi citizen's! A citizen serving in the Fleet, no less!" Michelle rubbed the bridge of her nose. "There's no way anyone believed me by the time he was finished."

"Councilmember Epimoe may have." Sam's voice was thoughtful. "She was the one who asked for your statement, after all. And she paid attention to what you had to say."

"Epimoe has influence, too," interjected Suji. "She isn't one of the Assistant Chairs, but she may as well be for the amount of respect she commands on the Council."

Michelle sighed. "It's all nothing but speculation at this point." She finished off her drink and set the glass down on the table. There were all the same cheers and camaraderie and joy in the air tonight as there had been last night, but she couldn't feel any of it for the gigantic lump of worry that had replaced every last one of her internal organs. "I don't want to ruin your evenings, but I would rather be back in my quarters, if you don't mind."

Sam laid a hand on her shoulder. She was getting used to the feeling of his hand there in her moments of need and was coming to understand that this was his version of a hug. She smiled tiredly up at him.

"I will walk you back." Suji stood and helped her down.

Sam lifted his tentacles in assent. "Then I will attend to some things that require my attention. Be of good courage, Mishel."

The encouragement fell bitterly on her ears. How could she? Still, she said, "I'll try, Sam." And she would, but she wasn't hopeful that more of her so-called courage would do her any good.

"What was I supposed to say?!" Jenqu hissed. "Its work was *flawless*! Sojak and half a dozen others examined it, too. I had to admit it."

Rimoli sighed. "Well, it doesn't have to matter now. Just make sure you hold up your end of the bargain when it comes to the verdict."

The Councilmember made a face like he'd just tasted something sour. "I have told you, I will do what I can, but my influence will only go so far."

The research scientist leaned into the monitor. "As long as it extends to six other members of the Council, that's far enough."

"Epimoe is... formidable."

Rimoli rolled back his tusk membrane ever so slightly. "So am I. Do not test me. I have nothing to lose if your shame comes out."

Jenqu's tentacles stiffened, but all he said was, "Someone is coming. I must go." And the screen went black.

A low growl issued from Rimoli's throat. This was not his favorite game to play, but if this was the only way to keep a lower life form like the Little in its proper place, then he would do it.

When he'd first learned of Vaomi's idiocy, Rimoli had been outraged. If Vaomi's attack had resulted in any other outcome, it could have been disastrous for his cause. As it was, Vaomi would forever be marked with the foolishness of his decision, but his recklessness ended up working out very well. As Vaomi had been telling Rim his version of events, it had taken all his self-control not to throttle the moron there in his medbay cot. But after Rim calmed down, when he began to see how he could use the encounter to his advantage, he heaped words of praise onto his poor, injured colleague and drew every last detail from him.

Between Rimoli's representation of Vaomi's 'sacrifice' and Jenqu's influence, it should be enough to get the Little in a cage in his laboratory, where it belonged.

It had better be, or Rimoli would be looking over his shoulder for that hotheaded Chief Engineer for the rest of his time aboard Yukesi.

"Enter," Hegoh answered the door chime to his office.

Sam walked in. The doctor looked tired and not at all as festive as one would expect on the second night of *Negoheh*. However, after the way Mishel's hearing had ended, it was exactly as festive as Hegoh was expecting.

"Sit down, Sam," he said, gesturing to the sofa along the wall rather than to the chair on the visitor side of his desk. As Sam took a seat, Hegoh brought over two glasses and a bottle of *yikgibe*. He poured them each a glass and sat down beside his longtime colleague.

Sam slugged back a large swallow. "That could have gone better," he finally said.

Hegoh hummed.

"What do you think? How do you think they're going to rule? Was all the good that came before enough to mitigate the disaster at the end?"

Hegoh hummed again. "It is hard to say. Had Rimoli said nothing, it is likely the deliberations would already be over and Mishel would be celebrating with the rest of us this evening. As it is, however…" Hegoh shrugged.

Sam grumbled. "I would like nothing more at this moment than to run him through with one tusk, then the other, then operate on him so he lives long enough to be ejected through a missile tube."

The captain of the Yukesi tried not to laugh, as it was unbefitting his station, and didn't entirely succeed. "Yes." He took a drink. "But Rim has the same rights as every other citizen on board, the same rights you have. He had the right to speak."

"He lied, Hegoh. You know it, I know it, but nobody can prove it. He *lied*. It is unforgivable."

Hegoh knew it. He also knew that, without proof, there was nothing official that he could do about it. "It is an accusation without evidence."

"I know it. Worse, *he* knows it."

Silence settled in as the two senior officers drank.

After some time, Sam broke it. "What's taking them so long?"

Hegoh had no doubt. "Epimoe."

Sam scrutinized him. "You have spoken with her?"

"No," Hegoh waved his tentacles. "But I know her. She is doing what she can to remind the Council of the first 85% of the hearing, and looking for reasonable doubt for the last 15%."

Sam continued to observe him. "How well do you know her?"

"Not as well as you're implying," Hegoh replied. *Though not for lack of trying.* Epimoe had given consent for him to woo her once his tour of Yukesi ended, if she was still uncoupled at that time, although that would be some years from now. "But enough to know that she is fair-minded and honorable. She will do her best to see that Mishel receives just treatment at the hands of the Council."

Sam nodded. "That was the impression I had, as well."

"The longer this goes on, the more hope we may hold out for Mishel."

Sam hummed. Then he refilled his glass and held it up in a toast. "Then may it extend through all of *Negoheh*."

Hegoh saluted him and drank. *Come on, Epi. Everything depends on you now.*

21

Michelle woke to a mild beeping noise coming from her communications console. With a groan, she checked the time and found that it was three hours before the regular day shift was due to begin. Which meant that she'd gotten about three hours of sleep.

After Suji walked her back last night, he'd offered to come in and keep her company, but she really wanted to be alone. It was harder than anyone knew for her to speak *Ijlenum* all day and night, harder than they knew to be the only one who looked like she did, who moved like she did, who received the stares, both innocently curious and prejudicially scornful, like she did. And after an all-day examination that ended the way that hearing had, all Michelle wanted was to let her guard down and really rest, as much as she could.

So she took off her fancy clothes, carefully hung them back up, and crawled into bed in only her underthings. She laid there for hours, staring at the ceiling, at the stars outside her viewport, at the inside of her eyelids, at nothing at all. She must have fallen asleep eventually, though she couldn't have said when it happened.

Michelle ached in her body, but even with all its recent injuries, it wasn't as bad as the ache in her heart. She missed *everything* about her life before. She missed the cramped little house on Mars. She missed fresh fruit. She missed using her own language. She missed hugging Phil, and kissing Dave, and watching both of them try so hard not to tell her how terrible her latest attempt to dress up protein rations tasted. She missed Dr. Morgan patronizing her, and she missed being buried up to her elbows in compost. She missed crying herself to sleep and waking up to Dave's gorgeous face in the mornings. She missed college and chocolate and coffee and alarm clocks and —

Alarm clocks. That beeping was still coming from her console.

Michelle swung her legs out from under the blanket and padded barefoot to the desk. She turned on the monitor and read the message.

"The Council has reached a verdict. Starboard Conference Room, 0730."

At 0720, her door chimed. Sam and Suji were right on time. Michelle was ready, and the three of them left her quarters and made their way to the conference room without a word among them.

It looked exactly as it had the day before. The captain was already seated; Sam, Michelle, and Suji walked in and joined him. Hegoh looked at her with an expression she couldn't read, then turned back toward the Councilmembers. Michelle tried to catch Councilmember Epimoe's eye, to gauge how things would go, but all the Councilmembers seemed to be concentrating on the tablets in front of them. Not a sound was heard in the chamber, not even from the onlookers. The only noise to disrupt the silence was the swoosh of the conference room door opening and closing twice after Michelle sat, first to admit Rimoli, then Lihku.

Then all was as quiet as the space outside as they waited for the clock to reach the appointed time.

At 0729, Michelle swallowed and reached out to either side. Each of her brothers held her hands in theirs.

At 0730, Senior Chairman Sijaj picked up the mallet and struck the gong. "This hearing, concluding on the ninth day of Hoyo, will come to order. Senior Chairman Sijaj presiding. This hearing regards the petition of Mishel the Little Being, sponsored by Captain Hegoh of Yukesi and Admiral Lezmu of Mejihi, requesting formal asylum among the Vinyi people.

"Mishel the Little Being, you will stand while the verdict of this Council is delivered."

Michelle made her way to standing on her chair, as she had the day before. She had to release Sam's and Suji's hands to do so.

"This Council has deliberated all through the night regarding your status and your fate, small one. It is well-known that we have never dealt with anything such as the situation you present to us, and each Councilmember has taken his or her duties toward you and toward the glorious Vinyi people seriously and executed them with the greatest solemnity.

"You were required to satisfy each of four characteristics

in order to successfully petition for asylum. A case was presented for each and the outcomes were thus.

"On the point of Sole Survivorship, this Council agrees unanimously that Mishel the Little Being is the only one of her kind."

A rush of air burst from Michelle's lungs. She hadn't realized she was holding her breath until then. She inhaled quickly and quietly.

"On the point of Sapience, this Council agrees unanimously that Mishel the Little Being is sapient."

Halfway. She was halfway there.

"On the point of Contribution, this Council agrees unanimously that Mishel the Little Being is capable of contributing."

Oh my god. Just one more. Just one more. Just this last one.

"On the point of Adaptation, this Council agrees seven members to six that Mishel the Little Being is unable to successfully adapt into Vinyi society without posing a danger to its citizens.

"Therefore, the asylum petition of Mishel the Little Being is denied."

Michelle felt the blood drain from her head. Her thoughts froze and she couldn't process what she'd just heard. *What? Denied? But… what happens to me now? What —*

"Mishel the Little Being will be immediately given into the custody of the Scientific Research Facilities aboard Yukesi, so that we may glean as much knowledge as possible about its species, until such time as Yukesi returns to Hoikke at the conclusion of its current commission. At that time, Mishel the Little Being shall be admitted to a planet-bound holding facility and housed there until it dies.

"This is the verdict of the Council."

And Senior Chairman Sijaj struck the gong one final time before the entire Council, with all its onlookers, disappeared forever.

It was as though all the air in the room disappeared when the Council did. Michelle couldn't breathe, couldn't move, couldn't think. *Custody of the Research Facilities... planet-bound holding facility... until it dies.* The words echoed in her head, sound without meaning ricocheting in her mind. Faintly, she heard some mumbling, voices chattering from a hundred miles away.

Denied. Her petition had been denied.

She was officially, legally, a non-entity. It didn't matter that she was sapient, that she was the only human alive, that she could contribute. She was dangerous and deemed unfit for Vinyi society.

She belonged to the lab now.

A familiar voice was calling her name, a voice that carried with it comfort and safety. "Dave?"

"Mishel, look at me."

A form came into focus above her, large and gray and worried. It was Sam. "Mishel. Mishel, do you see me? Can you hear me?"

"Sam." Michelle blinked and her surroundings came into focus. She was lying on the floor. "How did I get here?" She started to push herself up.

"You collapsed." Sam scooped a big hand behind her back and slowly helped her up to sitting. "It was the shock of the verdict, after all the stress of the hearing." He rubbed her back and helped her to stand. "Come, let us get you to the medbay."

"I don't think so."

Michelle looked toward the voice to see Rimoli looking smugly down at her, Suji standing in front of him, between him and her. "The lab needs to study and document the effects of shock on the Little's nervous system."

Suji did not move save for curling his tentacles and raising his tusks.

"Mishel needs to be cared for," objected Sam.

"The Little needs to be studied," rejoined Rimoli.

Nobody moved. None of them was willing to be the one who broke the stalemate and started a brawl.

Michelle gripped Sam's shirtsleeve tightly in her fist. She couldn't go to the lab. She'd never get out if she went to the lab. She'd never go home, never even get to look for home anymore, if she went to the lab.

Finally, the sonorous baritone of Captain Hegoh broke the tension. "Suji." He paused, as though finding it difficult to say the words that would destroy Michelle's hope.

"Suji," he said again, "Stand down."

Sam's head whipped around to face his captain. "Hegoh, you cannot let him take her! You *know* what he plans to do, you cannot do this!"

"Sam, you heard the verdict." Hegoh's voice was as hard as stone. "There is nothing else I *can* do. Lihku, escort Mishel to the Research Lab."

Lihku walked up to Suji, who had yet to move. The burly Battle Chief laid a hand on the younger man's shoulder and looked him in the eyes. A silent conversation transpired between the two, and Suji dropped his head in defeat and stepped aside.

Rimoli strode quickly forward, eager to lay hands on his new acquisition.

Then suddenly Lihku was there instead and Rimoli, behind him, flapped his hands in the air as though they burned. "*I* will escort Mishel to the lab," Lihku growled. He turned and looked at Michelle. "As ordered," he added softly, those two words carrying as much regret as Michelle had ever heard.

"Please," she whispered. She didn't know what was in store for her now, but there was no way it was good. "Please."

Lihku knelt in front of her and gently touched her bruised cheek. "I will ever be sorry for this, Mishel." And he wrapped his hands around her and lifted her off the ground with him as he stood.

"No." Michelle tried to wriggle out of his grasp, tried to employ the evasion techniques he'd taught her, but he was prepared for that. She wasn't getting away. Lihku didn't hurt her, but neither did he allow her any maneuvering room. "No, no, Lihku, please. Suji! Sam!"

Sam was pale. "We cannot stop it, Mishel."

"But we will *not* abandon you," Suji vowed, both a promise to her and a threat to Rimoli.

The researcher simply smiled at the engineer. Then he turned his gaze on her and Michelle's blood ran cold. "Come," he said, and looked her over from head to toe. "Let us get to the lab. I am eager to begin."

Alone in his quarters that night, Hegoh tossed back a shot of *gonu*. It burned going down his throat, and his only thought was that it didn't burn enough.

That poor Little. He had tried so hard to make a case, had so diligently mapped out the answers to the Council's requirements. Hegoh had been sure, absolutely certain, that the Council would see the validity in his arguments and grant Mishel asylum. How could they not? And now that he'd failed in a Council petition, what kind of impact would that have on their votes of confidence in his leadership? Would his compassion toward the alien end up hurting his career? His standing?

Damn politicians. He never would understand what motivated them. What harm would it do the People if this one lost, lonely creature were made welcome?

His communications console beeped. With a groan, he ran his hand over his face. He'd been Captain for long enough that he knew, as a basic fact of life, that he was always on duty. But dammit, could he not have thirty minutes to himself after that catastrophe?

The console beeped again, and when he looked over, he saw that the incoming communication was on his personal channel. He didn't have to answer to know who it was, and because he knew who it was, he answered. "What in the Pit happened today, Epi?"

Councilperson Epimoe shook her tentacles at him. She wore clothes from her own wardrobe rather than her formal attire, and she allowed herself to blow off some of the stress from the hearing. "I can't say for sure, Hegoh. But I am so, so sorry." Her voice took on a hard edge. "The Little didn't deserve what she got."

He sighed and sagged in his chair. "It was going well, wasn't it? It seemed to be from where I sat."

Epi raised her tentacles in confirmation. "It was. Mishel was very compelling. Had we voted before your researcher opened his mouth, it would have been nearly unanimous in her favor. But that researcher of yours…" She lowered her voice and looked around, despite being in the privacy of her own home. "I have doubts about his honor."

"He is one of the best in his field of study, but he is a *jik'loinhij*. Yet I have never been able to find any proof to support what my instinct tells me is true."

"Which makes him a cunning *jik'loinhij*. The worst kind."

Hegoh grunted.

Epi gave him a look of sympathy and continued. "I will be looking at some of my colleagues after this, as well, with an eye to the integrity of their actions. I will not name names without proof," she said with a wave of her hand, cutting off Hegoh's question before he could ask it. "But there may be some… inconsistencies that demand review."

He grunted again. He knew without her saying it that if she found anything he needed to know about, she would tell him.

"Don't have more than two," she said softly, nodding at the drink in his hand. "You deserve more, but…"

"But." He lifted his glass to her. She raised her own, they tapped their glasses on the monitors, and took a swig.

They sat in companionable silence for a few moments before Epi said, "I should go. I have work to do." She leaned back from the screen. "Again, Hegoh, I am truly sorry."

He nodded. He was sorry, too.

"Come home safe, won't you?"

Her words brought a small smile to his face, and he knew she was referencing his request to court her officially when he returned. "That's the plan."

Epimoe lifted her tentacles once and the monitor went dark.

Hegoh sighed and poured himself his second drink.

22

Blearily, Michelle scanned her surroundings. She could barely focus for the exhaustion, but despite being bone-weary she couldn't manage to fall asleep. The research lab aboard Yukesi could have been mistaken for most any research lab anywhere, at least to her untrained eye. Areas were compartmentalized and orderly, staff moved through the room efficiently and quietly, and the smell of antiseptic, apparently a universal constant, faintly tainted the air.

And there were a few empty cages. As far as she could see, hers was the only one that was occupied.

The gaps in between the bars were large enough for her to stick her arm out, but not her head. It was about one-fifth the size of her quarters, with no bed, no bathroom, and nowhere to see the stars outside. Instead, she had two blankets on a hard metal floor and a Vinyi-sized bucket in the corner, which she had yet to use. She had no books, nothing to write with, and nothing to do. She'd been left for at least hours, maybe longer, and would've paid her weight in gold for a glass of water.

At least I'm not tied up and naked this time.

Lihku had grudgingly deposited her here, tarrying for as long as he could until he had no choice but to leave. Since being locked in, nobody had come to check on her, to see if she was all right, to give her food or water, and she wondered if Sam and Suji could still be her family now that she wasn't actually a legal entity. Neither Rimoli nor his staff had touched her, either, but she couldn't relax, waiting for that shoe to drop. *"You know what he plans to do, you cannot do this!"* Sam's plea rang in her ears.

What can he possibly do to me that would matter now? She had nothing but the clothes on her back and the blankets at her feet. She had no family, no home, no freedom, and no way to regain any of those things. There wasn't much left to take from her.

A Vinyi Michelle had never seen before stopped in front of her cage, facing her but looking down at his tablet. He then looked up, reading a display on the outside of the bars, just above and to the left of the cage door. He took a few steps away, over to a small table that held a variety of vials and tubes. He picked up a beaker about half the size of his hand, filled with a clear liquid, and brought it back to Michelle's cage, making notes in his tablet.

He punched in a code, and a small opening appeared in the bars along the floor. He bent and pushed the glass container inside. "Drink this."

She eyed it warily. God, she was thirsty, and that looked like water, but…

When she didn't move, the Vinyi sighed. "You can drink it or we can inject it."

She met his eyes; his face betrayed nothing. Did he feel

any remorse for her situation? Was he enthusiastic about having a new test subject? She couldn't tell.

He made a note. "One more chance."

She was so thirsty. And so tired. And in a fucking cage. With a despairing sigh, Michelle walked over to the beaker and picked it up. She held it to her nose and sniffed. It didn't smell like anything.

The Vinyi wrote something down.

Still watching him as though he were a snake that might bite her at any moment, Michelle took a sip of the liquid.

Relief burst inside her mouth in an explosion of mint. The liquid was cool and soothing to her parched tongue and dry throat, and she made herself drink the rest of it slowly, though what she really wanted to do was swim in it. When she drained the last drop, the Vinyi said, "Put it back down on the floor where you found it."

She did.

"Step back."

She did.

He accessed the opening in the bars, retrieved the beaker, and closed things up again. He made a few more notes, then walked away, not looking back once. Michelle watched him for a minute, having nothing better to do, then went back to her blankets in the corner of her cell. She folded them up and sat down, leaning against the bars. It was uncomfortable, but it was that, keep standing, or lie down sleeplessly some more.

She picked at the edge of one of the blankets. It was soft between her fingers and felt fuzzy, even though it was completely smooth. She wondered what material it was made of, how it was made, where it came from. In fact, the more she rubbed, the softer it felt. Before long, it moved like putty, and she could pinch it and examine her fingerprints in it for a few moments after. She pinched the blanket's edge hard, and when she released it, not only had the blanket retained her fingerprints, but her fingers had bent where they had no joints, warping from the pressure she'd applied. She looked at the fingers of her left hand, at her thumb,. How could they be S-shaped without hurting? They weren't supposed to look like that.

A tingling in her legs got her attention, and she was surprised to see them melting into the metal floor. Shouldn't it be hot? Things melted when they got hot, didn't they? Was she hot?

The goosebumps on her arms told her she was not.

She was terribly thirsty again. Where was that lab guy? Maybe she could ask him to bring more of the minty water stuff. Why couldn't she turn her head? When Michelle slumped into the floor, her gaze turning up to the ceiling of her prison, she understood that she herself was melting.

Her flesh pooled on the floor, falling off her bones. Out of the corner of her eye, she saw her humerus, white and solid and strange and familiar, and then it too melted into the floor. She heard herself gurgling and realized that she wasn't breathing.

How could she? Her lungs had melted.

A vision of Dave at their wedding filled her mind, then an image of Phil as a little boy, sitting beside her on the sofa.

Then Michelle's consciousness melted, as well, and she was gone.

A thunderous vibration shook Michelle's head and rattled her teeth. Clanging rang in her ears, followed by the ruckus of voices, loud voices, shouting. Lions roared, tigers growled, and a bulldozer scooped her up into the tops of the mile-high trees of the jungle she was lost in.

The light pierced Michelle's eyelids, shooting all the way to the center of her head where a stabbing pain burned. She shivered. It was so cold. Michelle pulled the blanket up to her chin and snuggled into her pillow. She ached everywhere, and the pain in her head was enough to make her long for unconsciousness again.

The heavy thud of approaching footsteps jostled the hot poker in her head with each footfall. As they grew closer, grew louder, she became aware of a steady, persistent beeping. There were some chirps that were off-rhythm with the others, and the rhythmic ones stopped. The footsteps rumbled again as they left.

Michelle buried her face in the blanket, willing the footsteps to stay away and leave her alone.

It worked for a little while, but then more footsteps came back, multiples of them, some heavy, some lighter. She heard voices, then another set of chirps, and then the gentle ring of metal on metal.

She made herself open her eyes.

Her cage door was open.

But the way was blocked. Three Vinyi stood outside the cage, and one more had bent himself over and come in. Rimoli.

A whisper of hatred stirred in the bottom of her heart.

"Little." Michelle winced; he spoke loudly, abrasively, and her tender head couldn't stand it. When she didn't answer, the bastard raised his voice. "Little."

"What?" Her voice was thin, creaky.

"Good, you have regained command of language." He extended a hand to the technician behind him. When he brought it back around in front of him, he was holding what looked like a long metal spoon, if the bowl of the spoon were closed instead of halved. Rimoli held it by the bowl and pressed the tapered end of it to Michelle's temple.

The pain in her head instantly subsided. Moments later, the aches wracking her body waned and she took a deep breath, her muscles finally relaxing.

"There," Rimoli said, checking a handheld display. "That put you back to rights. Close enough, anyway." He stood and walked out of the cage. "Exam area 4," he told the Vinyi on the end as he walked away and out of sight.

Michelle did not consider her current state as being 'back to rights'. She was weak, possessed of that worn out feeling that accompanies the end of a long illness. The stranger entered her cell and, after a scan with a device that had a small display screen at the top, he picked her up, bridal style, and carried her out of the cage.

She didn't have the strength to protest.

He carried her through a maze of walls and half walls, making so many turns she was sure he must have doubled back on his own trail, until at last he laid her down. If Michelle hadn't known better, she'd say she was in a dentist's chair. And if she hadn't known better already, she would have figured it out when straps came out of the chair and secured her torso, wrists, hips, and ankles in place.

"Subject 94-001-L," intoned Rimoli as he readied a tray of instruments beside her head. "Test sequence 1." He paused, meeting her tired eyes with his own shiny black orbs. "Pain tolerance."

All she felt was pain.

The right side of her body was subjected to various levels and sources of heat. Rimoli and his team determined exactly how hot something had to be to burn her, exactly how hot it had to be to melt her skin, and how hot it had to be before her nervous system shut down and she passed out to avoid feeling it any longer.

The left side of her body experienced the opposite. Freezing cold was applied to her skin, causing burning pain, numbness, and frostbite. In some places, her skin swelled and burst. In other places, her body simply gave up. Her left little finger froze completely and broke off.

All she knew was delirium. All she wanted was to stop feeling.

She longed for death, though her mind was so far gone she couldn't name it.

Michelle didn't know when she was put back in her cage.

Michelle counted backwards from 100 in Spanish. The counting passed the time, a meaningless concept in a constant environment and random schedule, and the foreign language gave her mind something to do while she waited. She didn't know what she was waiting for, but she had nothing else to do.

Her finger, the one that wasn't there anymore, itched. Michelle refused to look at her mangled hand again, already haunted by the possibilities. What would be the next thing to go? A toe? Another finger? Perhaps an entire hand, or her nose, or an ear? Rimoli could take her apart piece by piece like a cheap toy, and there wasn't a damn thing she could do about it. Her powerlessness only served to feed her despair.

Heavy footsteps approached her cage. She pulled her legs under her into a crouching position. A weighted blanket of dread settled over her, forbidding any movement. Her stillness, born of instinct, deceived her, offering a hope based on a false assumption: that she had a chance to evade the approaching threat. Michelle stayed huddled like that, staring blindly at nothing, barely breathing, for a long time, far too long. When she finally realized that something was wrong, that she shouldn't still be here if the lab techs had come for her again, she blinked and slowly began to scan her surroundings without moving her head. She saw the boots first. They were close to the cage but fixed in place. Haltingly, Michelle dragged her gaze up the legs, to the torso, the arms, the face -

The face. The tentacles. Some damaged. One missing entirely.

Vaomi.

He had come to gawk at her in her humiliation. Saying nothing, he merely peered at her, staring, invading her privacy with his unwanted attention.

Michelle tried to draw herself into yet a smaller ball. She wrapped her arms around herself and ducked her face into the space between her chest and her knees.

The dribbling of a hot liquid on the back of her neck made her jump. Whimpering, Michelle tried scooting away from it, away from Vaomi's towering silence, toward the back of her cage. A quick glance up at her enemy and her face was splashed with the liquid. It was coming from Vaomi's second tentacle, fully extended and carefully aimed.

He was pissing on her.

She pressed all the way into the back of the cage, but his stream still hit its target. By the time he was finished, she stank of him, and the heat of it was beginning to give way to cold damp instead. Michelle shivered, cowering.

After an eternity, Vaomi broke the silence. "You will never be worthy to live among us."

When he finally walked away, she cried into her knees until the techs came again. Within moments, she was screaming in fear. Moments after that, the tenor of her terror changed from panic to pain.

Reality began to blur. Day and night lost all meaning. There was only pain and waiting for pain.

The lab techs came for her time and again, in an endless, brutal cycle, until there was only pain in between pain.

Michelle's mind, trapped and desperate in her tortured body, began to lose itself.

23

Sam had braced for what he'd find when he entered the lab, but as it turned out, his mental preparation was all for nothing.

Suji had been barred from entering the research lab after his furious reaction at seeing Mishel in a cage. In his fight to get to her, he had destroyed quite a few pieces of equipment and upset a number of in-progress experiments, not to mention sending Sam a number of patients. Hegoh determined that the replacement cost of the equipment was coming out of his service recompense, and Suji's expulsion from the lab was meant to keep the remaining experiments, and the researchers, secure. The only good to come from Suji's visit was Hegoh's order that Mishel be supplied with a mattress and pillow.

Since Suji was no longer able to enter the lab, Sam had dropped in unannounced once daily, but Mishel was always "busy assisting us in our research," as the technicians put it. As a result, Sam hadn't seen Mishel since the end of the hearing, when Lihku had physically removed her from the room just over two weeks ago.

Two weeks of daily visits, and he had yet to see Mishel. He had a feeling that Rimoli somehow always knew when Sam was on his way and he didn't want Sam to see the state of his newest lab rat. Otherwise, how would Mishel *always* be beyond his sight? Sam stopped booking time in his official schedule for the lab visits, in case Rimoli had somehow tapped into it, but Mishel was still kept hidden from his view. And Sam had no official recourse: she was legally, much to his disgust, the property of the research lab.

A tap on his door drew him out of his thoughts. "Mebeku," he greeted his assistant doctor. "Come in."

Bek lifted his tentacles and stepped inside Sam's office, closing the door behind him.

"What can I do for you? It isn't time for the consult already?"

"No, doctor." Mebeku sat in the chair directly opposite Sam. "All the examinations and physicals are on schedule. Everything is going exactly as expected."

"Well, that's good. So what's this about?"

"I have a friend who works in the lab, and I'll not name him. But he is concerned about the treatment Mishel is receiving in the lab."

Sam tensed. "How so?"

Mebeku took a breath, flexing and relaxing his hands. Bek was also fond of Mishel. "He is beginning to doubt that Mishel will live long enough to make it back to Hoikke."

Sam's tentacles went stiff as iron. The idea alone made his tusk membrane roll back aggressively. "What is happening?"

"Doctor... Samou, she is being experimented on for days

at a time by a round-the-clock team of technicians overseen by Rimoli and his aides. My friend has seen the data and is convinced that she is regularly being pushed beyond the limits of her physiology. She has been subjected to temperature tolerance tests, blood chemical adjustments, conductivity assessments -"

"She is being electrocuted?" Sam interrupted.

"Yes. And starved, bones are being broken and reknit, limbs severed and reattached, or sometimes just severed, and she is given inadequate time and care to recuperate from these atrocities."

Sam had lived many years, meditated deeply for most of those years, and had honed his ability to think calmly in the midst of anger, but thinking over the heat of his ire at this moment proved more than difficult. His mind's eye was filled with images of freeing Mishel and bringing her back here to care for her, of ripping that arrogant fuckwit Rimoli's head off his shoulders and feeding it to one of his experiments. "We cannot charge in as Suji did; it would leave her entirely alone," he murmured, thinking aloud.

"I agree." Mebeku's instant self-inclusion in whatever Sam was planning was a clear sign of Bek's feelings on the matter. "But neither can we let the situation play out as it will if left to Rimoli."

"No." If Mishel died in Rimoli's custody, Sam would never forgive himself, or the Head Researcher. "Yet, legally, she is no different than any other experiment under Rimoli's charge."

"I've been thinking about that," Bek said.

"And you think this will work?" Hegoh asked.

Sam pointed at the monitor. "Read it, Hegoh. Read the verdict as though you weren't there when it was issued, as though we have no personal interest in the subject. Rimoli, as the head of the Research Lab, was given *custody* of Mishel, not ownership. He may do what he likes to learn about her, but he is to deliver her to the holding facility on Hoikke at the end of our mission so that Mishel may die *at the holding facility.*" He slapped a hand on Hegoh's desk. "Rimoli may do what he likes *except* kill her. He has to ensure that she remains alive in order to be delivered to Hoikke at the end of the Yukesi's commission."

Hegoh's eyes scanned the text of the Council's verdict, then scanned it again slowly, one word at a time. Sam had a point. There was a clear expectation that Mishel would be delivered to a holding facility at the end of the Yukesi's current assignment. He slowly lifted his tentacles in assent.

Sam exhaled heavily before rushing to speak. "We have to act quickly. I have reason to believe that her life is at risk even now."

Hegoh stood. "Ready a place for her in the medbay. Lihku and a team of his will deliver her there if the situation requires it."

"And who determines if the situation requires it?"

Hegoh was already striding toward the door. "You do."

Sam was right behind him.

"This..." Rimoli sputtered. He was practically vibrating with impotent rage. "This is *not* what the Council meant! The Little is mine!"

"Whatever you may suppose the Council intended is irrelevant. What matters is what the Council *said*, and those terms are quite clear." Hegoh, with authority and size on his side, took an intimidating step closer to Rimoli. "Take us to Mishel."

Rimoli hesitated, opening his mouth as though to protest. Then he looked again at the small crowd invading his lab and decided against it. "It is in the middle of a delicate experiment," he objected weakly.

"I did not ask about her status. Obey my order, Researcher."

Sam's impatience nipped at his heels.

Rimoli turned and led them deeper into the labyrinth that was his domain. Sam followed Hegoh, who followed Rimoli, past lab technicians in small rooms, turning corner after corner until Sam wondered exactly how large the research facilities were. Lihku and two of his lieutenants fell in behind Sam.

At last, Rimoli stopped in front of a doorless room and petulantly gestured inside. Hegoh stepped aside to let Sam enter first.

Sam's heart nearly gave out at the sight of her.

Mishel was strapped to a table, surrounded by a team of three techs. They were monitoring her vitals as her body absorbed whatever was in that IV she was hooked up to. Sam didn't need a display to tell him that her vitals were terrible.

She was nothing but skin and bones, as though she hadn't eaten since the hearing. Her color was pale, as pale as when they'd first found her frozen. Her hair was half gone, with great sections of scalp clearly visible through it. Her chest moved shallowly, erratically. Her sunken eyes were closed, lips dry and cracked. Two fingers were missing from her left hand.

Sam swallowed the violence within him. "We are moving her to the medbay. *Now.*"

The technicians looked to Rimoli for confirmation.

Hegoh spoke. "You heard the doctor. Prepare a stretcher for transport."

They jumped into action at the captain's command, bustling around their section leader. Rimoli stood glaring at Sam. Mishel's body was moved to the stretcher and Lihku's men picked up either end. Hegoh left the room, followed by the stretcher and Sam, with Lihku bringing up the rear. Before Sam could completely leave the room, Rimoli intercepted him, stopping him in his tracks. "I will have it back. It belongs here."

That hard truth burned in Sam's gut. "Yes, you will have her back, and you will continue to do all manner of unspeakable things to her. I cannot stop it. But you will not - *you will not* - kill her. The Council has ruled."

Rimoli's tentacles curled, a challenge.

Sam bared his tusks as Lihku stepped closer, hand on his weapon.

The researcher backed off, though his glare would killed them both if it could have. "I will have it back as soon as it is no longer at death's door."

It was a fact, but Sam didn't have to like it. "You will have her back when I say you may." He rammed his shoulder into Rimoli's hard enough to bruise on his way out.

Sam and Bek were bent over Michel's still form when Suji burst into the room. "You have her!"

Juyukku, one of the medical assistants, stopped Suji from entering any farther. "She is not well. They are still working on her." He pushed gently on Suji's shoulders, steering him backwards out of the operating room as the engineer strained to see around him. "Go wait. Dr. Samou will call you when he has news."

Suji stopped pressing forward, but glared at Juyukku. "I'm not leaving the medbay."

"Then wait outside so we can concentrate!" Sam shouted.

Suji clamped his mouth shut and stepped back until he was just outside the operating room foyer.

Sam understood the younger man's impatience; he felt it himself. Sam was impatient for the procedure to be over and for Mishel to start healing; he was impatient to return to Hoikke where she would at least be treated decently and would be far away from Rimoli; he was impatient to disembowel the researcher and string him up by his own entrails as a *Negoheh* decoration.

Mishel had been severely abused. She was burned and frozen, electrocuted and drowned, starved and dehydrated. As Sam began working on repairing the most threatening damage to her sensitive systems, others of the medical team created their best semblance of artificial replacement limbs, in this case, fingers for him to reattach as best he could. As that was one of the least of her problems, however, the reattachment would occur near the end of the procedure.

After the first hour, she was hydrated again and her

breathing was steady. After the second hour, damage to her heart tissue had been repaired and her digestive system was on its way to healing. The excess fluid in her lungs had been expelled; the nanobots Mishel already had there were healing the damage those organs received almost as soon as the damage had been done.

That meant that the drowning had been done recently.

After the third hour, Mishel's body was correctly processing nutrients again and her nervous system was stabilizing. By the end of the fourth hour, two new artificial fingers had been added to the tattered remnants of her left hand.

Sam reviewed her status, going over all the displays, and finally was satisfied. "Apply the neuron stimulator," he directed Bek.

Mebeku set a small metal curve on top of Mishel's forehead. Sam aligned the pulses to stimulate neurons in the ventrolateral preoptic nucleus of her hypothalamus; that should help induce sleep. He and Bek applied stimulants to her pineal and pituitary glands, as well, to promote deep, consistent sleep and gently speed up her healing.

Then he stood up straight and just watched her.

"This is the second time she will live because of you," Mebeku said softly.

"Because of us," Sam corrected. After a weary sigh, he said, "Go. Rest. You have done more than your share today."

Bek laid a tender hand on Mishel's arm. "I'm glad she's here. Rest well, Doctor."

"And you."

Sam waited until Bek left before pulling a chair over to Mishel's bedside and lowering himself heavily into it. Carefully, he took her small right hand in one of his, sat back, and closed his eyes. The steady beeping of her vitals monitor was his lullaby.

Michelle's eyes fluttered open to a ceiling of soft white rather than the near black metal of her cage. When she realized that the ceiling, this exact section of ceiling, was familiar to her, an irony danced in her brain despite the exhaustion that permeated every facet of her being. It seemed to be her destiny to forever be waking up in the medbay.

She closed her eyes again and took an internal inventory. Sore. Worn out. Desperate for rest. But there was no active pain. *Sam must be giving me the good stuff. Pain is inevitable, unless you have drugs, I guess.*

Her mind ruthlessly played a macabre slideshow from which she couldn't tear her gaze, reliving for her the various tortures she had been introduced to in the last... how long had it been? It was forever, but there was a Before Forever, because wasn't there a time without pain?

Michelle was sure there was. Maybe.

Or maybe not. She didn't really know. Pain was her constant. Her body tensed, ready for the strong hands she couldn't resist manipulating her like a marionette. She braced for the petrifying terror and heavy burning of inhaled water, the sharp spasms of existence that were part of sharing her body with increasing jolts of electric current, the blinding pain of broken bones, the nerve panic that lived forever in burned skin that never completely ended... she saw all of it again and again, felt all of it again and again, unable to break away and think of anything else.

Had she ever been anywhere else? Ever felt anything other than fear, hopelessness, and pain?

Michelle opened her eyes again. She wasn't in her cage now. Was it over? Was she safe now? She couldn't believe it, couldn't feel the hope flutter in her chest, but the abject horror that filled her soul was replaced with a cautious void, a still malleable nothingness currently shaped like despair.

A movement in her peripheral vision made her jump. They were coming for her again, coming to take her to another death.

But it wasn't a lab tech. It wasn't The Bad One. But it *was* someone familiar, only someone who didn't scare her.

As he approached her, a name broke the surface of her muddled consciousness. Mebeku.

The rush of adrenaline subsided, leaving her warm and shaky. "Bek."

He walked over to her and laid a gentle hand on her forehead. How long had it been since someone had touched her without the intent to harm? She couldn't remember. "It is good to see you again, Mishel."

"Bek..." Michelle trailed off. A kaleidoscope of emotion roiled within her. She didn't know what she wanted to say, so she said nothing.

He quietly ran his hand over her head, caressing her scalp. "It is good that you are here. Your only job here is to rest and be quiet."

"Bek," she said again, trying to communicate something that wasn't even clear to her.

He lifted his tentacles. "I'll call for him. You relax." And he stood and walked to the wall where a communications console was located. She couldn't hear what he said, but he returned in moments and just held her hand, lightly brushing a finger over her knuckles.

Something old and familiar stirred in her belly. Someone else used to brush her knuckles like that. Someone who loved her. She couldn't think, couldn't remember.

When the doctor entered the room, a sense of safety wrapped around her like a fluffy winter coat and another name came to her. "Dave."

He looked sad as he sat in a chair next to her. "Samou," he corrected.

Michelle felt a puzzle piece click into place in her mind. "Sam," she said, and smiled. Of course it was Sam.

Sam smiled back in that unique Vinyi way. Looking into his gray, tentacled face bordered by tusks on either end of his mouth, Michelle's throat tightened in fear. *First the faces, then the pain,* she thought frantically. *First they come for you, then they try to end you.* But this face was different. Sam's face wasn't cold, detached, or angry. Sam's face was somber and sad.

Sam was sad. Why was Sam sad?

"Sam," she said, unable to find the rest of the words she wanted right now.

"Rest quietly, Mishel," he murmured. "You can rest quietly here. We will watch over you."

"Phil." Michelle desperately latched onto Sam, hoping he knew better than she did what she was asking.

Sam met Bek's eyes and said, "Call for Suji."

"Suji!" That was right. Not Phil. And Sam, not Dave. Who were Dave and Phil? They were good. They were safe.

A ray of soft light broke through the dark prison of her mind. Phil and Dave were from Before. Suji and Sam were from Right Before. Hell was Now. Or maybe this was After..?

"Is this After?" she asked Sam.

His tentacles quivered as he carefully caressed her cheek.

"Not yet."

Tears filled her eyes and he went blurry. "Why not?"

He grunted. "I do not know, *Rikube*. I do not know."

Michelle's life came back into focus for her with each passing hour. Either Suji or Sam, if not both, remained always at her side. Sam broke the ugly truth to her, that her reprieve in the medbay was temporary. She wasn't rescued. Sam and Suji hadn't found a way to save her. She was still condemned. She was only here to heal, then she would be sent back to the lab for Rimoli's experiments to start all over again. Once he tested her into a state of near-death again, she would come back to Sam for him to heal her and return her to Rimoli's custody yet again. The cycle of torture, near death, life, healing, and back to torture would never stop, not as long as she were on board Yukesi. Possibly not even after that. Who knew what happened at a 'holding facility', after all?

When Sam reluctantly answered an assistant's call and stepped out to check on another patient, each of his fading footfalls pierced her as a nail in the coffin of her hope. "It's over, isn't it?"

Suji's outermost tentacles hugged the bottom curve of his tusks in a gesture of calm and comfort. "What do you mean? What's over?"

Life. Freedom. Looking for my family. Being normal. Everything. A future of endless days in the lab, then days in some holding facility on an alien planet that, no matter how nice, would be a prison. "I am. I'm over."

He shook his tentacles from side to side. "No. You

mustn't accept that. I do not."

She stared at him incredulously. "You don't? *You* don't?"

Suji shook more adamantly. "No. I cannot."

Michelle gaped, then laughed. It wasn't a laugh of joy, or of humor of any kind. It was scornful, as dry and harsh as the landscape of the planet on which she'd left the loves of her life. "You don't get to have an opinion about it, Suji. You're not the one going through it."

He just stared at her, nonplussed, as she went on. "You might have the choice to 'not accept it'," she scathingly mocked. "*I'm* the one who's being broken. You can sit in your quarters and talk to your wife and new baby and 'not accept' what's happening to the Little Being you discovered all you want. And while you're doing that, I'll be in the lab losing body parts, getting pissed on and being tortured to death then brought back to life to be tortured until I die again. But hey, you go right ahead and feel all the righteous denial you want to in the comfort of your quarters all wrapped up in the love of your family."

Family. Michelle ran out of heat abruptly, defeat crashing over her. She was doomed to a solitary existence of abuse and torture until she lost either her mind or her life, or probably both. She turned her face away. "Tell Pekoe I said hello." Michelle didn't even attempt to soften the bitterness of her bite.

"Mishel," Suji pleaded. "You can't give up. You've come so far and fought so hard, through so much, too much to give up."

She pulled away from him without moving a muscle. "Oh, I think I've earned the right to give up if I choose. You don't know, Suji. You can't know. You're among your own people. You haven't been ripped out of your own life to be humiliated into nothing more than a curiosity to be played with until the stuffing falls out." Michelle thought again, as she had countless times before, of Dave and Phil and Mars and Earth and home, of the life she had before the Faceless, the life that she had lost forever. But this time, unlike the countless times before, no tears sprung to her eyes. No ache filled her heart, no longing moved her.

Michelle Arensen was officially empty.

Time was a thing in the medbay. The lights dimmed regularly, suggesting it was time to sleep, and brightened a while later, simulating the fresh start of a new morning.

It was, of course, bullshit.

Suji still came to see her, twice a day like clockwork. But since her outburst, he had been a little less warm, a little less inclined to offer words of support and encouragement. For her part, Michelle offered no more words at all. If Suji cared, he cared. If not, then he didn't. Either way, it didn't change anything for her. She was still only a lab rat ultimately at the mercy of an actual mad scientist.

Total bullshit.

Sam, on the other hand, seemed to be trying even harder to reach her, to bolster her in her hour of need. She didn't bother responding to him, either. What was the point? So she could experience her next excruciating pain with a cheerful attitude?

Bull-fucking-shit, as Petra would have said.

Ah, Petra. She would have been braced for this. She would have known it would all turn out like this. She would never have let naiveté, false hope, stupid fucking *optimism* distort her view of this new world. Well, Michelle was admittedly late to the party, but she was picking up the lyrics to the song stuck on replay.

Everything was pointless, misery constant, death inevitable and, likely, right around the goddamn corner, waiting for the opportunity to jump out at her and wrangle a frightened squeal from her before it ripped her to shreds.

Yeah, maybe Before. But not Now.

Not anymore.

The doctor himself entered the room. Every morning, he ran through the same routine: Sam came into the room with a variety of instruments on a tray. One by one, he either used the instruments to scan her and learn some undoubtedly fascinating detail of her vitals, or he injected her with them, filling her with medicine or vitamins or nutrients or painkillers. And every morning he talked to her.

Credit where credit was due, Sam had a great bedside manner.

Michelle had come to hate it.

He set the tray down on a mobile table that he positioned near her. "Good morning, Mishel. It's time for your morning exam, then breakfast." He paused, giving her time to answer if she were going to, then carried on in the face of her silence as though she had. "Your stomach is growing stronger. I think you're ready for *qaiguj hujhehu* this morning, but if it doesn't sit well, I'll give you something to ease the nausea and we can go back to simple grains for the rest of today."

Sam scanned her with one of the oblong devices. He studied the results, frowned, and studied them some more.

Michelle knew exactly what they said.

She was better. Her life was no longer in jeopardy and

her health was strong enough to be considered stable if not hardy. As her records were shared between the medbay and the lab each day, Rimoli knew as much about her state as Sam did.

He was going to take her back any day now and Sam wouldn't be able to stop him.

Sam sighed heavily. "You're healing even better than expected, Mishel." He sat in the chair that was almost always at her bedside now. "I wish you wouldn't," he admitted quietly.

That did it. "It's your own damn fault, isn't it?" she demanded.

His tentacles jumped in surprise. After days of silence, this was perhaps not what he'd been expecting from her. He scrutinized her, as though trying to determine if she was joking or not.

As if there were anything funny about this situation.

"You knew, Sam. You knew *exactly* what was going to happen and you fucking did it anyway."

The doctor's typically amiable expression hardened. "Did what? Healed you?"

"Yes."

"Of course I healed you, Mishel!" He goggled at her. "I'm a doctor. That's what I do. I heal the sick and, when I'm fortunate, I save lives. When I'm very fortunate, I save the lives of those I care about."

She snorted. "Well, goody for you. I'm so pleased that *you're* fortunate. Me, I'm fucked seven ways from Sunday."

Sam grunted. The figure of speech was, she was sure, baffling but her tone left nothing about her meaning in doubt. "I know you have to go back," he replied, "but you have a chance now. You're healthy again -"

"A chance?" she interrupted. "A chance for what? For a sadistic bastard to torture me to death? You think I should be grateful that I'm healthy enough to go through even more hell? I should be happy that I'm ready to lose more body parts? Thanks so much for that, Sam."

His shoulders sagged; Michelle couldn't find it in her to be even a little sorry that she'd caused it. "Mishel, we had to get you out of there. His 'tests' were about to kill you."

"Then why didn't you just let me die?!" It crystallized for her in that moment. She was willing to avoid going back to that torturous existence by any means necessary.

"What?" Sam's tentacles curled in disgust at the thought. "Because I care for you! Because we all care for you! We failed you in front of the Council, I will not fail you now!"

"You're not doing me any favors, sending me back there! You think I'd rather be there, in agony all the time, than at peace? You think you're doing something good, patching me up to send me back there? *You're not helping me, Sam! You're helping him!*" In the back of her mind, Michelle heard her vitals monitor beeping an alarm.

Sam drew a sharp intake of breath. He directed his attention to the alarm, reviewed and dismissed it, then returned his focus to the conversation. The moment away had given him a chance to gather his wits. "I cannot know how much agony you have experienced, Mishel. But do not think you are in it alone. Every day that you are down there, in his grasp, is a day that I am regretting every failure of mine in losing you your freedom. Yes, you are the one undergoing the unimaginable. But you are not the only one it hurts."

"Fuck you, Sam," Michelle said quietly. "You don't know hurt."

"No?" He leaned on the edge of her bed, bringing his face close to hers. "You are not the only one who has ever fought a war, Mishel. You are not the only one who has ever lost pieces of herself in every way possible."

Michelle waved her new fingers at him. "I'm the only one fighting this war."

Sam sat back, considering her. "Perhaps you have not fought a war like this one before. If that is so, then you do not yet understand." He held her half-fake hand in one of his huge ones. "Wars end, Mishel. You must survive until this one does."

She pulled her hand out of his hold. "Go away, Sam." She turned her face to the wall. "If you want to help, then leave me alone and let me die next time."

The gentle giant hummed. "I will go away, but I will never leave you."

The mattress dipped with the light weight of something he set on the bed before he stood and walked out of the room. When his sounds got lost in the other sounds of the medbay outside her room, Michelle turned to see what Sam left with her. It was a tablet. Despite herself, she picked it up and activated it. When the screen came to life, she stared.

It was a scrapbook of sorts. She scrolled through the table of contents. There were letters to her from Sam, Suji, even Bek and Lihku. Her favorite Vinyi stories were here. There was even a section of pictures. The first one on display pulled at the heartstrings she thought had snapped. It was a candid shot of her, Sam, and Suji at her first and only *Negoheh* feast. Suji was laughing, mouth wide open, ridiculous brown nest of 'hair' on his head. Sam was resplendent in his costume, a wide smile on his face. She sat in between them, small and fragile, protected. She, too, had been captured mid-laugh, her face glowing with happiness.

A part of her soul so small she'd not known it was there gently awakened. Tenderness ached within her, causing a not entirely unwelcome pain. She'd forgotten that pain could be healing as well as devastating.

With the faintest suggestion of a smile, Michelle extended a finger and gently traced Sam's and Suji's faces. Then she closed her eyes and hugged the tablet to her chest.

She was still holding it close when the explosion sent her flying across the room.

24

Michelle shook her head, trying to stop the ringing in her ears only to realize it was the alarm klaxon wailing. She pushed up to all fours before shakily getting to her feet. A medical assistant ran by, yelling at the top of his lungs; it sounded like an elephant trumpeting *Ijlenum*. Michelle pressed herself up against the wall to avoid being trampled by him. She watched him dash around the corner into a corridor that she had never been down, then made to step forward.

Another explosion rocked the ship and knocked her off her feet. A metallic thud on the wall next to her caught her attention. She was still gripping the handle of the tablet Sam had given her. Her artificial fingers had clasped it and wouldn't let go.

Again, she regained her footing and stumbled toward the main door leading from her semi-private area into the main medbay. She peeked out. Medical staff were running everywhere even though Michelle couldn't see anything wrong, anything different. She spotted Mebeku barking orders in the far corner opposite where she was. Other Vinyi scrambled to obey him.

Sam's voice suddenly filled the air. "Battle stations. Incoming casualties."

Another loud boom made the floor underneath her sway. This time she kept herself upright. *Battle stations?* Goosebumps covered her skin.

The Yukesi was under attack.

Sam charged around the corner and spotted her in the doorway. "Mishel!" He took a giant step toward her and shoved her backwards. She rolled into her room, tumbling end over end until she collided against the foot of her bed. When the world stopped spinning, she looked to where she'd last seen Sam.

The door was closed.

"Sam!" She had to help. She could help; there had to be something she could do. She grabbed the handle with her right hand and pulled.

He'd locked it.

"Fuck!" She was locked in. Everything in her rebelled. She got locked inside her cage in the lab, her own personal hell where she was a prisoner, an experiment. Here, with Bek, with Sam, Michelle refused to be locked in.

Another explosion and the floor, walls, ceiling, *everything* gave a great shudder. She dashed to the cabinets and opened the one after another, rifling through their contents to find something she could pick the lock with. The fact that she had no idea how to pick a lock was something she'd deal with in a minute.

There. Michelle picked up a sharp, tapered metal object nearly as long as her forearm. That might be a scalpel. Or maybe a laser. Or something. Next to the scalpel-like tool lay a variety of syringes and spray injectors. The long needle of a syringe might be helpful, too.

She pulled a bundle of bandages out of a drawer, wrapped her tools in them, and stuffed the mass into one of the Vinyi-sized pockets of the altered outfit Suji had brought her. She was about to turn away and head for the door when she spotted a tube of nanobots, like the ones in her lungs, on the shelf. Without thinking, Michelle reached out and stuffed the bot tube in her other pocket before running for the door.

When she got there, she had the same problem as the last time she'd been locked in a room: she was too short to reach the locking mechanism. The shouting had grown even louder on the other side of the wall and there were now screams adding to the cacophony.

Casualties.

Desperately, she searched for a stepstool. Finding none, she instead sprinted to her bedside and pulled with all her might on Sam's chair. It was on its side and chattered and jumped around as she tried to move it, so she stopped her efforts and took a few moments to right the giant piece of furniture. Now, once she got it to the door, she could climb up onto it long enough to toy with the lock and get out. Or so she hoped.

By the time Michelle got Sam's chair into position, she was sweating rivulets. She clambered up onto it and began randomly punching buttons, hoping she'd maybe get lucky. She was overdue for a little good luck, after all. But the door refused to open. She dug into her bandage pocket, pulled out the scalpel, and set about prying the control panel off the wall.

The screams and the shouts increased in intensity again

as the medbay doors opened and shut, opened and shut, admitting more and more patients.

She had to get out there.

Precious minutes ticked by and nothing, absolutely nothing, happened to her door. Moaning in frustration, she shifted her hold on the scalpel and brandished it like a dagger, stabbing at the damn electronic guardian.

Sparks suddenly flew out of it. Michelle shrieked and ducked, losing her balance and falling off her chair, arms pinwheeling, the tablet Sam had given her still firmly stuck in her left hand. She landed hard on the ground as yet another explosion rocked Yukesi. When she got her bearings, she noticed two things. One, the chair she'd worked so hard to pull over to the door had rolled away to the other side of the room. Two, the door was open.

Not by much, though. There was a small gap, only a couple of inches, just enough for her to glimpse the chaos that had taken over the medbay. She tried pushing on the door, pulling on it, wedging her foot in the gap and trying to leverage her body weight against it. Nothing worked. She could see, but she couldn't help.

Sam was bent over a patient on a bed, his shirt smeared with the faintly reflective silvery blood of his patient. Bek was much the same, at a bed three stations closer to the door. Medical personnel were swarming the place, everyone attending everyone else, and that pernicious silver stain marred every last one of them.

My God, how many casualties have we taken?

She was stuck. She couldn't help.

Wait. She was stuck in here, in this room *that had plenty of supplies in it.* She couldn't help, but maybe...

She dashed back to the nearest cabinet and flung it open.

There were all kinds of things in here, things she couldn't identify, but if they were here, maybe they could be useful. Michelle scooped up an armful and ran back to her small door gap. One handful at a time, she tossed the supplies through the gap as far as she could.

A medtech she had never met caught the movement out of the corner of his eye. He saw the supplies, then looked up at her. He strode over, picked up three of the items she'd tossed out, and gave her a quick salute with his tentacles.

She squared her shoulders. OK, it wasn't much, but if this was the only way she could help, this is what she would do. She bent down, grabbing more handfuls and tossing them out onto the pile she'd started. More medical staff noticed and began coming over to grab what they needed. When Michelle had nothing left to toss out, she ran back to the cabinet to gather another pile.

She did this three more times, and each time the existing pile dwindled to almost nothing as she tossed the last of what she had out to the people who needed it. She was just about to turn away to gather the next round of supplies when the main medbay doors opened.

Michelle froze in her tracks, her blood pounding.

At least a half-dozen walked through the medbay doors. Michelle's mind reeled.

They weren't Vinyi.

She'd never seen anything like them before, never even *imagined* anything like them. They were snakes, giant cobra-like creatures, not quite as large as the Vinyi but far larger than she. They wore armor, some kind of metal that glinted deep blue in the lights of the medbay.

A medical assistant looked up from the patient he was suturing. He jumped, dropped his suturing tool, and shouted a warning to the others. Before he could finish his cry, he was gurgling, dangling off the ground by one of the snakes' giant fangs.

It ran clear through his skull.

He jerked and spasmed like a freshly caught fish, and the medbay exploded with movement. Michelle had thought it chaotic before, but that had been the urgency of a well-trained medical team doing as much as they could to save multiple lives. This... this was a group of doctors fending off an attack by a squadron of trained soldiers.

The Snakes moved faster than Michelle could follow with her unaided eye. It was as though they just suddenly appeared in front of one Vinyi, then another, piercing each one with as many of their six sharp fangs as it took to kill him. The medical staff mounted a defense as best they could, but this was the medbay, not the armory. They took up their scalpels and lasers, but they had been caught off guard, unsuspecting, interrupted in the all-consuming act of saving another's life.

The Snakes swarmed in, taking Vinyi lives in rapid succession. Seven had died before the rest of the room truly understood what was happening.

One of the Snakes suddenly appeared in front of Bek. Michelle cried out a warning, her small voice lost in the din of the battle. Bek dodged a fang thrust and swung a medical tray at the beast, catching two of the fangs at once in it. He pushed it up, exposing the Snake's belly. He pressed a spray injector into it.

It only appeared to piss the Snake off.

The Snake pulled back and hissed. It shook the tray off its fangs and moved in again.

Other battling bodies got in the way of Michelle's view. She couldn't see what was happening to Bek. She couldn't follow what was happening to anyone. There was thrashing and shouting, so much silvery blood with its distinct rose scent, and she couldn't see anything, much less *do* anything.

Two bodies flew into the wall not six feet from where she stood anxiously peering out. It was a Snake and -

"NO!" The cry escaped her without her being aware of it.

Sam was wrestling for his life.

He had a grip on the two largest fangs being thrust at him, and his immense strength was keeping the creature at arm's length. He swiped at the serpent with his own tusks, but the lithe body of the alien dodged his attack easily. It coiled its tail around Sam's ankles. He kicked one foot free and swiped at the beast with his tusks again. The Snake's tongue flicked out, and to Michelle's horror, two more fangs emerged from its sides.

"SAM!"

The Snake bent itself into Sam and pierced his tough hide with its two body fangs. Sam screamed, but took advantage of the Snake's proximity and pierced it with a quick swipe of his left tusk. The Snake shrieked a hideous sound that ran down Michelle's spine. Moving faster than should have been possible, it coiled itself up and around, encircling Sam's neck and head, and squeezing. It gripped him more and more tightly until Sam couldn't move his head.

The Snake had neutralized the only weapons Sam had.

Michelle beat furiously on the door, trying to break it down, shove it open, *something* to get out there to help him.

As she watched helplessly, the serpent plunged all six of its fangs into Sam. Once, twice, three times, four times, over and over again. Sam's body jerked and pulled with every plunge and removal of the vicious weapons. Still he fought, swinging with his fists, trying to kick with his legs.

The Snake kept stabbing.

Sam's fists stopped swinging.

The Snake stabbed.

Sam's legs flopped onto the bloody medbay floor.

The Snake stabbed.

Sam's body jerked and danced.

The Snake stopped and released him. It turned and haltingly slithered away, sloppily, like a tire gone flat.

A high-pitched wailing filled Michelle's ears. She wished it would stop. She covered her ears and realized the wailing was coming from her.

Sam wasn't moving. He was still, so still, lying in such a large puddle of blood.

No, no, no, no no nononono... Michelle couldn't look away, but neither could she comprehend the truth in front of her.

Sam was dead.

Michelle couldn't move. Sam was *dead*.

Snakes had entered the medbay and killed Sam. They were killing everyone. The screams from the battle were beginning to decrease in volume, the number of fighters beginning to dwindle.

With a jolt, Michelle realized that she had to get out of there. She had to leave, leave Sam behind, leave Bek behind, leave them all and run, hide, get away. But how? She couldn't get out of this room, that's what she'd been trying to do in the first place.

The realization knocked the wind out of her. Sam locking her in had saved her life. If she had been out there when the Snakes came in, she would be dead already. She'd *wanted* that, wanted to be dead when all there was in her future was the lab and the torture and Rimoli. But she hadn't wanted anyone *else* to die. She never wanted *Sam* to...

The vision of Sam struggling against the Snake was burned indelibly into her memory. Seeing him killed, being helpless to do anything but watch, had been the worst torture she'd ever endured, and she'd endured plenty.

She still couldn't wrap her head around the fact that Sam was gone, or that everyone in the medbay had been slaughtered, or oh God where was Suji, and Lihku, and Kalik? Amidst all the chaos, in her head and around her, one fact stood out crystal clear: she had to run.

Michelle quietly backed away from the door as quickly as she could. She scanned the room frantically, looking for a way out. The only way in or out of this room to the main area was that damn door that wouldn't open.

But what if she didn't want to go to the main area?

She sprinted over to the bathroom in the corner and dashed inside, closing the door behind her. Michelle sat on the commode, trying to think. She couldn't hide in here forever; the Snakes would get into her room and they would find her here. But where could she go? Where else in her medbay room would lead her out?

When she caught sight of the service tunnel cover under the sink, she nearly cringed. It couldn't possibly work. They'd catch her there wouldn't they? Wouldn't they look in such an obvious place? She closed her eyes and took a couple of deep breaths, trying to recall the ship's schematics that Suji had shown her. There was a network of service tunnels that led to every area of the ship. They were small and efficient, meant for maintenance drones and remote controlled repair technology rather than bodily exploration. The hulking Vinyi couldn't physically access them.

But as the Council had gone to pains to point out, she wasn't Vinyi.

Michelle got on her knees and used her scalpel to pry off the tunnel access cover. The sounds of battle no longer reached her ears. She wouldn't allow herself to think about what that meant. As quietly as possible, she set it aside and poked her head into the wall.

The tunnel was larger than she thought. She'd have to stay on all fours, but she would have plenty of room to maneuver. Maneuver and do what, she didn't know, but right now, she just needed to try to stay alive. Sam would have wanted her to.

Michelle crawled into the dark tunnel and turned around. She grabbed the cover and notched it back into place. She took the time to re-secure two of the four corners, just enough to keep it from falling off and alerting anyone to her whereabouts. She put the scalpel back into the bandage pocket, turned around, and crawled slowly into the darkness.

25

Going by feel, Michelle inched her way along the tunnel on her hands and knees. The prosthetic fingers of her left hand still would not release the tablet, so even if she knew where she was going and could see perfectly, she would still have to go slowly to avoid a telltale *thunk* every time the tablet hit the metal of the tunnel. As she crawled, she tried to bring to mind the schematics she'd studied of the Yukesi, but unfortunately, the service tunnels had never been a focus of her attention. From somewhere in the recesses of her mind, she remembered a book she'd read years ago about someone trying to find their way through a maze who had always kept one hand, the same hand, in contact with the wall of the maze, knowing that, eventually, it would lead them out.

She would try the same thing. When she came to her first intersection, she turned right, keeping her right hip next to the wall. She would crawl into the belly of the ship until she felt reasonably safe, and then maybe she could use her tablet to access the ship's database and find a map of the tunnels.

But first, she had to get to a place where nobody would notice the glow of the tablet's screen or hear her shuffling around.

She came to two more intersections and turned right each time, never letting her right hip stray far from the metal wall of the tunnel. It was warmer in here than it was in the medbay, and the adrenaline rush was starting to wear off. Her movements were slowing, becoming more sluggish as her drowsiness grew. When she finally felt like she'd gone far enough to remain unseen, Michelle sat with her back against the wall and activated the tablet.

The screen opened to the picture of her, Sam, and Suji from the *Negoheh* feast. Her heart twisted at the sight of Sam and agonzied over Suji, wherever he was. She rubbed her eyes with her right hand and swiped the screen clear. She activated the link that would connect her to the Yukesi's reference database.

Access code?

Shit. Her access code. What was it? It had been over a month since she'd last logged in, and she'd become a legal non-entity since then. What if they'd deactivated her code? She wouldn't have any idea where she was or how to figure out a way out of this mess. She'd have to rely solely on luck, and Michelle knew by now that her luck was shit. So... what was her access code? It would've been something easy to remember, something she knew well.

Something from Before.

She tried Dave's birthday, day, month, year. *Error: more characters required.*

She tried Dave's birthday immediately followed by Phil's birthday, same format. *Error: code exceeds maximum characters.*

Well, hell. What could it -

Then she remembered. Michelle entered Dave's birthday, day and month, then Phil's birthday, day and month. She'd dropped the years to make it fit.

The reference file table of contents appeared on her screen. Michelle pulled up the schematics of the Yukesi, highlighting the service tunnels. It was a maze, but it had never been intended to be used this way, so there would have been no point in making it navigation-friendly. Because she had followed the 'always touch the wall' rule, she was able to figure out where she was despite the lack of signage or other landmarks. The good news was that the service tunnels did, indeed, run all throughout the ship. There was nowhere in Yukesi that she couldn't eventually get to from where she was right now.

Michelle sighed and let herself relax against the wall. All right, one hurdle down. So, now that she could go anywhere she wanted... where should she go? She scanned the schematics again. The armory? At the moment, she was armed with a scalpel, so getting hold of a pistol might be a good idea. Then again, with her diminutive size, she'd have to make it the lightest, least powerful of all the available weapons and then still use two hands to work it, so maybe that wasn't such a great idea. What about engineering? Suji would have been in engineering, and Michelle desperately wanted to know how he was. But what else could she accomplish in engineering? Even if she could figure out a way to sabotage the complex engines, would it give the Vinyi an advantage?

Then it hit her. She needed to do what she was good at. She needed to get to a communications console. She couldn't run the engines or fire the big guns, but she could operate a communications console and send a distress signal.

What else could she do to help when help arrived?

Looking at the schematics some more, an idea began to take root and grow.

Michelle mapped out her route, memorized it, and set off for the Records department.

Michelle peered through the grate into the room below. It was silent and dim, and the floral scent of Vinyi death filled her nostrils, even at this height. The floor of the tunnel was at ceiling height, which put it a good twelve feet or higher off the ground. She scowled at her left hand.

If she was going to make this work, she was going to have to let go of the tablet one way or another.

She tried willing her hand to open yet again, and, yet again, nothing happened. She stretched the rest of her fingers, flexed and wiggled them, but the two new additions retained a will of their own. She set her hand down on the floor and used the fingers of her other hand to try to pry them open, but she couldn't budge them.

Reluctantly, she pulled the scalpel out of her pocket. With such dim light from below as the only light source, the blade didn't glint and shine like it had in the medbay. It didn't need to for Michelle to know where it was.

She moved her hand close to the grate to make the most of the scarce light. She took a deep breath and brought the blade over to the base of her outermost finger.

Don't kill the dog to get rid of the fleas, Mishel. Sam's voice rang clearly in her ears. He had been teaching her sayings, colloquialisms, in the days before her hearing. Her rejoinder of *don't throw the baby out with the bathwater* had horrified him, far more than *cutting off your nose to spite your face*. That one he found entirely appropriate.

A sardonic smile twisted her lips. *No cutting off your fingers to spite your hand, Mishel,* she told herself, and changed the angle of the blade. Wedging it under the tip of her finger, she used the harder, more resistant metal as a lever and pried her fingertip off the tablet's handle. Then she worked the blade to the next joint and pulled it up, as well. After only a few minutes, she had worked her fingers open and set the tablet aside. She'd given herself some some cuts (it was a scalpel, after all), but she still had all her fingers, the natural and the new.

Quickly, Michelle bandaged her fingers and opened the grate into the Records department. There were communications consoles all over the ship that she could have used to send a message, but there was a specific one here that mattered more than any other. It was the Vinyi equivalent of 911, or the US President's red phone, or maybe the Batsignal. If she could get to it, send the message about the Yukesi being boarded by the Snakes (she assumed the Vinyi receiving the message would know who she was talking about), it would automatically go where it needed to go and get whoever's attention it needed to get.

If someone had already sent a beacon, well, great. But if not...

Carefully, she poked her head out and looked around, ensuring that she was alone. She swung her legs around so that they dangled from the ceiling, then flipped over onto her belly and began lowering herself down. She had lost much of the muscular strength she'd had before being imprisoned in the lab, but she still remembered the body mechanics, how to move the way Lihku and Kalik taught her.

It wasn't graceful, but she managed to shimmy down the bandages she'd tied together into as long a rope as she thought she needed. It didn't go all the way to the floor, but by the time she got to the end of her makeshift rope, the floor was only a couple of feet away. She let go and dropped into a crouch the moment her feet hit the floor.

It was hard to hear over the blood rushing through her ears, but she was pretty sure she was still alone.

After a moment, Michelle stood and scanned the room, searching for the emergency console. According to the map, it should be in the northwest corner of the main area.

There! She rushed to the machine. It wasn't quite what she was expecting. For something so important, the emergency broadcasting station was fairly nondescript. It had fewer lights, fewer switches, far less going on than on the other consoles in the room. Given that it had a dedicated purpose, she supposed that made sense.

It wasn't even on, much less sending a cry for help. The Snakes had moved fast. Michelle turned the key and activated the console. She switched the machine to text-only mode; she couldn't take the chance that a Snake might hear her voice. As of now, she thought it was possible that they might not even know she was on board, though once they discovered the message being sent, they'd know someone was unaccounted for.

She had to move quickly.

She typed a short message stating that Yukesi had been taken over by Snake warriors, there were a very large number of Vinyi dead, and they needed help desperately, as soon as it could be dispatched. She reviewed it once to make sure there were no errors, because confusion was the last thing a plea for emergency assistance needed. Then she directed the console to send her plea, and when she received confirmation that it was on its way, a shiver ran down her back.

Now if only the cavalry would arrive before it was too late.

She ran back to her bandage-rope and shimmied her way into the tunnel, replacing the grate behind her.

One more stop, then she could find somewhere to hole up and hide until they were rescued. Michelle opened her tablet and planned out her route.

This grate was located on the wall near the floor, like the one in the medbay bathroom had been. Michelle sat silently, listening and cautiously peering out into the room. Her palms were slick with sweat, which was only going to make this harder, but try as she might, she couldn't completely control her nerves.

One would expect the Records department to be empty during a hostile invasion. The Weapons Control room, on the other hand, ought to be occupied and guarded. At least, that's what Michelle would do if she were taking over an enemy ship. It turned out she was half-right. The room wasn't occupied, but there were two enemy guards outside the open door to the Control room. She had a clear view of the armory on the other side of the threshold.

They would absolutely hear her if she tried to open the circuit box for the Weapons Console now. It was too near the exit of the tunnel into the main room. She needed the guards to go away, she needed a distraction. But what? And how?

She pinched the bridge of her nose, sighing softly, then slowly unwound the bandage rope from her pocket just in case. Then Michelle picked up her scalpel and hovered it in front of the secured lid of the circuit box before setting it down again.

She still didn't have any idea how to distract the guards. By the time she traced a path through the tunnels to somewhere outside the room and raised a distraction, then got back in the tunnels and back here to where she wanted to be... there was no way she could move fast enough to execute her plan. Could she kill the guards? Michelle quashed that plan in short order. *Sam* couldn't kill the single one that attacked him; she would be handing herself to them on a platter.

But then, he'd been caught off guard. She had time to plan. Too bad she didn't even know anything about killing *regular* snakes, much less giant super Snake space invader things.

The decision was abruptly made for her. From the other room, the swish of the Armory doors opening barely preceded the appearance of two more Snakes. The one on the right was dragging a Vinyi by the ankles behind it, cinched in its tail. All four Snakes charged into the Weapons Control room. The two new ones dragged the Vinyi up to the control console, released him, and, still using their tails and bodies, stood him up in front of it.

Now she could see his face. Kalik was battered and bleeding, with one eye swollen shut and one tusk sitting crooked in his head. He swayed as he stood and his head lolled.

Oh, Kalik, what have they done to you? Kalik, who had made her strong, who had pushed her so far her boundaries grew, who had supported her and encouraged her and given her the body of a fighter, was beaten so severely he was barely conscious in the grip of his captors.

The Snake holding him hissed, then pressed a brooch he wore on his weapons harness. He hissed again, and then a metallic voice sounded in the room.

"Give us the ship's weapons."

Michelle's mind raced. They hadn't gained control of weapons yet. The console was access protected, so only those with proper security clearance could adjust power flow, route control to various stations throughout the ship, or even shut them down entirely, which might be exactly what happened. If the Snakes didn't have access to any of Yukesi's weapons systems, someone must have locked them out when the aliens began boarding.

A sense of pride filled her chest.

Kalik merely stood there. Michelle wasn't sure he'd even heard the Snake, he was so far out of it. Faster than she could track it, a Snake tail came up and struck Kalik across the face with a smack so hard it nearly rattled Michelle's own teeth. The flat metallic voice spoke again.

"Give us the weapons."

The Vinyi soldier raised his one good eye to the Snake, curled a tentacle, and spit on the side of his captor's face.

Suddenly, Kalik screamed, a wail of pain that brought tears to Michelle's eyes. She pressed her knuckles over her mouth to keep herself silent. The Snake had extended one of its hidden body fangs into Kalik's arm, piercing the soft part of his elbow and driving it straight up the length of his arm until she could see the point of it poking through the hide of Kalik's shoulder. The Snake then ripped its fang out, tearing another scream from Kalik's throat and bringing him to his knees.

The Snake leaned in.

"*I make the words one more ask. Give us the weapons.*"

Kalik, gripping his destroyed arm, calmly looked up at his attacker. He opened his mouth to speak and nothing came out. He closed his mouth, swallowed, and tried again. "Go fuck yourself with a shock stick."

Tears blurred Michelle's vision.

A rapid movement, a grunt from Kalik, and it was over. The Snake had plunged its fang into Kalik's good eye until it came out the back of his skull. Kalik's body crumpled to the ground, blood pooling around his head.

Michelle clamped her hands more tightly over her mouth.

Kalik's killer hissed at the others, then all four slithered from the control room, into the armory, and out the doors.

They were gone. All the Snakes were gone. If Michelle was going to do this, she had to do it now. Her movements were sluggish, clumsy, through her shock. Until today, she had never seen anyone killed. She was there when Katherine died, and she'd certainly seen Adam's body, but murder? She'd never seen it happen before, and now she'd seen it more times than she could count.

Twice to people she cared for.

Despite the warmth of the tunnel, Michelle felt cold all over. Shaking, she crawled past the access grate and reached the circuit junction. She wanted to burst out of the tunnel, kneel at Kalik's side, cry and mourn, but there was no time. The Snakes could be back any minute, and she intended to fuck their plans up beyond all hope. If the Snakes gained access to the Yukesi's weapons, they would fight back when help arrived. If she wasn't completely off-base, there was already one Snake ship out there that would put up resistance; their rescuers didn't need to defend themselves from the Yukesi, too.

Michelle wedged her scalpel underneath the lip of the cover and wiggled it until it was good and stuck. There wasn't enough room for her to deftly manipulate her scalpel to remove the cover, so instead, she leveraged all her weight and pushed on it with everything she had.

With a loud pop, the lid swung open hard on its hinges, slamming into the metal wall. Michelle froze and waited, listening. When there was only silence from the Control room, she returned her focus to the circuitry and wires running through the box. She knew as much about electricity as she did about killing snakes, but she *did* know that electricity and metal didn't mix. So she wrapped her hand in bandages, reached in, and pulled at the first place she saw where a bundle of wires ran into a covered node.

Nothing happened. Whoever did this work secured those wires well and good.

She planted her feet against the wall, grabbed with both hands, and yanked with all her might. A shower of sparks was her reward and a handful of unattached wires her trophy.

She did it three more times, until the circuit junction resembled frayed yarn more than any kind of orderly operation. Satisfied, Michelle sat back, unwrapped her hands, and started to scramble back down the tunnel. As she crossed the access grate, she stopped, her gaze locked on Kalik's corpse. There was no time to mourn properly, but she placed a hand on the wall, reaching toward him.

First Sam, and probably Bek, now Kalik. And Suji's fate was still a mystery, as was Lihku's.

She was going to do everything she could to stop these

FOUND

bastards.

26

Michelle headed toward her quarters. Given that it had been a closet prior to its conversion into her living space, chances were good it was at least unoccupied, and possibly had even been left entirely alone. Exhaustion began to wear on her, and she needed water. She could get it from the console in her room, if the console still worked.

She'd cross that bridge when she came to it. Right now, she just needed to get to a water source.

As she crawled through the darkness, her thoughts kept returning to Sam and Kalik, Dave and Phil, the Council hearing, Rimoli and Vaomi, even the Faceless, and Petra, Bonnie, Kate, and Ingrid. The universe was a cold, hard place, with loss and grief the normal state of things. Michelle hadn't realized it before, but now, after seeing that even a seemingly impervious people like the Vinyi can be brought to ruin in the blink of an eye, she understood. It was said that 'only the strong survive', but that wasn't true. There was no telling *who* would survive, or why, or how.

Sam should have survived. He was strong and kind and good, but he didn't survive. The way he went out, though, spoke volumes. The way Sam went out, and Kalik, and Petra, too… that was where the truth was. You had no choice but to take what life dished out. The only choice anyone had was whether to flex your own personal power or not, to pick yourself up, dust yourself off, and keep swinging, or to lie down like a bitch and give up, dying with a whimper. Pain and humiliation and certainly death will get you in the end, but life was in the struggle, in the fight.

Crawling through a tunnel she had no business being in, hungry and thirsty and tired and traumatized, Michelle resolved that she would live powerfully until she drew her final breath.

Which could be anytime now, considering the circumstances.

She came to a bend in the tunnel, but while the path should have turned right, it went left instead. Michelle frowned. Had she missed something? She was certain she was supposed to turn right now. Damn it. She must have taken a wrong turn somewhere, and now she had no idea where she was. Well, the Yukesi didn't go on indefinitely; at some point, she'd come across a room and then she could get her bearings.

Cautiously, she followed the bend in the tunnel. She moved as quietly as possible, listening and looking for anything that might give her an indication of where she was. At last, in the distance, light from an access grate in the floor set a small section of the tunnel aglow. As she approached, she could hear noises drifting up from below. Grunting. Moaning. The slap of flesh on flesh. A deep voice, muffled.

A chill ran through her when she heard the flat electronic voice of a translator.

Slowly, so slowly, Michelle crept up on the grate and peeked through it. Her stomach churned at the sight that greeted her eyes.

It was the mess hall. But all the tables were pushed to the side, stacked up haphazardly against the wall. The chairs were scattered around the room, and the *Negoheh* decorations still stubbornly twinkled, out of place amidst the disorder in rest of the room. A number of Vinyi, at least a dozen, were lined up along one wall, bound and on their knees, facing the room. Michelle scanned the group. Her heart leapt up into her throat. Suji was among them. His face was battered and swollen, his arms and torso streaked with blood, and the end of his right tusk had broken off. But he was upright, and if looks could kill, his glare alone would have been enough to get them all out of this mess.

The Vinyi prisoners were guarded by four Snakes who vigilantly patrolled in front of and around them. The Snakes were looking in the same direction as the Vinyi.

Michelle followed their gaze. Hegoh sat tied to a chair in the center of the room. He looked terrible. He was practically coated in silver, and the strength of the floral scent left no doubt that Hegoh was not the first to bleed profusely in this room. A Snake was hissing in his face about something Michelle couldn't quite hear, the hiss and the translation overlapping. Hegoh replied with something the Snake didn't like, because it slashed him across the temple with its fang, unleashing a new stream of blood. Hegoh grunted, but otherwise remained stoic.

The Snake slithered over to another Vinyi, one in the row of kneeling captives, and waved a fang under his tentacles, looking back at Hegoh and taunting the captain of the invaded vessel. Casually, it sliced off one of the tentacles of the helpless Vinyi, who screamed once, then clamped his mouth shut, doing his best to emulate his Captain. The Snake's hood widened and it slithered back to Hegoh.

It hissed as it approached, and suddenly jabbed a threatening fang under Hegoh's jaw. The room gasped sharply, a reaction Michelle almost echoed. Instead, she clamped her hands over her mouth and watched in horror as the Snake leaned in and hissed again.

For Christ's sake, Hegoh, just tell them what they want to know! The cavalry is on the way!

But Hegoh didn't, and finally the Snake had had enough. In one smooth motion, it drove the fang up through Hegoh's head until the sharp white tip popped out the top of his skull. His bound body shimmied and jerked against its bonds as the Snake pulled its fang back out, then finally went still.

Tears Michelle refused to cry burned her eyes. Her nails bit into her palms as she clenched her fists in helpless fury. *Jesus fucking damn it.*

Two other Snakes untied Hegoh's corpse from the chair and threw it to the far side of the room. Then they reached for Suji and Michelle went light-headed.

They dragged him to the center chair and tied him to it, sitting in the blood of his friend and captain. The Snake that killed Hegoh approached Suji and began hissing at him.

Michelle saw red. She had heard of that happening to people, but she had never experienced it herself until this moment. They would *not* take the life of yet another person she cared for. She refused to let it happen.

There was no time to wait to be rescued. As quickly as she could without making noise, Michelle scurried away from the mess hall grate and dashed toward the Armory.

Michelle only made it about halfway through her route when it occurred to her that the Armory was very likely to still be guarded. Unlike Records, there was an actual risk present in leaving the Armory unguarded. Charging in there would be profoundly stupid. But she couldn't just let Suji die! Where else could she get her hands on a weapon?

She pulled up abruptly as the answer came to her. Where did she get her hands on a weapon the last time?

Michelle activated her tablet and rerouted herself to the Training Hall.

When she got there, she found that the access grate was nestled in the southeast corner of the room at floor level. All she could see from her space in the tunnel was a pile of sparring mats, but she couldn't hear a peep coming from the room. Then again, how loudly did Snakes breathe? The Hall might be full of them; she'd never know.

Unless she left the tunnel and entered the room.

Worried about what Suji was going through at the same moment, Michelle tried to stealthily hurry through the process of unlatching the grate. She pulled it inside the tunnel so that it couldn't be used to block her escape route if she needed to get out of there fast. She crawled out and surveyed the room before standing up. She was alone, and the ceremonial shortswords were hanging exactly where they'd been before, at the end of the opposite wall. Not knowing how long her luck would hold but not trusting it for a second, she sprinted to the swords, pulled one off the wall, and started to dash back to the tunnel when something caught her eye.

There was a dagger on display underneath a

warhammer. That hadn't been there before. It was closer to her size than anything else she'd seen; even the so-called short swords were long enough to be nearly full-length in her hands. She grabbed it, too, and hurried back to the tunnel entrance.

When she got there, she paused. How was she going to silently crawl through an all-metal passageway with a sword and a dagger? Michelle mentally shook herself and slid the weapons in first, crawling into the tunnel after them. *First things first.* She replaced the grate. If nobody looked carefully at the wall, nobody would ever know she had been there.

Now, how to transport the blades? The dagger was easy enough; she slipped it into one of her large pockets. Next, she wrapped the sword in bandages to muffle the clang of metal on metal, and began sliding it along in front of her as she hustled back to the Mess.

They were going to hear her.

As Michelle crawled through the darkness, she realized that the Snakes were going to hear her when she started unlatching the grate to the Mess Hall. She'd lose the element of surprise completely and would probably be captured and killed before she could even get a swing in. Frustrated, she sighed heavily as she crawled. *OK, so I go in through the kitchen, instead.*

The galley was in a room nearly the same size as the Mess, immediately adjoining it. Part of the wall had been removed entirely so that traffic between the two areas could move freely, but the rest of it was separated from the general eating area.

Michelle couldn't remember exactly, but she hoped the galley's tunnel access was in the enclosed area.

She made the detour and rolled her eyes when she arrived at the grate. Thankfully, it *was* in the enclosed portion of the galley. Unfortunately, it was also about 14 feet off the ground. *Because why not?* She couldn't see anyone in the room, but she listened carefully for any sound of movement nonetheless. The only sounds were the faint noises of hissing, the *whump* of a body being struck, and groaning.

Suji.

Quickly, Michelle unlatched the grate and tied off her bandage rope, tossing it out so it trailed down roughly a third the height of the wall. She made sure the dagger was still in her pocket then tied the sword to her back and began to shimmy down the rope. When she got to the end, she held tight with both hands and walked her feet down the wall as far as she could go. The 14 foot drop was now reduced to only three or four feet between her and the floor.

She released the rope and landed as softly as she could, tucking herself into a ball and rolling on impact. Her right ankle objected a little, but a quick rotation showed that it wasn't injured, just annoyed. *If we live through this, you can have a day off,* she promised it.

Another smack rang through the room, and because she still couldn't see anything, Michelle didn't know whether to be proud or worried that Suji didn't moan afterward. She got down on all fours, thinking the Snakes would be less inclined to look for faces below knee height, and cautiously peered around the corner.

Suji's head lolled as though he were unconscious. The Snake, using his tail, grabbed Suji's face and yanked his head upright. The Vinyi did not respond.

Michelle hoped Suji was only unconscious.

There were two Snakes near him, and two guards for the remaining five prisoners. Michelle ruthlessly ignored the butterflies in her stomach. These were not good odds, but what else was there to do?

Fight back, or lie down with a whimper.

She would fight. She would die, but she would fight. For Suji, for Sam, for Kalik, for the Yukesi, for herself.

She pulled her head back around the corner and stood up. She untied the sword from her back. With it in one hand, and her dagger in the other, she stepped around the corner.

27

Michelle saw the scene in profile. The Snake's face was close to Suji's. It was pressing one of its fangs into the underneath of Suji's chin, just as it had with Hegoh.

"No!" shouted Michelle, and she hurled the dagger at the Snake.

Knife-throwing hadn't been something she'd studied with Lihku so the throw was terrible. The dagger bounced right off the Snake's tough scales and bounced on the floor a couple of times before skidding to a halt. But it accomplished the minimum objective: the Snake, surprised, backed off of Suji. It snapped into an upright posture.

Every face in the room except Suji's turned her way.

Shit. Four Snakes seemed daunting even in theory, but now, with all of the glaring at her in stunned surprise, Michelle knew way down in her gut that she was about to die.

She glared back at the lead Snake. It was going to kill her, but she was damn well going to make it earn the privilege.

She lifted the sword to shoulder height in challenge. "Get off this ship."

The Snake at the leader's side hissed, and a metallic voice said, *"What is it?"*

Suji's abuser slithered just a few inches in her direction. They stared at one another for a moment, then the Snake hissed. *"Dead."*

Shit. Michelle clenched her jaw and settled into combat ready stance.

Time and motion slowed down as the Snake moved toward her with its characteristic speed. Michelle lowered into a ready stance and started to swing, hoping to avoid its fangs as much as possible and slice into it as it arrived.

It never got to her.

As the Snake's hood began to loom large in her vision, when it was only an arm's lengths away, it was suddenly tackled aside by a giant gray freight train that smashed into it with the force of a meteor.

One of the prisoners had finally broken the link in the cuffs chaining him to the others.

His violent defiance spurred the others to action. With deafening roars, the rest of the prisoners leaped to their feet and used their restored freedom to charge their captors. They tackled, they slashed with their tusks, they kicked and trampled underfoot. The Snakes were handicapped by surprise, first by Michelle's appearance, then by the rebellion of those they thought they had broken. The bonds still holding hands behind backs began to snap with the extra pressure they were now under, freeing arms, fists, spurring those who attacked their captors to strike with the ferocity of berserkers.

Amidst the chaos, Suji sat motionless in the chair.

Michelle sprinted toward him.

The floor shook as a Vinyi and a Snake fell together, directly in her path. The Vinyi had thrust one of his tusks into the Snakes open mouth, piercing it through the roof so that now his tusk was stuck. She followed the pair as they rolled over and over, wrestling for top position. The next time the Vinyi was on top, Michelle aimed for the Snake's open mouth and plunged her sword downward with all her strength. She felt the crunch of bone giving way as the sharp point of her weapon drove through the serpentine skull and into the floor.

The Snake went limp.

The Vinyi tore its tusk out of the Snake's face and let out a victory roar. Michelle tried to retrieve her sword, but it was stuck in the floor. The Vinyi she had just helped turned around and grabbed the handle of it with his still-bound underhands. He pulled and, with a jerk, freed her blade. He held it out to her; she took it and grabbed his arm in thanks. He fleetingly grasped her wrist before running to assist one of his fellows.

Michelle rushed back to Suji. He was covered in his own blood. The noise of the battle being waged behind her faded as she grabbed him by the shoulders, calling his name.

He was unresponsive and cold to the touch. He was barely, sporadically breathing. His face was nearly unrecognizable, he'd been beaten so savagely. A large wound in his chest was spilling blood with every pump of his heart, and he had gone a very pale shade of gray.

She was too late. No amount of first aid was going to save him. After all of her effort, and all of his, Suji was going to die anyway.

"No." She whispered the denial, willing him to be all

right. She'd lost everyone and everything. She thought of Pekoe, of their new baby, of Suji's laugh and joy and determination, and she rebelled against the idea of his death. But there was nothing she could do.

She sank to her knees in front of him, and as she did, something metallic in her pocket clanked against the leg of the chair. A glimmer of hope flickered in her chest as she reached into her pocket and saw what had made the noise.

The nanobots. She still had the nanobots.

Michelle had no idea what she was doing, but desperation drove her more than logic. Quickly, she took the syringe out of its canister, pointed the needle into Suji's chest wound, and depressed the plunger until it wouldn't go any further. Then she tossed it aside and laid a hand on either side of his face, willing him to wake up.

An explosion flung her through the air. She crashed into the wall, hitting the back of her head hard, and slid down to the floor.

She didn't know how long she had been out when she pushed up off the floor. Her ears were ringing and her head felt muddled, stuffed with cotton. For a moment, she looked at her hands on the floor, unable to place where she was and why. A moan to her left got her attention and it all came back to her in a rush.

Suji was lying on the floor, his chair on its side, one of its legs broken off. A quick scan of the room revealed that the Snakes were gone, except for the body of the one she'd killed. The mess hall doors swooshed as the last two Vinyi in the room charged out into the hall. During that brief glimpse of the hall, Michelle could see nothing but an empty hall. The sounds, though, filled her ears instantly. The zing of weapons fire. The shouts of warriors colliding. The rattling impact of bodies being shoved against walls or pummeled into the floor.

The sounds of battle.

Heart pounding, Michelle scrambled to Suji's side. He was groaning, struggling meekly against his bonds. "Suji," she said, looking around for the sword that had been torn from her grasp, "I'm here. Suji." She laid a hand on his face. "Can you hear me?"

His eyes were both swollen shut but he turned his head slightly in her direction. "Mishel?" His voice was thin and thready, bearing none of its usual ebullience.

"Yes." Her throat clenched. He was alive. He was conscious. "Yes, it's Michelle." Finally, she spotted the glint of the dagger she'd thrown at the Snake lying on the ground a few yards away. "I'm going to set you free. I'll be right back."

Suji groaned again.

Michelle ran over and picked up the knife. A burst of light outside the viewport got her attention. Two ships, configurations she recognized from her studies as Vinyi battleships, were firing on a ship she'd never seen before. *Must be the Snakes' ship.* The Snakes were firing on the battleships as well as on Yukesi, but it was beginning to get the raw end of that deal as it was rocked by blasts more and more often.

"The cavalry's here, Suji!" she shouted.

A buzzing sound from behind her had Michelle whipping around, brandishing her dagger in front of her. The Snake corpse on the floor was disappearing in waves of light. In moments, it was gone, along with the buzzing. She turned to look back out the window. The Snake ship had turned around, its stern facing the Yukesi.

They were leaving.

Her heart glowed with its own fire as she went back to Suji and began cutting the cords that bound him to the chair. She had just cut the one holding his overarms in place when a blinding flash from outside made her gasp and cover her eyes. It faded as quickly as it had arisen. Michelle looked out the viewport.

The Snake ship was no longer leaving. There was nothing left of it but small pieces of free-floating debris.

A vicious satisfaction filled her. She cut Suji's cords with renewed vigor.

He muttered her name. She leaned in and rested her forehead on his. "You're going to be fine, Suji," she said. "We all are."

28

TWO WEEKS LATER

Michelle calmly strode down the hall. The Council's headquarters were ornate and stately, with high ceilings even by Vinyi standards and plate glass windows that let in all the light of the bright, clear day. Michelle paused and pressed her palm to the glass. Hoikke's sun wasn't quite as yellow as Earth's, but it lit up the ocean just as beautifully.

When the battleships arrived to rescue Yukesi, the Snake ship tried to destroy the patrol cruiser before making a run for it. But right as the Snakes fired, one of the battleships struck it and the shot that was meant for the Yukesi's engine room instead struck one of the research labs. The labs were located only two floors below the mess hall; that had been the explosion that sent Michelle flying across the room.

Unfortunately, Rimoli wasn't in the lab when it blew up. Somehow, he had been one of the roughly 40% of the crew that survived. As though she needed more proof that it wasn't the good or the strong, but the lucky who survived.

It had taken the better part of a week to get back to Hoikke with as much damage as Yukesi had taken, but return they had. A Council-led investigation into the attack was underway before they'd even set their return course.

Testimony from surviving crewmembers as well as records logs reflected that the Snake ship had employed some kind of invisibility technology that nobody knew existed. The Snakes, who were officially called *Jik'loinhij*, and the Vinyi had a bitterly adversarial history, but nobody had seen a Snake in years. The working hypothesis was that when the Snakes saw the Yukesi, they decided to use it to test their new technology. The invisibility had, of course, been a stunning success: the Snakes had begun boarding the Yukesi before anyone even knew they were out there, and the first place they took over was the bridge. One of the first things the boarding party did was shut down external communications so that no distress calls could be sent. They didn't know about the dedicated console in the Records department, so no guards had been stationed there.

It turned out that Michelle had, indeed, been lucky, despite everything.

She hadn't been the only one.

The doors to the Medical Wing slid open to admit her. "Hello, Ene," she greeted the nurse behind the desk.

Ene smiled at her. "He's awake and ready."

Michelle smiled back her thanks and walked to the end of the hall where Suji's room was. When she arrived at the open door, she raised her fist to knock and announce her presence, but paused she noticed that he wasn't alone. Pekoe was sitting in a chair next to Suji, who held their newborn son Senhku in his lap. Her hand rested tenderly on his back, and his soft gaze caressed his wife and his son by turns. Michelle was about to turn around and creep back down the hall so that she could return and announce herself well before getting to the door when Suji looked up and saw her.

"Mishel!" he boomed, and she couldn't help but grin at the familiar buoyancy in his voice that she had so missed in their darkest moments. He was still recovering, and would be for a few more weeks, but he was well on his way. The nanobots had done their job and healed the worst of the damage before any of it could become fatal or permanent. The rest of the time in the Medical Wing had patched him up nicely.

He stood, handing Senhku back to Pekoe, who also stood as Michelle entered the room. "Looking good, Su," she teased him.

He wore his dress uniform, and his tusks were sharpened and polished to gleaming. "One of us ought to," he rejoined, causing Pekoe to smack him lightly on his overarm. "What?" he asked her innocently.

Pekoe ignored him and sat down on the end of his bed, resting Senhku on her lap. "Say hello to your *hojhke* Mishel, son."

Legally, Michelle couldn't be *yejorep* to Senhku, but that hadn't stopped Suji and Pekoe from asking her anyway. When the Yukesi had first landed, all surviving crew, including her, had been taken to this very Medical Wing for examination and treatment. Michelle's main problem had been dehydration, though the doctors here had also made an adjustment to her prosthetic fingers so that now they worked as well as her natural ones. All in all, she only had to stay for a couple of days before she was issued a guest room (outfitted with a lot of stepstools and other boosters) in the

Hospitality Wing.

On her second day in Medical, Councilmember Epimoe came to see her. She had taken a seat in one of the visitor chairs in Michelle's room with all the grace and elegance she expected of the Vinyi woman. "I am pleased to see that you are well."

Michelle inclined her head. "Thank you."

Epimoe merely observed her for a few moments, then she waved a dismissive hand in the air. "Oh, to the Pit with it. I'm meant to be here in an official capacity, which requires a certain amount of formality and protocol, but the fact is… I'm sorry, Mishel. I am heartbrokenly sorry."

Michelle blinked, surprised by the change in the Councilwoman's tone.

"The outcome of your hearing should never have come to pass as it did. Crafty, dishonorable people played on old prejudices and used the Council to legalize an injustice. I tried to stop it, but even I was not powerful enough to stand against the collective fear of change."

Epimoe stood and began to pace. "Not then, anyway. Now? Now is a different time. You," she said, stopping to face Michelle, "have put our judgment to shame. Your actions saved the Yukesi from destruction. And while many fine Vinyi died -" The Councilwoman's voice cracked, and Michelle wondered who aboard Yukesi had mattered to her. "Every last crewmember who survived owes his life to you."

Her words hung in the air as silence settled between them. At last, Michelle gave Epimoe a half-hearted shrug, not knowing how to express what she was feeling. "It was the only right choice to make."

Epimoe laid a hand gently on Michelle's left foot and squeezed. "You are not a lab subject, Mishel. You have the heart of a Vinyi. I will re-petition the Council on your behalf given your recent heroics. You will stay in quarters here until we have rendered our decision."

And she swept out of Michelle's room as elegantly as she'd swept in.

That had been almost two weeks ago now, and Michelle was still waiting. In the meantime, there were other items of business to attend to.

Like the overly plump tentacles on a newborn baby boy who was her *juzejhku*. She smiled at the butterball squirming on Pekoe's lap. "Hello, Senhku." She leaned in and nuzzled his cheek. Senhku's hide smelled like sandalwood, not a scent she had ever before associated with infants. Vinyi children were born without tusks and didn't develop them until around their tenth year, so Senhku's head was soft, covered with a layer of baby fat, and almost perfectly round.

He looked up at her with his shiny black marble eyes, innocent and trusting, and just like that, he made himself a place in her heart.

Suji softly cleared his throat. "We should go."

Michelle gave Senhku's cheek one last caress then stepped away. "You're right. Are you ready?"

"Yes." Suji leaned down, brought his head alongside Pekoe's, and they intertwined their outermost tentacles. "We'll see you there," he said.

"We'll be there," she replied with a gentle knock of her tusk on his.

And Suji and Michelle left his room and exited the Medical Wing.

"Lihku!"

Michelle hadn't seen the brawny warrior since the Council hearing. She read his name on the list of survivors, but seeing him in the flesh was altogether different than merely knowing he was alive. Now, here he was, larger than life on the crowded stage of the Grand Hall in Council Headquarters.

He looked her way and grinned. "Mishel!" He extended his underarms and wrapped them around her when she threw her arms around his waist as far as they would go. "It is very good to see you, *Rikube*."

She laughed delightedly at the nickname, then pulled back to look up at him. She couldn't see any lasting damage, any new scars, but she knew that the medical team here was highly skilled in both healing and reconstruction. "Are you all right? Did they hurt you badly?"

Lihku sobered as he rested a hand on her shoulder. "Not as badly as they did many others."

She nodded solemnly, images of Sam and Kalik flashing in her mind's eye.

Suji stepped forward and clapped Lihku on the shoulder. "Good to see you, Captain."

Her eyebrows arched. "Captain?"

Lihku lifted his tentacles. "When the Yukesi has completed its repairs, I will be its Captain. I can only aspire to lead the crew as well as Captain Hegoh did."

"When the *Jik'loinhij* first boarded, Lihku was the one who had the presence of mind to shut down weapons control from the bridge. Because the *Jik'loinhij* couldn't access weapons, they couldn't proceed with their plan to rendezvous the Yukesi and their own hidden vessel with other unsuspecting Vinyi crews," explained Suji.

"So it was more than just a test of their invisibility shielding, then?" she said. "It was actually an attempt at an incursion."

Lihku nodded. "A tentative one. But they will try again."

Suji squared his shoulders. "The next time, we'll be ready."

The new Captain patted Michelle's shoulder. "So we will."

She was taken aback by the strength of her yearning to be with them on the Yukesi, back among the stars, when it returned to patrol. But she was still waiting on the next Council hearing, so her future was, yet again, in the hands of others.

The movement of someone approaching drew Michelle's gaze. *Speak, or I guess think, of the devil.* Senior Chairman Sijaj had made his way across the room to speak to them.

"Captain," he greeted Lihku before turning to Suji. "Commander."

"Senior Chairman," they replied in unison, saluting.

He acknowledged the salute before turning to Michelle. She met his gaze stoically, recalling the last time she had seen his face. "Mishel," Sijaj greeted her, and saluted.

She was stunned. It was unheard of for the Senior Chairman to make obeisance to anyone other than the king. Yet here he was, honoring her, in front of Suji and Lihku and anyone else who happened to be watching. Caught completely off-guard, she winged it. Michelle made an awkward half-bow and said, "Senior Chairman."

Apparently she did all right, because he lowered his salute and said, "You were done a grievous wrong." He paused, then began again. "*We* did you a grievous wrong.

Please attend a Council hearing regarding the re-petition of your legal status tomorrow at 0930 in the Main Chamber of the Legislative Wing."

Well, that seemed promising. "I'll be there, Senior Chairman."

Sijaj then looked at Lihku and Suji. "Please attend, all of you."

Suji nodded at Lihku, who answered for them both in the affirmative.

"Good." Sijaj sighed, satisfied. "Now, let us take our places. The ceremony is about to begin."

It was Michelle's first Vinyi memorial service.

It wasn't a typical ceremony, to be sure. The surviving crewmembers of the Yukesi were seated on stage, looking out at an auditorium filled to standing room only with the families of both the survivors and the deceased. Senior Chairman Sijaj strode to a small, raised dais in the center of the front stage and opened the ceremony with a prayer to the gods.

Michelle knew little about Vinyi religious beliefs, but she followed Sijaj's prayer and opening statements well enough to understand that the dead were thought to continue to exist, though on a different plane, in a different manifestation of existence than what we currently experienced. The people the dead had been were gone forever, but their energy, their spirits, recombined and coexisted in another abstract, difficult to imagine, way.

"It is fitting," he said, "that we remember each of them,

individually and collectively, as they lived and as they died." He looked in Michelle's direction. "Will the Captain of the Yukesi step forward and lead us in the path of remembrance?"

Lihku stood, leaving her side, and made his way to the center dais. "Let us stand to honor our noble dead."

Everyone in the Grand Hall rose to their feet.

A soft but triumphant tune filled the air as pictures of the lost crew were projected onto various screens around the room. As each face filled the screen, Lihku named them, and each time he called a name, though the crew on the stage continued to stand straight and tall, various Vinyi in the audience would take a knee to identify with their fallen loved one. Sometimes they were clustered together, other times, they were spread throughout the hall. Sometimes it was only a handful of people who knelt, other times it seemed a third of the auditorium went down.

But someone knelt every single time. Nobody was on their own here, among this people.

Michelle thought of Dave, and of Phil, and she realized with a jolt that it was the first time she'd thought of them in a meaningful way in at least the past couple of weeks. They had crossed her mind, but between enduring the lab, crawling through the access tunnels, watching her loved ones tortured and killed, being tended to by the medicals, and recuperating from all of it, she hadn't stopped for long enough to really think of her own lost family. Even when she had been still, her mind had continued to race.

Now, though... now she had a moment. She wouldn't see their pictures on the wall, but she could see them in her mind and feel them in her heart. Michelle directed her gaze to the slowly changing Vinyi photos but saw Dave and Phil instead. She felt her heart skip a beat and her throat constrict.

She couldn't do this. She wasn't ready to say goodbye.

With a brief shake of her head, Michelle refocused on the crewmen being named. With more than a hundred names to go through, this part of the ceremony was going to take a while. Most of them she didn't know. Too many of them she did, their images provoking pain and loss, and different degrees and types of sorrow.

Kalik.

Vaomi.

Mebeku.

The faces continued to scroll slowly by until finally one appeared that lodged her heart in her throat.

Sam.

Her face began to crumple, and it took everything in her to firm it up. She would not cry at his memorial. She would honor him at this moment, in this place, by refusing to give into the grief and loss, by pushing back against it, by standing strong and resolute and firm.

She could barely see his image through her tears, but those tears did not fall, and she did not cry.

Thank you, Sam, for everything. I will never forget you, my friend and brother.

The back of Suji's underhand lightly brushed her upper arm. She inhaled deeply, brushing her shoulder against his hand in response.

They still had each other.

The last image to grace the screen was that of Hegoh. Michelle thought of when they'd met in her quarters, how he had presented the Council with all the arguments for her asylum, how hard he had worked and how kind and good he had been.

When they were finally allowed to be seated, Michelle stepped back up into her chair feeling beat up and wrung out. Lihku returned to his seat and very briefly laid a reassuring hand on her knee before placing it on his own.

Senior Councilman Sijaj was back on the dais. "In the midst of all this darkness, there is light." He gestured to the crew on the stage. "Had it not been for the brave actions of every Vinyi..." He cut himself off. "...the brave actions of every crewman seated here, the Battle for the Yukesi would have ended quite differently. It is likely that there would have been no survivors. It is likely that the commandeered Yukesi would have been used to launch surprise attacks on other Fleet vessels, causing more damage and even greater loss of life. Instead, the *Jik'loinhij* were repelled and destroyed, to the testament and glory of the courageous, victorious Vinyi people."

Sijaj turned to face the crew. "To the brave men... the brave *crew* of the Yukesi. Your people salute you."

The auditorium stood as one and saluted the stage.

On either side of her, Lihku and Suji saluted back. Michelle repeated her clumsy half-bow from earlier.

The families in the audience took their seats again, and the Senior Chairman dismissed the gathering with a benediction beseeching the succor of the gods of honor.

Michelle didn't know much about the gods of honor, but as Suji's hand came to rest on her shoulder, she leaned into his arm and decided that she would accept all the comfort she could get.

29

The Legislative Wing was less ornately decorated than the rest of Council Headquarters. Here, an understated elegance dominated by skillfully crafted stone lent an air of dignity and solemnity to the atmosphere. Michelle and Suji entered the Main Chamber together at 0927. At the near end of the Council table, a less ostentatious version of the one in the hologram aboard Yukesi, stood Lihku and Epimoe, deep in conversation. Across from the Council table, a smaller table sat, facing the Councilmembers.

With only three chairs, it was obvious who would be sitting there.

Suji apparently had the same thought. They looked at one another at the same time and, with a gesture toward the small table, he asked, "Shall we?"

Michelle nodded her assent, and they took their places. She sat in the center chair, where the stepstool was already arranged, with Suji on her right.

Lihku lifted two tentacles to Epimoe in a formal gesture

of parting and walked across the room to join them.

"Well?" asked Michelle as he sat. "What is she saying? What do you think?"

The captain smiled softly at her. "I think I have never been so proud of a pupil of mine in my life."

A shy smile slowly spread across her face. Lihku's praise filled her with warmth and she sat a little taller.

"Hey," Suji objected. "I was one of your pupils, too."

Lihku regarded the younger man impassively. "I remember."

A bark of laughter escaped her as Suji chuckled.

A door on the far end of the Council table opened and the thirteen members strode in, led by Epimoe. They all sat; Michelle nodded a greeting at Senior Chairman Sijaj. He discreetly wiggled a tentacle at her in response.

The sound of trumpeting elephants filled the room, heralding the start of the proceedings. As the cacophony faded, Sijaj stood. "This hearing, opening on the first day of Rizkiku, will come to order. Senior Chairman Sijaj presiding. This hearing regards the review of the legal status of Mishel the Little Being, sponsored by Councilmember Epimoe and Captain Lihku of Yukesi."

Sijaj sat, arranged his robes, and looked to Epimoe. "Councilmember, you may begin."

Epimoe got to her feet. Between her bearing and her formal ensemble, she could have been mistaken for one of the gods of honor. "Thank you, Senior Chairman, fellow Councilmembers, and esteemed guests."

She regally walked around the end of the table and stood in the center of the room, commanding everyone's attention. "Earlier this year, on the ninth day of Hoyo, this Council made one of the greatest missteps in its long and honorable history. On that day, the petition of Mishel the Little Being, requesting asylum among the proud and noble Vinyi people, was denied. I am confident that we, the Council of Hoikke, acted in the best interests of the people, sought the wisdom of the gods, and made what we deemed to be the wisest and best decision.

"On that day, however, fellow Councilmembers, we erred.

"We refused Mishel the Little Being asylum, relegating her to the status of research subject." Epimoe scanned the faces of the Council. "We bestowed on her the legal status of a laboratory experiment, believing her to be too unskilled and uncontrolled to successfully integrate into our society in a meaningful way."

Epimoe turned to face Michelle. "We have never before been proven so profoundly, foolishly wrong."

The soft jingle of the ceremonial bells on Epimoe's shoes as she walked barely reached Michelle's ears. "Mishel endured our error. Alone, she endured pain, humiliation, and torture. She was debased and abused, almost to the point of death.

"Then she saved the Yukesi."

Suji's chest swelled with pride.

"Mishel used her diminutive size to her advantage, going where the rest of Yukesi's crew could not, doing what they could not. She avoided capture, sent a distress call that summoned the battle cruisers Hijh'kaok and Vaikke, and sabotaged ship's weapons so they could not be used against the help she summoned. What is more..."

Epimoe turned to face her again. "When a crewman, her *yejorep* brother, Commander Suji, was on the verge of death at the hands of the *Jik'loinhij*, Mishel emerged from hiding, armed with nothing but two small blades and the courage of a seasoned Vinyi warrior, to defend him."

She looked dryly at the Council. "As you can plainly see, her efforts were successful."

It hadn't happened quite like that, but given that events had been twisted against her the last time she sat before the Council, Michelle considered that maybe Epimoe's spin on events now was less embellishment and more justice.

"The records of the Yukesi and the testimony of multiple members of her crew, including witnesses to her brave stand against the *Jik'loinhij*, support my statements. Due to these events, Captain Lihku and I are in agreement with regards to our petition and recommendation.

"We submit to the Council that Mishel the Little Being should not be granted asylum."

Michelle blinked and frowned as Suji tensed beside her. What? *Not* granted asylum? And Lihku went along with this? She stared up at him, baffled.

He stared straight ahead, not meeting her eyes.

What the hell is going on right now?

Epimoe once again turned to face Michelle, and the compassion on her face confused Michelle even further., until she spoke. "Instead, we submit to the Council that Mishel the Little Being should be granted full citizenship."

Michelle gasped. A *citizen*? They wanted to make her fully, legally Vinyi? She gaped first at Epimoe, then at Lihku. He glanced down at her with a happy smirk that made Michelle feel a bit embarrassed that she'd thought that he'd thrown her under the bus, even for a moment.

Epimoe saluted the Council. "Thank you, fellow Councilmembers, for your consideration. Senior Chairman, I yield." She went back to her seat.

"Thank you, Councilmember Epimoe." Sijaj surveyed the other members of the Council. "Does the Council require any clarification at this time?"

Nobody did.

"Then this matter is put to a vote."

Every Councilmember reached for their tablet, tapped the screen a few times, and set it back down on the table in front of them. There was no adjournment for debate, no discussion or contention.

"The Council has voted."

Michelle's heart began to race. That was either a very good sign, or a very bad one. Under the table, she reached over and grabbed Suji's forearm.

"Mishel the Little Being, you will stand while the verdict is read."

She stood up in her chair.

"Mishel the Little Being, it is the unanimous verdict of this Council on the first day of Rizkiku that you are, from this moment henceforth, a legal citizen of the Vinyi Empire, with all the rights and privileges thereto appertaining."

Michelle thought she might float up into the air.

"This Council humbly offers you our most sincere apology for its earlier treatment of you, and our most sincere hopes for a bright and honorable future for our newest, and most unique, citizen."

A citizen. She was real. She was a real person again. She could be Senhku's *hojhke*. She would never be compelled to undergo lab experimentation again. She could participate in society as a fully functioning member. She could finally belong, not always be an outcast. She could officially start a new life, here, among the Vinyi, as a Vinyi.

Michelle could make herself a new home.

"Congratulations, and welcome, Mishel. Do you wish to say anything at this time?"

She swallowed tightly. They had welcomed her into their society, as different and unusual as she was. They were making a place for her. But the sound of her name from Sijaj's mouth rang like a bad chord in an otherwise lovely song. None of the Vinyi had ever been able to quite say her name correctly; it simply didn't fit in their mouths well.

Michelle wanted everything to fit. Becoming Vinyi was going to be an exhausting undertaking; she wanted to go all in.

"Yes, Senior Chairman."

Sijaj gestured to her. "You have the floor, Mishel."

There it was again, that discordant note. "Thank you, Senior Chairman." She cleared her throat and squared her shoulders. "You have done me a great honor today by welcoming me into your society. It will be my privilege to work hard to create my place in it and to better the lives of those around me by my efforts."

An approving murmur ran through the Council table.

"But I have a request, Senior Chairman, if I may."

Sijaj lifted a tentacle in acquiescence.

"If I am to live as a Vinyi, among Vinyi, *become* Vinyi, I would choose to be known by a Vinyi name."

From the corner of her eye, Michelle caught Suji's head whip around in surprise. A burst of whispering rose and fell from the Council table.

Sijaj curled two tentacles, intrigued. "And what name would you like to make your own?"

Michelle turned her face to the left and winked at Lihku before facing Sijaj again. "If it pleases the Council, I am Rikube."

She didn't have to be looking at him to feel the warmth of Lihku's grin.

"Does the Council require any clarification or have any objection?"

Nobody moved.

In what was almost certainly a break from protocol, Sijaj gave her a large smile. "Then it shall be. Welcome, Rikube of the Vinyi."

And with a bang of the Senior Chairman's gavel, Michelle became Rikube.

Lihku and Epimoe, knowing exactly what was going to happen in the hearing, had arranged a small but festive celebration in a room just down the hall in honor of Rikube's new citizenship. Suji's family was there, as was Lihku's, who Rikube had never met before, along with multiple members of the Yukesi crew. It didn't take long for news of her new name to spread, and it was received with as much happiness as the news of her citizenship.

She fielded congratulations after congratulations, and with each well-wisher, Rikube thought she couldn't feel any more elated. Then along came the next one and her joy continued to increase. A table on the side of the room was replete with food and drink, and cheerful music was being piped in from somewhere, a pleasant backdrop to the upbeat chatter in the rich mahogany-colored room.

She looked around, amazed and pleased and gratified. The only thing missing was her Mars family. *If only Dave and Phil could see me now,* she thought wistfully.

"Mish... Rikube," said Lihku, coming up to her as Zibru, one of the Yukesi crew who had been in the mess hall that fateful day, walked away. He smiled. "My apologies. An old habit that may take a little time to break."

"Oh, I understand, believe me." She didn't know how long it was going to take before she started responding to her new name as instinctively as she did the one she'd had since birth.

"As you are aware, citizenship not only has rights and privileges, but responsibilities, as well."

She nodded.

"Including the responsibility to earn your way."

She nodded again. "I was wondering about that. I still have so much to learn," she said, spreading her hands wide and shrugging. "Other than crawling around in tunnels, what can I do? Do you have any ideas?"

Lihku chuckled. "I have many ideas, but they all come back to one common theme. Rikube, will you accept a post on Yukesi when it sails out again, under my command?"

Her jaw dropped. "Really?"

Lihku tilted his head at her, puzzled. "Yes, of course. Did that sound like a joke?" He shook his tentacles. "That would have been a terrible attempt at humor. Not funny at all."

She laughed. "No. I mean, yes... I mean, no, not a funny joke and yes, yes, yes, I would love to come back to the Yukesi. I just can't understand why you would have me when I have no skills yet."

He patted her upper back fondly. "Rikube, skills can be taught. A courageous heart, on the other hand, cannot. You already have the hardest part well in hand."

She bowed to him. "It would be my honor to serve under you, Captain."

"Good," he said, then imitated her earlier wink. "We will do great things together, you will see."

Rikube thought of all the hours spent training with him, all the frustration and setbacks and effort and, in the end, reward from all their hard work. "We already have."

Lihku grunted.

Suji came up alongside her and tapped her shoulder. "Excuse me, Rikube, Captain. May I steal the guest of honor away for a moment?"

"It is probably good that you do so," Lihku replied. "Being Captain comes with far more social obligation than being Battle Chief did. One of the drawbacks I'll have to get used to." And he grumbled quietly as he walked toward a Vinyi she didn't recognize.

Suji steered her toward where Pekoe was waiting in a corner of the room. Suji's wife greeted her with a warm smile. "Congratulations, Rikube."

Rikube beamed. "Thank you, Pekoe. Where is my *zejhku*?"

"Oh, Senhku is happily ensconced in the care center." Pekoe held up the glass of *gonu* she held. "I love my son, but from time to time, it's nice to hold something a little lighter."

Suji laughed and touched one of his tentacles to Pekoe's. "You deserve as much lightness as life can give you, my shield."

Pekoe gazed fondly at her husband, and unless Rikube was much mistaken, Senhku wouldn't be an only child for long.

"But this moment is about our newest citizen and surprise heroine," he said, pulling Rikube into a hug. "Pekoe and I have something for you."

Rikube stared at them. "Wait... did you know about the verdict in advance, too? Did *everyone* know except me?"

Pekoe laughed. "No, we had no idea about the verdict."

"We had planned on giving you this today, anyway. It just turns out that now we have an even better reason to do so." Suji grinned as he handed her a small box. It was a small plastic box that reminded Rikube of the Negoheh gifts that Suji and Sam had given her.

Sam. Her heart twisted as she thought of how proud, how happy, he would be right now.

She pried open the lid and stared. Her chin began to tremble, and she firmed it up, reigning in the powerful wave of emotion that swept over her. She reached in and lifted out the Sword of Mercy brooch.

Suji's voice was soft. "I know it's not the one Sam gave you. I don't know what happened to that one. But maybe you can wear this one and think of him all the same."

She sniffled; she couldn't help it. "Oh, Suji. Pekoe." When she looked up at them, it was with shining eyes. "Thank you. Thank you so much. With one gift, I will remember the love of *both* of my brothers."

Pekoe reached out and gently squeezed her shoulder. "We should do our best to surround ourselves with reminders of the love in our lives. Now you are just starting out, but you will be swimming in reminders one day, I'm certain."

Rikube reached up and squeezed Pekoe's hand. "I feel as though I already am."

30

TWO YEARS LATER

Rikube sat and took off her shoes, first rubbing the sole of her right foot, then her left. Zibru had worn her out today. She had been the example, time and again, of how to execute evasion techniques in a hand-to-hand combat situation. Two years of dedicated training and practice had given her a sculpted, capable physique and polished fighting skills. There were very few situations she couldn't get out of now, and Zibru used her as an example for the others to follow. Of course, the shoe was on the other foot when it came to striking; she was pretty ineffective at actually trading blows without a weapon, but, at her size, what else could one reasonably expect?

She removed the sword brooch from her collar, stripped down to nothing, and stepped into the shower. Her quarters had come a long way from their early days and now even her bathroom had been fitted to her smaller proportions. Vinyi didn't shower. Their hide secreted an enzyme that turned the germs on its surface into a subdermal layer of microbial protection. For all the ways she had adapted to Vinyi culture, however, she still needed to bathe. Captain Lihku had given permission for Suji and his team to design and install a shower in her bathroom, and there was nothing Lihku could have done that would have earned him her loyalty more.

The hot water flowed over her, taking her aches and fatigue down the drain with it. When she finished, Rikube dried off and pulled out a long white dress that she tied about her waist with a silver sash. Then she walked out into her living area and lit two candles, setting them on her low table.

So much about life on Yukesi was different now. She split her time between Records and Security, meeting the demands of a job Lihku convinced the Vinyi military to create just for her. And she was doing it well. She was contributing to society, as was her responsibility, and she was enjoying it. She enjoyed the love of her *zejhku*, Senhku, who at two years old was just starting to explore and have thoughts about the world around him in a way that he could communicate to her. She had become a part of Suji's family, he and Pekoe feeling like her own brother and sister. And she had made friends of her own. Lihku had exercised his authority as Captain and refused Rimoli's application to rejoin the Yukesi, instead appointing the highly capable, deeply honorable, and absolutely hilarious Immin to the post. Rikube gratefully counted Immin among her closest friends.

Everything about her present had taken shape nicely, and Rikube was hopeful about her future. So it was time now to part ways with her past.

She dimmed the lights so that the candles were the brightest things in the room. She sat cross-legged on the floor at the table. From her vantage point, the candles were framed by the starscape outside her viewport. She breathed and meditated for some minutes before slowly, gently opening her eyes. She began reciting names of those in her past who had mattered to her, who had impacted her, who had preceded her into death, seeing in her mind's eye each one as she spoke their names.

Adam.

Katherine.

Petra.

Hegoh.

Kalik.

Mebeku.

And Sam. Always Sam.

Reluctance formed a pit in her stomach as she knew what had to come next. Rikube closed her eyes again, breathed deeply in and out, calming herself. Then she opened her eyes and focused on the first candle.

It was time.

"Dave," she said, speaking aloud a name that she had only whispered to herself for years. "David Matthew Collins, I love you." Even after all this time, his face appeared in her mind's eye as clearly as ever. "I have loved you forever, and I will never cease to love you. But the time has come to accept that our paths have diverged."

Rikube didn't cry these days, but here, in the privacy of her quarters, in her last address to her lost husband, the tears rolled slowly down her cheeks, one by one, and she did nothing to stop them. "I hope, with all my being, that you lived a joyous life, full of light and love, and there will always be a part of me that is so, so sorry I missed it, so sorry that I couldn't grow old with you."

Images of Dave at sixteen, when she'd first met him filled her mind's eye. Then at graduation, at college, at first Katherine's funeral, then Adam's. She saw him all dressed up and nervous the evening he'd proposed. She saw him in his tuxedo, dashing and gorgeous and breathtaking, as they exchanged vows. She remembered him naked and glorious, the feeling of the two of them coming together, *being* together, closer than she would, or could, ever be with anyone else. "You have been the strength of my life, the shelter of my heart, and the very core of all that is good. You will always be a part of my soul, and I will never, ever regret a moment we spent together. I will never fully stop missing you. And I will never, until the day I die, forget you."

She cupped a hand behind the flame. "I love you, Dave. Goodbye."

And with a trembling breath, she blew out the candle.

Rikube sat and cried, allowing herself to feel the loss of everything she'd held so dear for so long. Then she moved on to the second candle.

"Phil." Her already shaky voice broke. "Philip Edward Arensen, I love you." She thought of her little brother, from the baby he'd been to the chubby-cheeked toddler to the awkward, gangly teen and finally, to the young man he was becoming on Mars. "I miss you so much. I wish things had gone differently. I wish that I had been able to stay there with you like I promised, that I could have been there with you as you grew into manhood, maybe falling in love and raising a family. Or not. Whatever life you lived, I hope you were, above all, happy. I hope, with all my being, that you lived a joyous life, full of light and love, and Phil, I am so, so sorry that I missed it all. But the time has come to accept that our paths have diverged."

She had to take a few moments to bawl before she could continue the ceremony. "You were always a light in my darkness, a joy in my sorrow, and I will never stop missing you. I will never, until the day I die, forget you."

She cupped a hand behind the second flame. "I love you, Phil. Goodbye."

In between sobs, Rikube blew out the second flame.

She buried her face in her hands and wailed, her body heaving, until she ran out of tears.

When the tempest finally passed, she blew her nose one last time, wiped her eyes, and took a deep breath. She looked up, beyond the candles, the wicks of which had stopped smoking, to the field of stars behind them in the window. She stood, picking up the candles and placing them on a high shelf, above the picture Senhku had drawn for her. In silence, she contemplated the candles and the love they represented. She had lost Dave and Phil, but she had never lost their love, no more than they had ever lost hers.

Pekoe had been right. It was important to surround herself with reminders of the love in her life. It was important to remember that love was such a powerful force that, once given, it was hers to keep forever, even if the original giver was lost to her long ago.

Rikube sighed deeply. Her eyes ached, but her spirit felt lighter. Now she could begin to live fully in the here and now, finally feeling at peace with her past. With the reassurance of the love she had in her life, in her heart and soul, she turned and looked to the endless vista of stars in front of her.

To her future.

Acknowledgments

FOUND, my debut novel, would not exist if not for the dedicated efforts of some very dear people. I offer my heartfelt thanks to each of them.

To Jenny Cicotte, without whose gentle persistence nobody other than me would ever have read a word of this story. You read FOUND when it was its worst version of itself, and you still believed in it, and in me.

To Marthese Fenech. Your mad editing skills combined with your *goodness* not only made this story stronger, but encouraged me to keep going with it when I wasn't sure the effort would be worth it. FOUND is what it is because of both your professionalism and your kindness.

To Karen Stevens, scientist and expert grammarian. Thanks to you, not only did I nail the pH scene, but everybody's name is spelled correctly and (most of) the commas are where they ought to be. Dave's not the only one who's glad to know Dr. Aiani.

To Tracy Otterholt, whose enthusiasm for this novel breathed new life into it and into my desire to publish it. It's so easy to lose confidence during your first publishing journey. You restored mine.

Above all, my endless gratitude to my husband, Mike. You believe in me more than I do in myself, in every single area of my life, without exception. Your unwavering support is the launchpad from which I reach for the stars, so this story set among them is dedicated to you.

All my thanks.

Milton Keynes UK
Ingram Content Group UK Ltd.
UKHW021554230824
447235UK00011B/367